Escaping The Shadows

Women Of Strength Series (Book 4)

Lucy Appadoo

Dedication

I dedicate this book to those struggling with injustice and violence. You are not alone.

Contents

PROLOGUE

"Hurry up, Samuel." She huffed. "We have to get away from here. Quickly." The woman wiped sweat from her forehead as she sprinted over loose stones, dry brush and rough terrain, clutching a large handbag. The small trees and dull brown and green vegetation caught in her unwashed hair as she gripped her son's hand and ignored the bright sun burning her skin. They needed to get away. God only knew what they would do to her if they found them escaping. But it was impossible to know which way she was going. This place was deserted, and she had no idea where civilisation started.

The snapping of twigs alerted her to something behind, but she refused to turn around. The seconds she'd waste looking around would make her lose precious time, and she had to keep going, despite Samuel's breathlessness and sweaty brow. What she had seen couldn't be unseen. She had been deceived and had then made a hasty decision without enough information. Now she had to protect her family and get out of this ghost town.

Her legs ached as she pulled Samuel over dips and around boulders until they came to a sign. One arrow pointed behind her to Corral del Sastre, and another to the left to Font Antiga. Where in the hell would that direction take her? She had no choice, as she couldn't turn back. If only she knew this part of the Spanish countryside, but her decrepit husband had never taken her outside of Madrid. He was a cheapskate and preferred to cheat on her with other women, ignoring the needs of his wife and son. For all she knew, he might have orchestrated all this just to avoid paying child support.

Samuel fell over a rock, grazed his knee and stopped. Quickly turning around, she saw a spot hidden from the path by overhanging trees. She helped Samuel hide in it and then peered back the way they had come. She let out a long-held in breath of relief. No one was following. They were safe for now.

Quickly, she bent over and assessed Samuel's knee. She rummaged in her back pocket for a tissue and wiped away the blood. "There. Just scrapes. Not too bad. Can you walk?" Samuel nodded. "Great. We must keep going. They can't find us."

Renewing their trek but at a slower pace, she held tight onto his hand and headed towards Font Antiga and wherever that would lead—hopefully back into the city, where she would alert the police. Would they do anything about it? Remembering the way they'd ignored her husband's violent episodes more than once, finding domestic violence acceptable made her physically sick. Because they hadn't believed her there was no record of the abuse. So she'd kept it to herself, ashamed of her own weakness. She wondered again whether he had tricked her into coming to this deserted hellhole.

The woman had managed to swipe two bottles of water, and once she was sure that no one was following her, she'd stop for a much-needed drink. Ignoring her parched throat and burning bare skin, she urged Samuel to move faster. Up ahead, figures came into view, but could she trust them? Were they who she didn't want them to be?

"Let's hide behind this tree. I don't know who's up ahead." She prodded her son to a safe position out of view and waited. Two men and a woman headed in her direction, but she couldn't see them clearly enough to recognise them. Who were they, and what were they doing in the middle of nowhere?

Chills ran down her spine as they came closer to the tree. Surely, they hadn't seen her. Eyes darting, she lost all breath and started to shake. Her surroundings blurred as she realised there was nowhere else to go without being seen. All she could do was wait it out until they left.

She breathed freely again as they turned away. With calming breaths, she placed a hand on her heart and patted Samuel's head. "I think it's okay to go now, darling. They've gone." He smiled.

Taking a step forward, she rubbed her son's hand with the tissue to remove the sweat, feeling the uneven indentations of the pebbles and twigs he had fallen on. The blood on his knee had dried up, too.

The sun was setting and storm clouds gathered. She prayed it wouldn't rain. It would make it that much harder to escape.

She froze in mid-stride upon hearing an ominous sound. It couldn't be, could it? She hoped it was her imagination, but Samuel heard it, too. No one seemed to be around. The bushland was deserted again.

When her son let go of her hand and covered his ears with his hands, she knew this was it. "Samuel, run. Run and don't stop. Please. Get away from here." He shook his head, terror in his eyes. "I love you, but you have to go. Now." She gave him her bag.

The second click of the rifle made her turn around. She put up her hands. "I am coming back. Don't worry." She glanced at her son, who had dashed behind them while she side-tracked the newcomers. He had to save himself.

Staring down the barrel of the rifle, she felt the bullets tear into her chest, grateful she could save her son. Only blackness and peace enveloped her after realising she'd made the worst mistake of her life.

CHAPTER 1

Eva leaned over her student while guiding her finger across the page of a book. "Great work, Mateo. But sound it out." Her eyes briefly flickered over to the teacher and her friend, Francisca, who sat opposite another student flailing his arms as he shook his head. Laying a hand on his shoulder, Francisca whispered words of encouragement that led to her student jotting notes into his book. She had calmed him down.

Groups of students huddled over their books as Francisca walked along the matte floorboards between the shelves of readers, down to the rows of computers sitting on a bench. Tables and padded chairs were placed haphazardly around the room.

Eva leaned back, watching Mateo close the book he had been working on and picking up a spelling workbook. For an eleven-year-old in primary school he had a broad frame and stubby fingers. "Now write these English words into your book so I can test you on them tomorrow. Practise them."

He nodded. "I can get them all right, Miss. I can."

She threaded a hand through the long, glossy brown waves that fell down to her lower back while turning to ensure that he was holding his pencil right. "Of course you can. You'll get plenty of practice."

She thrived on her work as a special education teacher, working with students who presented with autism like Mateo, or who had intellectual disabilities, attention deficit hyperactivity disorder, or Down's Syndrome, to name a few. The school was private but supported those with special needs, so not every student in the room needed special intervention.

Eva's affinity for her special needs students made her feel safe. She could relate to them because she also had a disability: a glass left eye. Over the years she had adapted to her vision, and could still drive a car despite limits to her peripheral vision. Plus, she had developed an acute sense of hearing.

The quiet chatter ceased at the end of the day when class ended, and she waved to Francisca. "I'll see you later."

"Hmm. See you in a bit," she said, her emerald-green eyes brightening.

Eva waved goodbye to Mateo and waited for the remainder of the children to rush out of class like a swarm of bees. She headed down the corridor to her desk and placed documents into her in-tray. A few other teachers sat at desks across from her, heads bowed to concentrate on planning for the next day. She sat and scribbled down case notes to plan for her next lot of students tomorrow. Rubbing her shoulders, she put down her pen, stacked papers, then checked her phone to see that an hour had passed. *Time to leave.*

While picking up her satchel and handbag, she felt Francisca's hand on her shoulder and faced her. "I'm leaving. Are you ready?" Francisca's short, petite stature contrasted with her strong character. Her faded chestnut-colour hair style suited her warm and relaxed nature, as if she didn't have a care in the world. If only Eva felt that way.

"Sure. I'm ready." On their way to the exit, they waved goodbye to passing students and teaching staff. "Have you heard anything about Samuel and Lola?"

Francisca shook her head. "Nothing from the teachers or principal, and I'm worried. They've been missing for at least three weeks."

Eva's throat suddenly felt parched as she felt her shoulders stiffen. "What do you think happened?"

"I wish I knew, but the police obviously have no leads, or we'd hear about it. I know poor Lola was stressed out by Samuel. Who wouldn't be, with a boy who's mute? It's having to communicate in different ways. I know she was stressed to the max, girl, and that damn husband of hers left them in the lurch. Bastard."

Eva recalled a parent-teacher interview when Lola's husband dominated the interview and cut her off in conversation. The woman couldn't get a word in. Something about the man had rubbed Eva the wrong way, and she could imagine him being aggressive. But would he resort to kidnapping, if that's what this was? What if something more sinister had happened?

Scorching heat blasted their cheeks as they stepped out the door. "We only just started the term, and suddenly they disappear after coming to school for only a few weeks. I wonder if it's the husband," Eva said.

Francisca shrugged. She had been a primary school teacher for six years, while Eva had started working at the school only four years earlier. Eva had worked at another private school at the start of her career and wouldn't dream of doing anything else. "Who knows? She might've gone on a trip without telling anyone. Might not want to be bothered. Probably sick of stressing over school stuff, homework, and other mothers talking about her mute child. That poor woman had to put up with a lot of damn shit from those who don't know what it's like to deal with trauma. That's why Samuel doesn't talk." She took a breath. "Samuel's aunt is on our system, too. Andreina. We've kept in touch, but she still has no idea where they might be. I'd feel sorry for her if she was a nicer person, but she's colder than an iceberg."

"Hmm," said Eva. "I guess if something happens, she'll be the first to hear about it, so you need to stay on Andreina's good side." Francisca nodded. "A lot of the kids are challenging but beautiful," Eva continued. "I can't imagine how hard it must be for those mothers who don't have that support. I know Samuel had behavioural issues, but I thought he was getting better."

Francisca nodded. "Damn straight, girl. Some of them are doing it on their own." She retrieved her keys from her handbag and watched as one of the mothers, Isabela, rush towards her car, huffing.

Eva headed towards her. "Isabela. Are you all right?"

Her wavy blonde hair flew in the gusty wind as she threaded bright red manicured nails through it. "What?" The bright designer blouse and skirt, as well as her stiletto heels, contrasted with her dark mood. Her husband was a wealthy business owner, and Isabela liked to buy nice things to suit her status as the rich wife.

Francisca joined her friend. "You're here late. Where's your son, Joaquin?"

Isabela's green eyes darkened, but despite her sadness she still appeared beautiful and younger than her thirty-five years. "Oh, my husband picked him up today. They attended a sports meeting, so I decided to catch up on paperwork to prepare for the reading groups next week." Her hands fidgeted and her feet shuffled on the ground. "But I have to go now and get dinner ready for when they return. Bye."

The women waved to her as they headed to their own car. Eva thought that Isabela must have been missing Lola, her closest friend. But she didn't want to broach the subject of Lola with her, given that she'd been depressed for the past two weeks. Why burden her when there was still no news?

Eva stepped into Francisca's convertible and waited for her friend to start the motor to drive to the apartment they shared. "Poor Isabela. She must be missing Lola like crazy. But she always looks busy and distracted."

Francisca turned to her as she sped towards Plaza de Espana where they lived. "It's the nature of voluntary work and so many kids, girl. But you're right. It must be hitting her hard. I'm sure the police will find them soon." She curled a brow. "But at least she's got her gorgeous, sexy husband to console her. What I would give to have a man in my life." She turned into their underground car park. "It wouldn't hurt for you to meet someone. It's time, don't you think, girl?"

Eva's throat tightened as she flashed back three years to her ex-boyfriend, Leo. He'd been abusive. "I don't think relationships are in the cards for me, Francisca. I'd much rather focus on the kids and my friends, and that includes you. I won't be meeting another abusive man who treated me like my father did. No man worthy of my time will ever exist, and I've made my peace with it."

Francisca nudged her on the shoulder. "I understand it was hard, Eva, but you deserve a man who will shower you with love and gifts. I'm sure he's out there somewhere."

"I doubt that will ever happen."

Eva stared through the window and thought about how she wouldn't go there with anyone. She'd lost too much confidence to try again with someone else, and life was full of worries and negativity. She preferred to stay in her own little bubble.

CHAPTER 2

Tomas gripped a bottle of beer as he stood on his apartment balcony scanning the streets of La Latina. Cyclists rode by behind cars down the narrow roads, slowed down by trucks distributing goods to the many and varied shops and cafes. Tourists and locals sipped coffee and snacks surrounding the groups of apartments alongside his, with the plaza opposite. Smells of engine fumes and dust filled his nostrils. Muffled voices and car horns resounded.

His friend, Gonzalo, ran a hand through his blond, curly hair as he stood beside him overlooking the mayhem below. If trouble ensued in the street, as it did occasionally, his bodyguard physique and legs like tree trunks would scare those who didn't know him.

A vibration from his back pocket brought Tomas out of his reverie as he set his drink on the nearby table and pulled it out. Clicking on the text, he smiled. "Good news," he said. "That boy, Juan, we transported to the hospital is going to be fine."

Gonzalo nodded. "It was lucky we brought the dude to the hospital when we did. Got it in early or he could've died."

He reached back for his beer bottle. "Exactly. The drugs they gave him helped to reduce the level of mercury in his system. Hopefully there'll be no lasting effects." He had seen a few cases of mercury poisoning over the last couple of years, but the victims didn't know the cause. "I know we get mercury from seafood or fish, but why have a few that we've seen had so much of it in their system? It's happened a few times lately."

"It has, Tomas. Luckily, they survived. But our job is to be emergency medical technicians, and as far as I'm concerned, we're giving them medical attention. Nothing more we can do, man, so don't stress. I'm sure it'll pass."

"I am not stressed. Just curious," said Tomas.

"Could've fooled me." He chuckled. "I know your dad did a number on you when he ignored your medical needs, but you pulled through. That's the important thing. We save them, but we can't save them all."

Tomas shivered. "Right. If it wasn't for my mother nursing me to health, I would've been dead." The memory returned: the sweaty texture of his father's hand over his mouth, his smelly breath as he hovered over him, the stuffiness of a smelly van, and the empty hole in his stomach. He shuddered at the idea that his father had been willing to sacrifice his son for the sake of survival. One less kid to manage. That had been only one of a series of traumas in his childhood life.

He had been rescued from that fate when his father died unexpectedly. An ache in his chest reminded Tomas how he wished he could have given his father a piece of his mind, to make him understand the pain he'd caused his son. He had been a monster.

"I know, man," Gonzalo said. "You've had a lot of shit to deal with, and I for one don't know how you can deal with the victims sometimes. I'm surprised you haven't burnt out."

Tomas sipped his beer. "What can I say?" He beamed. "I love helping people. It keeps me sane and gives me this rush, you know. I couldn't imagine doing anything else."

"Yeah, you sure helped Lucia when she thought she was having a heart attack."

He scoffed. "Don't even talk about her, Gonzalo. She was a piece of work." Thinking about his ex-girlfriend brought short breaths and a burn into his chest. She had left him without notice, just sending him a text about leaving. Who did that? No warning, no indication that she was running off. It had hurt like hell. He had been desperately in love with her and refused to go through the pain of new love again.

The flashing lights of an ambulance made him flinch, and passersby stopped walking to watch. Cars pulled over to the side to let the ambulance pass. Tomas wondered who the victim was and whether they'd survive the trip to the hospital. It irked him when drivers wouldn't pull over to the side to let the ambulance pass, as a second's delay could be the difference between life and death.

Sometimes the deaths he'd witnessed made him feel helpless, as if he had to help the whole world. But Gonzalo was right—he couldn't save everyone. He couldn't make them magically breathe again when he'd tried everything.

When he couldn't save someone, Tomas always replayed the scene in his mind as if he could've done something differently. What if he had been quicker with the injection or had checked the airway more thoroughly? What if he hadn't taken an extra breath rather than act in rapid succession?

He wasn't God, but hell, sometimes he wished he was. There were times the deaths and domestic violence cases killed him inside. He couldn't stand it to see women being abused in all manner of ways, nor men, for that matter.

Gonzalo broke into his thoughts again. "Have you heard from her lately? Know what she's up to?"

"I heard through mutual friends that she's married now. Didn't take her long after our breakup a year ago. Most likely, she left me for her new husband. I think she might've been cheating on me, too. But hell. I loved her, Tomas. I thought I'd die when she left me. It was like no pain I'd ever experienced."

"Onwards and upwards, man. Let's just party a bit more and have fun. No point getting serious when you can forget about her with other women. It's the cure for heartache. No strings attached."

Tomas laughed. "I'm not you. I can't sleep with any woman and be fine with it. I have to get to know someone before I'm comfortable. I used to like to wine and dine them, but I'm done with that. There is no way in hell I am getting serious with a woman again. I want to trust, but it's hard when I still feel I'm a magnet for women who leave. Hell, I'm a magnet for anyone to leave, so I might as well be alone."

Gonzalo tapped him on the shoulder. "You are not alone, man. You've got me and your other friends who are there for you in a heartbeat. I love you, Tomas."

He gave Gonzalo a reassuring smile. "I love you, too. You're a great friend, but no one can help get me rid of this baggage. It weighs me down, and I don't know how to fix it."

"It's not about fixing it but managing it and moving on. You need to find the right woman. A woman who understands you and can love you like you deserve. She's out there somewhere, bro."

He shook his head. "No such woman exists, and I can't be bothered anymore. I'm done with relationships, and I'm done with this conversation. I'm going inside." He turned around and swung open the door, huffing his way back indoors.

CHAPTER 3

Tomas swung open the passenger door of the ambulance, stepped to the rear of the vehicle, and together with Gonzalo pulled out the stretcher. Heading towards the familiar Urgencias sign, he wheeled the young boy into the hospital entrance while doctors and nurses surrounded them.

Tomas faced the physicians. "A young boy of unknown identification has cuts, grazes and bruises all over his body, signs of dehydration, treated with oral rehydration sachets and liquids. Appears to be mute, as the boy doesn't speak. Semi-conscious state. Stress fractures and a pulled hamstring. Could be a runaway."

"Any internal damage? Drug use?" asked a tall doctor with a dimple on his chin, as he leaned over the patient. The boy trembled as the ophthalmoscope trained on him, his eyes opening and closing.

Gonzalo shook his head as they continued to wheel the boy towards a ward, passing hurried medical staff. "No signs of internal damage or drug use, but you guys might tell a different story. He obviously needs tests and a contact person to identify him."

The doctor nodded. "Thank you, guys. We will take it from here."

Tomas's heart clenched tight at the thought that such a young boy had possibly run away, malnourished. Something about the boy suggested he'd been traumatised, but how? Where did he even come from? The sores and wounds on his feet suggested he'd run a long distance.

Gonzalo leaned in towards him. "Let's get these case notes done, man." He scanned the patient record form over his friend's shoulder while Tomas scribbled his notes. A few minutes later, he asked, "Anything else you want to add?"

"Possible trauma due to symptoms of anxiety, too," Tomas said. "I could see it in his eyes. Something spooked the poor guy. Let me finish the form while you grab us coffee at the vending machine."

"Fine, but hurry up because we can't hold off on dispatch for too long. There aren't enough of us EMTs, man."

Tomas nodded. "No worries. I'll get it done." He promised himself he'd come and see the boy tomorrow, on his day off. The young guy pulled at his heartstrings, as if he could relate to him on some level. The fact that he was mute could have indicated he stopped talking due to an incident. Domestic violence? Witness to a murder?

Why did he always get ahead of himself when he didn't know the facts? Always needing to find a connection between everything and everyone.

Five minutes later, Gonzalo returned with a coffee cup and handed it to him. "Here you go. Are you done?"

"Sure am. Thanks." Tomas hesitated. "Why don't we go check on the guy?"

Gonzalo shook his head. "No, man. Come after hours. Our day's not quite finished yet." He started to walk with his friend, passing wards, the reception area and more sick people on stretchers. "Why do young children always affect you, Tomas? You can't get attached, dude. It's not healthy."

He shrugged. "Don't know. It just hits me, that's all." Gonzalo didn't know what his father had done, as he preferred to keep it quiet. What was the point of bothering others about it when people didn't live up to his expectations?

Tomas would make sure he'd visit the poor boy later today, after his last case. He couldn't wait until tomorrow. He had to make sure he had family who could take him in. Otherwise, he'd be stuck in a foster home or worse, if the medical staff couldn't locate his parents.

***

Passing several ambulances, Eva stepped inside the hospital with Francisca, dodging the hustle and bustle of medical staff and civilians as they made their way towards the reception area. Sounds of monitors going off, flashing warning lights, and rapid footsteps made her wish she was anywhere but at the hospital. She could have slipped on the glossy flooring through the narrow corridor if she focussed on how much she hated hospitals. But when the police had given them news at school about Samuel, she had breathed a sigh of relief.

"Are you okay?" asked Francisca, increasing her pace.

"Of course. I'm excited about Samuel. Thank God he's okay." Francisca gave her a reassuring smile as she prodded her friend into the ward.

What she didn't expect to find was a man wearing a high-visibility jacket and pants and a lanyard around his neck, leaning towards Samuel. Was he an EMT?

He looked up as the two women arrived to see Samuel with an IV lead in his arm and bandages on his foot. His body was covered with multiple cuts and bruises. But he smiled as soon as he saw Eva and Francisca, shifting in his raised hospital bed.

The man walked over to the window to give them space. Eva bent over Samuel and hugged him tightly. "Oh, Samuel. It is so good to see you." The poor guy tried to wipe away tears as he shed them. "It's okay. You're safe now. Where's your aunt?" He pointed to the door, indicating that she'd just stepped out. "That's okay. We'll speak to her later."

Francisca squeezed his shoulder. "You're a sight for sore eyes, little man."

Eva turned at the sound of a voice.

"I'm Tomas, the EMT who brought Samuel in this morning. I thought I'd check in on him at the end of my shift."

Eva took in his short blond hair with gorgeous waves. He was tall, and his clear blue eyes penetrated her own as if he was trying to figure her out. A large, muscular hand threaded through his small beard, giving him a rough and rugged look. Dimples on his cheeks gave him an innocent expression. She tried to ignore the tingles in her chest and the flush in her cheeks. "Hello. I'm Eva and this is my friend, Francisca. We work with Samuel at his school."

"Do you know what happened?" asked Francisca.

Tomas moved in closer, his eyes focussed on Eva. "We got a call from dispatch, saying a young boy of unknown origin had enlisted the help of an elderly gentleman who called 112 on his behalf. The man assumed he was a runaway. He was in Cortes. That's all we know. The boy had his mother's handbag with him, which was how the police tracked down his aunt."

"Have the police questioned you?" asked Eva.

He nodded. "My partner and I spoke to them briefly, but no sign of his missing mother yet. They said they'll continue the search for her whereabouts."

Francisca scoffed. "I won't hold my breath. She won't be on their list of priorities."

"I won't disagree with you there," said Tomas.

Eva's heart raced when Samuel's eyes became as wide as saucers, his body quaking and his mouth opening and closing. He hugged the blankets closer to his body and hid underneath them, shielding his face. She gazed at him and wondered if their conversation about his mother had triggered him. "Samuel. What's wrong?" She grabbed his hand and swallowed. "Look at me. Please." Slowly, he relaxed his breathing and turned the other way.

"Can I speak to you outside?" Tomas asked Eva.

Francisca nodded. "You go. I'll stay here with Samuel."

Eva made her way to the corridor outside the ward and waited for the man to follow. What was so important that this strange man had to pull her out at such a time?

CHAPTER 4

Eva took a closer look at the EMT's face, ignoring her parched throat and tingles up her spine. This wasn't the time to feel anything for a man she didn't know when poor Samuel was distressed. "What is it?" The woody and lime scent of his cologne sharpened her senses.

He swallowed. "This isn't the first time he's acted this way." She angled her head, curious. "About ten minutes before you arrived, he behaved the same way. Scared like anything. As if he'd seen his worst nightmare. Something's traumatised him, but he refuses to write anything down or give us any clue."

"Have you let the police know?"

"It won't make a difference. They only look at hard evidence, and so far, I don't know what's triggered him. I wonder if he knows where his mother is, but is too scared to say anything. Do you know why he doesn't speak?"

Eva shifted. "Domestic violence. His father was abusive towards Lola. His mother." His eyes looked past her a moment. "But I wish I knew what happened to the poor woman. She and Samuel have been missing for three weeks, and I'm starting to think we might never hear from her again."

He sighed. "That explains it. I've seen a lot of cases of domestic abuse, but some of them don't live to tell the tale. I hope they find his mother and that she's okay."

"Yes. He's only twelve years old, and no one at that age should lose their mother." She curled a brow. "It must be hard for you to see these cases, day in and day out. How do you do it? I'd go crazy with worry and would never sleep if I had to witness so much abuse."

"It has its good and bad days, but I can unwind in my spare time. We have psychologists we debrief with, and I have a great team around me."

She nodded. "That's good." Their eyes locked when they reached an awkward silence. Eva cleared her throat. "I'd better get back in there and see how he's doing." Tomas followed her back to the ward, their shoulders brushing as they walked alongside each other. "Where's his aunt?"

"She went to grab a coffee and said she'd be back in half an hour." He whispered before they entered the ward.

"I can't tell if she's in shock, but she's not a very warm person."

"I've never met her, but Francisca has at the school he attends, and she mentioned the same thing."

Tomas bit his bottom lip, which sent a shiver up her spine. "Andreina mentioned his father is coming back from an overseas work trip. No doubt those two might be fighting for custody. But if he was abusive, he shouldn't get custody."

Eva stepped back inside the ward. "So true." She beamed at Francisca, who was reading Samuel a children's book. She pulled up a chair next to her friend and Tomas stood behind her, listening to the story until the end.

When Francisca closed the book, Tomas said, "I'd better go and get some rest before my next shift first thing in the morning." He touched Samuel on the arm, but he flinched and pulled away his arm as if he didn't want to be touched. "Sorry, man. Didn't mean to upset you. I'll come visit you tomorrow night again, Samuel." He turned to Francisca. "Great to meet you." His eyes lingered on Eva. "Nice to meet you as well. I might see you tomorrow."

"Bye, Tomas. Thank you for being here," said Eva. She wondered why they were able to touch him, but Tomas couldn't. Was it something about men he didn't like, or was it because he was a stranger?

"With pleasure." When he left, Francisca whispered in Eva's ear, "That guy has it bad for you."

She flinched. "What? Don't be silly."

"Oh, no. I know these things, and you feel the same way."

Her face warmed and her breath caught. "Ridiculous. Don't you think we have more important things to focus on?"

She nodded. "Of course. You're right, but I know what I saw."

Eva shook her head and made small talk with Samuel as she flashed back to the way Tomas' eyes had lingered, and how his presence made her feel something. But she had no plans to think about any man when she had Samuel to help.

***

Efren felt sick as Marco gripped him by the arm while watching the entrance to the hospital, the warm wind brushing against his face. The man crept like a shadow, with a blade in his jacket pocket. Efren didn't know who that boy in the hospital was, but Marco had a special interest in him. He wouldn't explain why.

"Get inside the car," Marco said as he entered the driver's side. Efren stepped inside, but Marco kept watch over at the ambulances, noticing a young man who had entered the van.

"What's going on?" Efren asked when Marco sped off towards their home. "Why are you watching those men in the van?"

"That kid inside the hospital is Samuel."

He remembered meeting him briefly. "I didn't know him that well."

"He's special, like you. He wouldn't be in the hospital if his mother hadn't brainwashed him and turned the boy against us. She never understood our real mission, Efren. It's important we stick together."

"Where's the mother now?"

He shrugged. "Not sure, but it looks like she might've abandoned her son. I wouldn't put it past her to have hurt him, which is why he needs medical attention."

Efren had met Marco at the market while browsing through herbs for his mother. The man offered him grand things and taught him important life lessons. It wasn't as if his mother was ever home, working three different jobs. His father wasn't around after killing himself. Gutless prick.

Marco was like the father he'd never had, and after attending a few meetings he'd made his decision. If he wanted a better life, freedom, and a sense of security, he was better off with Marco and his chosen spiritual community.

CHAPTER 5

A huddle of sheltered outdoor restaurants on uneven ground and lilting voices surrounded Eva and her companions on Saturday afternoon. Overhanging trees and the apartment buildings that encircled the city of Plaza de Santa Ana towered above them as they had dodged tourists and locals, who held up their phones or iPads. Hurrying waiters carried dishes and drink orders to tables set in the middle of the square.

Eva sat with her friends, Blanca, Kim, and Sofia, around a rickety round table while her sister, Daniela, gave her a strange look from the opposite side. What was on her sister's mind? Did she know about Samuel, even though she hadn't told anyone yet?

If only they could find his mother and find out what had happened to him, but the police couldn't get any information out of him.

A young male waiter handed them menus. "Would you like drinks to start with?"

"I will have a sangria, thank you," said Eva.

Blanca leaned forward, her vibrant green eyes and well-defined features matching her nurturing and caring nature. She had been through an ordeal as a child, and it had shaped her into someone who truly related to people as a journalist. She worked with Daniela's boyfriend, Rafael, at the same newspaper. "I'll have your house wine. Thanks."

Kim scanned the drinks menu then smiled at the waiter, brushing a hand through her shoulder-length jet-black hair. She had a sweet beauty and quiet nature. She had arrived in Madrid from China as a child, and had recently started employment as a youth worker, in addition to intermittent work as a yoga teacher. "I will have the Vina Cuerva, thank you so much."

Sofia worked with Daniela as a dance teacher. She was a take-charge kind of woman who was protective of her six-year-old daughter as a sole parent. She gripped the menu with long, dainty fingers, showcasing her bright pink nail polish. Her dark brown eyes fixed on the waiter. "I'll have a sangria, too. Much appreciated."

Eva's sister, Daniela, curled a brow as she pondered her choice. "What to have, what to have. You know what, I'll have your house wine. Thanks." Eva envied Daniela's trim and taut figure as a professional ballet dancer and teacher. Her preference was to tie up her dark long, brown hair into a high bun. Eva and Daniela had been through trauma growing up, and they were close as a result.

She felt like the mother hen when all of them except for her and Sofia were in their late twenties. Eva was thirty while Sofia was thirty-two.

As they scanned the menus, Daniela rubbed her hands. "Cannot believe, woman, that you're getting married in two months. Hell, how are you feeling about it? Any doubts?"

Blanca laughed. "Of course not. I love Carlos so much, it hurts. I've got to do the last fitting a month before. I hope I don't put on weight after that. I am so anxious about the dress and how it's going to look. Oh, and there's the seating to organise, and ... I don't know, so much to still do."

Kim tapped Blanca on the shoulder. "Take a breath, Blanca. You will get through it. If you need extra help, I am readily available."

"Thanks, Kim. I love you, but I'll be fine."

Eva's heart warmed at the way Blanca's need for organisation and structure made her anxious most times.

"I thought I was the anxious one, but you're worse than me."

Sofia laughed. "What about your pessimistic nature, Eva?"

"I know. I'm a work in progress, Sofia." She hated that sense of insecurity and dread she usually felt. Would it ever go away?

Sofia threaded a finger through her hair. "Aside from that, I can see something's on your mind, so spill."

Daniela's eyes seared into her sister's. "Yeah, Eva. I second that. What's going on? You look distracted."

The waiter returned with their drinks and set them on the table before pulling out a notepad and pen. "Are you ladies ready to order?"

Daniela spoke up. "We'll go with the canapés: the ham, fish, and cheese to share. Also, the Spanish omelette, and prawn with potatoes." Her eyes darted. "Anything else, girls?" They shook their heads. "That's it. If we want more, we'll order later."

The waiter nodded. "Of course." After he walked off, Blanca returned to the topic of conversation. "Have you heard something about the missing boy and his mother?"

Eva's body shivered despite the warm air. "Samuel's in the hospital, but the mother's still missing. We don't know what happened or where he's been. It's a mystery. He still won't talk." She explained more, including her encounter with the EMT, Tomas.

"Why do you think this EMT's taken an interest in Samuel?" asked Blanca.

She shrugged. "I don't know, but I imagine in his line of work he'd grow attached to some of the victims. It's normal to get attached, especially when it's a child. I can't imagine how he deals with the trauma he must see. The suffering, misery, and hell on Earth."

Daniela's eyes widened. "Oh, you like the guy, Eva. I can see it in your eyes."

Eva's heart ran rampant. "Don't be silly. I don't even know the man. He did mention wanting to visit Samuel tonight, and I might, too. But we'll most likely miss each other."

Sofia had a lightness in her eyes and touched Eva's hand. "He sounds nice."

Eva scoffed. "Yes, he is nice, but that's it. I'm not looking at getting into anything. Relationships never work for me. I'd rather stay in my bubble and focus on my kids and all of you. It's enough for me."

"Hey, I thought you wanted to get your thriller book published. How's that going?" asked Blanca.

Eva shrugged. "Hmm. It's hard to focus on writing when I worry about my mum on her own and, the parents who are struggling at school. I worry about what's going to happen to Samuel and if his aunt can help with his needs. Not to mention worrying about you guys. Daniela with your challenges at the school. Sofia with finances for your daughter. Blanca with your wedding, and Kim with the crises you manage at the youth centre. Some of them, even violent."

Kim threw her hands up in the air. "You cannot be serious, Eva? I know you worry a lot, but this is too much. Life is about navigating through problems. It's what makes us who we are, and you do not need to worry about us. We can manage unless we ask for help. Is that clear, young lady?" She reached forward and held her hand. "You need to look after yourself and make sure you're happy. I love my job, so don't worry. Please work on helping yourself and focus on what you can control."

Daniela clapped. "I couldn't have said it better myself, dear sister."

"Me too," said Blanca.

Eva took a breath, knowing she had to ruminate less and do more. But she couldn't help being realistic. If they thought she was being negative, then each to their own. "Okay, Kim. It's noted. Now enough about me. Let's talk about something else."

Sofia gave her a reassuring smile. "Yes. Did I tell you that my daughter won an award at school? I am so proud of her."

Eva's heart lightened as she leaned in and clasped her hands, thankful to have the spotlight off her. She loved hearing about Sofia's daughter, which distracted her from her own worries. But what if they were right? What if she had felt a slight tingle when she had met Tomas? But not only was he out of her league, she didn't trust in relationships. Her ex-boyfriend had been nice too, until he wasn't. Who knew what a person's true colours were?

CHAPTER 6

Efren stood alongside Marco in the countryside, watching the exchange between the market seller and a female customer. He was miles away from home and missed his mother. But Marco assured him he'd spoken to her about this intense spiritual journey before returning home and that she was fine with it. But was she truly?

"These special, relaxing herbs consist of passionflower, lavender, and rhodiola. Even a tinge of chamomile to relax the mind and body," the seller explained. "Specifically, to address anxiety symptoms, even depression and anger management."

"I don't know," said the customer, who complained of a fractured elbow. "Have these been tested? Do you have any reports about their effectiveness?" The woman's son, who appeared to be ten years old, shuffled his feet and whirled around until his mother touched his shoulder. "Take it easy, son. I won't be long."

"Of course, we do. Here you go," he said, handing over a sheet of paper covered in small print.

The young lady scanned it over with a hint of doubt. "I'm not sure."

"The herbs will not only help with the fracture, but with behavioural problems too. I can see your son's hyperactive, right?" She nodded. "Does he sleep well?"

The woman curled a brow. "No. We need to review his ADHD medication."

"Okay. This will help. Guaranteed."

Her eyes softened and her shoulders relaxed. "All right. How much?"

He handed her a sticky note. "This is the cost."

The lady rummaged into her purse and pulled out a fine bunch of Euro notes. Meanwhile, her son kicked rocks towards passersby, who glared in his direction.

The seller rummaged into a bag and handed over small change. "Here you go."

"Thank you," the lady said.

"No. Thank you," he said. "Oh, before you go, I thought you might be interested in this." He handed her a flyer. "We have classes on spirituality, specifically about exploring the spirit and bringing inner peace. Finding peace and harmony within ourselves. It's amazing how much this can change your life. It can be helpful for you and your son. Have a think about it. We might see you at one of our meetings. We hold them regularly to discuss these course options."

"Sounds interesting," the woman said, then waved goodbye and walked away.

Marco touched Efren on the shoulder. "We'll give you more knowledge to sell these online and at the occasional market. It's important you know about our products, too."

***

After lunch, Eva got off the train at Plaza de Espana and strolled down the tree-lined street. Flowers contained in garden beds swayed in the warm breeze alongside lopsided trees and tall ferns, with fallen dry leaves scattering in the wind under the shade of sheltering branches. Monuments and statues honoured Spanish history. Engines revved, motorcycles hummed, and footsteps resounded from those walking by. She was thankful for public transport as she hated driving on the congested roads which escalated her stress. Her car was usually parked underground, close to home, and she only used it when she needed to travel far.

She never got tired of seeing the many buildings and apartments on her way home and wondered if she'd ever consider buying a house, rather than staying in an apartment. Having left her mother's house a year earlier made her rethink her decision of late, as her mother hadn't been well for a couple of months, but was now healthy.

Walking parallel to the highway, Eva didn't envy those driving in the congested traffic but rather savoured the natural beauty and landscape of Spanish gardens and the fresh air. She was all for less pollution and limited driving.

She passed a man-made fountain surrounded by a huddle of plants and trees with several timber benches. She listened to the calm ripple of water.

Eva climbed down a set of stairs, approaching a sign that read "Magnificent apartments for rent." She passed businesses, a café, three restaurants, a hairdressing salon, and a pharmacy. Services close to home.

As she neared her building, she felt a prickle across her shoulders. Was someone watching her? She scanned her surroundings but saw no one. She was getting paranoid in her old age.

Eva headed inside the building to the elevator, pressed the button for the first floor and stepped inside. She put a key into the lock and entered her home, dropping her bag on the rug and sitting down on her ash-black two-seater sofa.

She took her laptop from the matching black coffee table and rested it on her knees. Bringing up the thriller novel she'd started, she stared at the screen for five minutes but struggled to focus. All she could think of were Samuel and Tomas. Why couldn't she get the man out of her head when she'd only met him once? Because he was nice, that was all. Nothing more to it.

Brushing away thoughts of Tomas, she flashed back to the light in Samuel's eyes when he saw her. It was as if a great burden had been lifted from his shoulders. The poor boy was malnourished and dehydrated, but also terrified of something. Whatever he had run from was still the centre of his focus, but she didn't want to go back to her own painful story thinking about it. The way she had acquired her glass eye. Her sense of dread. Shame. Degradation. Sheer terror. No, she wouldn't go there.

Eva hated feeling insecure in her world, with little trust, and a sense of not feeling valued by the opposite sex. Her mind was always flooded by negative thoughts that kept her cautious in everything she did. She remembered her kidnapping a couple of years earlier, being locked in a dingy room, never knowing whether she'd survive.

Her phone buzzed in her bag. She rummaged for it and clicked to answer. "Esmeralda, hi. Is everything all right?" She had a soft spot for the school psychologist, who had helped parents and children find their way.

"Hey, Eva. Of course. Nothing to worry about. I wanted to see whether you'd caught up with Samuel and how I can help. I know you two are close."

"Thanks, Esmeralda, but I'm fine. Do you know what happened to Samuel?"

"I wish I did. The police are still investigating. Hopefully they'll locate his mother and get her back home safely."

"Samuel needs time to recover and heal, but he's afraid of something."

"Hmm." Esmeralda exhaled. "I thought I'd give you a heads-up and let you know he'll need more time off from school. I'll work with him at the hospital and when he returns to school. Not sure when he's scheduled to leave, but play therapy could help with his trauma."

"No doubt from that horrible father of his. Apparently, he's coming back from overseas and might fight for custody."

"Fat chance of that. I'll fight tooth and nail against it, even if I have to stay all night with the judge to convince him. After what he's put poor Lola through and exposing Samuel to violence, he will not see his son ever again," said Esmeralda.

Eva admired her tenacity. "I hope you're right. But we need to see what he's planning."

"Are you going back to see Samuel in the hospital?"

Eva gripped the phone tight, a lightness in her chest at the idea she might see Tomas again. *Stop it.* "I plan to go after dinner tonight and see how he's doing."

"Great. I believe the more familiar faces he sees, the quicker he'll recover, and the quicker he'll talk."

"Well, he did meet an EMT yesterday who took a bit of an interest."

"Oh, really? That isn't unusual. The EMTs often want to see how their victims are doing. It's admirable, really."

"It is. I agree. But Samuel took a liking to him. He seems to trust him after he brought him to the hospital. But what a tough job."

"Indeed. Anyway, I will let you go and see you at school on Monday. We'll talk more about his progress then, and ways to ease him back into class."

"I look forward to it, Esmeralda. Thanks again for calling."

"Pleasure." She ended the call and put on her walking shoes for another quick visit to the fountain.

CHAPTER 7

Tomas stepped inside the hospital with Gonzalo. The woman he'd met yesterday rose from her chair and straightened up her blouse, revealing cleavage as she straightened her posture. Samuel lifted a hand to slap it against Gonzalo's then Tomas's. Despite Samuel's smile, a hint of sadness understandably rested in his eyes, as if he'd been through much more than a twelve-year-old should.

"Hello, boys," said his aunt. He couldn't remember her name. She appeared abrasive and aloof, with her pointy nose, sharp eyebrows, hair wound tight in a bun, and her fringe pulled back. Her smile changed her appearance to give her a little appeal. She had to be in her late thirties.

Gonzalo nodded at her. "Andreina, was it?"

The woman licked her upper lip and offered her chair to Gonzalo. "Yes, that's right." She knit her brows and faced his friend. "Hello, Tomas."

How did she remember his name easily? They'd met yesterday for only a few minutes before she left for coffee. Gonzalo was also a stickler for remembering names, particularly women of an older age.

Samuel rested his bandaged arm on the bedsheet. His aunt spotted blood dripping, and she picked up his arm, but he shoved her away with a shake of his head.

"Samuel. We need to stop it from bleeding. Remove the bandage. It looks quite ratty, darling. The wound needs cleaning." She pressed the buzzer by the side of the bed.

More blood droplets stained the sheet, so Tomas handed him tissues. Samuel was wiping the blood from his bandage when a nurse with a large frame hurried into the ward. "What do we have here, dear Mr Martin?"

Tomas gasped. *Martin? As in Lola Martin?* It couldn't be, could it? When he'd spoken to the police, they only talked about Samuel and never disclosed his mother's name at the time.

Andreina squared her shoulders. "You need to change the wound, Nurse. I cannot believe that bandage hasn't been changed. It's filthy. What kind of establishment are you running here when you don't change his bandage? Ludicrous."

The nurse pressed her lips together and scrutinised Samuel's arm. She ignored Andreina who hovered over

Samuel. "Darling. We need to change your bandage. It's bleeding. We can't let it get infected. I'll be back."

"The nerve of the staff, letting this go on," Andreina said after the nurse left. "I think I'll have a word with the doctor here. Excuse me, boys." She got up and scurried out of the room.

Tomas chuckled. "Wow. She is a challenge."

Gonzalo whispered to Tomas. "It's kind of turn-on, man." He stood on the other side of the bed. "I like a woman who goes after what she wants."

Tomas couldn't believe he liked this woman. But then again, he'd always had an attraction to older women. "Okay. Whatever floats your boat." His mind turned to Lola. "Did the nurse say that Samuel's surname is Martin? Is his mother's name, Lola?"

Gonzalo angled his head. "Ah, yeah. Why do you ask?"

The nurse returned with a set of bandages and a wet rag. She attempted to remove the old bandage, but Samuel pulled away and wouldn't budge when she picked up his arm gently. "We need to check the wound, darling. Please let me take it off."

Tomas approached. "Listen, Samuel. How about I change it for you?" The boy still shook his head. "I had a wound like this once, and it got so infected I had to go to the hospital and take lots of medications. I felt sicker and almost died. Please, let's change the bandage." Samuel nodded slowly. "Okay then. I will do that."

When he heard footsteps behind him, Tomas' body perked up. But when he saw who it was, his shoulders sank. Andreina was back. For one moment, he had a fleeting thought it was Eva.

Ten minutes later, Tomas' heart skipped a beat when Eva stepped into the hospital ward with a spring in her step. He imagined running a hand through her long, glossy hair that ran down to her lower back. The sadness in her expression intrigued him.

When Eva turned to Samuel, he sat up in bed beside his aunt resting against the bed, reading a children's book. He smiled brightly, his hands resting on his lap. "Hi Samuel."

The cold woman stood up with her hand out. "Hello. I am Andreina, Samuel's aunt. And you are?" Her look matched her personality.

"Hi, I'm Eva, Samuel's special education teacher."

"Right. The boy still hasn't said anything. There is no news to report here."

The boy? He had a name. Tomas shrugged in Eva's direction. "Samuel's happy to see her. Can't you see he's excited?" Andreina kept staring at Eva.

Eva cleared her throat, her face turning red. "I understand, and there is no pressure from me, but I want to make sure he's got all the support he needs." She approached Samuel on the other side and wrapped her arms around him. He hugged her back.

"Hmm. I am here, and Samuel knows that." Andreina pointed to her chest, her anger evident in her glare. She stroked his cheek as if to show she cared.

Why did this woman behave this way with Eva? She was still rude towards him, but not as resentful as she was with Eva. Why judge someone before she knew them? But wasn't he doing the same thing? Judging this woman who must have had her reasons for being protective of her nephew.

"You can finish the book. I don't mind listening," Eva said.

Andreina picked up the book and resumed reading. Tomas shut out her voice, feeling a strong need to wrap his arms around this teacher. She appeared fragile with her trembling hands and awkward stance.

He approached her with a heavy feeling in his chest. "Would you like to grab a coffee at the cafeteria?"

She nodded. "Sure."

Tomas walked alongside her down the corridor, passing hurried medical staff carrying piles of manila folders or wheeling patients to wards. Chatter from nearby wards distracted him from the scent of Eva's musky perfume and fresh soap smell. He wanted to reach out and feel the softness of her clear skin and thread his hands through her hair, but he brushed those thoughts away.

Hating the silence as they entered the elevator, Tomas asked, "Are you okay?" He leaned forward and pressed the button to go down.

Eva chuckled as if nervous. "I don't know what I did to the woman, but she was a bit harsh, don't you think?"

"I agree, but I think she's just protective of Samuel. She's grieving, too, because she doesn't know where her sister is. It's still a mystery." They walked out of the elevator, passed multiple wards and cleaning closets until they reached the cafeteria. "What kind of coffee do you like? I'll go get it."

"Thank you." She hesitated. "A weak cappuccino." She pointed. "We can sit over there." She made her way to the table while he stood in the queue with at least ten people in front of him.

CHAPTER 8

Efren made his way alongside the rear of the cabin towards a sectioned-off vegetable patch. He carried a basket of packeted seeds, coriander, dill, rosemary, oregano, chives, and basil, which could be blended into soups and assorted meats.

Others around him bent down low as they pulled out weeds around the garden beds and glided a mower along a patch of lawn. Still others picked fresh flowers for an aromatic scent in the dining areas of the cabins.

The mild wind tickled his cheek. Putting down the basket, he pulled up his sleeves, dug into the dirt with a garden trowel, and planted the seeds before covering them back up with the soil. He wiped the sweat from his brow as he toiled for the next hour, planting a row of several metres of herbs alongside vegetables. He smiled to himself as he got up and walked back towards the cabin.

Marco headed towards him. "Great job, Efren. Looks like we'll have plenty of organic herbs and vegetables for our famous Spanish feasts. You deserve a reward."

He raised a brow. "I do?"

Marco nodded. "Miguel's looking for a fellow soccer player near the portable building, down there where the goal posts have been built. Juan's injured his foot. But stay away from that nearby building, as it's currently occupied."

"Sure," said Efren, shrugging his shoulders. He ran towards Miguel who was on the other side of the field, approached and gave him a slap on the hand. His new friend was short and slim, a little older than Efren at seventeen.

"Thanks, man," said Miguel. "But go get proper soccer boots in the compound. It rained last night, so it's muddy."

"But Marco told me to stay out of that building," said Efren.

Miguel flailed his hand, with a flash of darkness in his eyes. "The soccer boots are just inside the first room, but make sure you don't go anywhere else."

What was he hiding? "Sure," he lied, as his curiosity got the better of him.

Efren ran inside the sunken building, scanning the area for boots in the first room. Stacks of boxes and bunk beds surrounded him. Hangers of clothing, artwork and dining tables scattered the room for the use of those who lived and slept in this building. The smell of body odour made him wince.

He rounded the corner and came across another room filled with chest of drawers, unopened bottles of liquid, buckets, Buddha statues, gas bottles, and tiny bowls. This must be where they made the herbs. Curious, he opened one of the drawers and pulled out bottles of liquid with sticky labels. These must be the herbs they sold to the public.

Footsteps sounded close by. Quickly, he hid behind a cupboard and waited, as he was breaking the rules by being here. He peeked.

One of the leaders, Ana, rushed inside and pulled open the drawer with the vials of liquid. Picking one out, she ran towards a door and shoved it open. It creaked. "Oh, hell. You couldn't hold it, could you?" She sighed. "If you try anything, I'll kill you. Open up. This'll give you the buzz you need."

He heard a choking sound. "Please. No."

"This is what happens when you don't listen. That should teach you for rejecting Armando. You'll stay here until tonight for your punishment."

Efren's heart raced as he watched Ana rush outside. He snuck into the room, opened up the door and spotted the girl huddled in a corner. He held onto his nose against the stink of urine and faeces. The poor girl was chained by her ankle to a chair nailed to the floor. Her head hung low and she was crying but had her back to him. He wanted to reach out, but he shouldn't be here. She'd be released tonight, but even if she had rejected Armando, did she deserve this harsh form of punishment?

***

Tomas carried their two cappuccinos to their table, his heart skipping a beat at the way Eva stared into her lap. She appeared wistful yet preoccupied. From the way her hands shook and how she kept glancing back over her shoulder, he wondered if something had happened while he was in the queue for the last ten minutes.

"Here you go," he said, placing the mug in front of her.

She gave him a reassuring smile. "Thanks." Her hands glided over her upper arms as she hugged her body tight.

"Are you all right? You look worried." He hoped he wasn't crossing any boundaries as they barely knew each other, but a part of him felt like he'd known her for years.

He'd also noticed her glass eye, and wondered how that had come about.

Eva hesitated. "I'm … fine. Fine." She picked up her mug and sipped. "Tell me about you, Tomas. I am curious how your second visit with Samuel went."

Tomas wasn't about to give her his spiel about his childhood or how he might have known Lola before. Or even how he could relate to Samuel, understanding trauma only too well. He couldn't say any of that to this beautiful woman who drew him towards her like a magnet. She was a stranger.

But hell, the way she bit her bottom lip in thought or the way she rubbed the base of her throat endeared her to him. "I'm worried about the little man. He's obviously been through an ordeal and the police have yet to find his mother."

Eva knit her brows. "I'm sorry. I didn't mean to sound rude or invasive, but I was concerned. I worry about him, too."

He nodded. "The police will hopefully get to the bottom of it." He'd had enough of the dreary stuff. "Tell me about your job at the school."

She shrugged. "Nothing much to tell. I'm a special needs teacher who offers remedial education to secondary school students with disabilities, like ADHD, autism, dyslexia, and intellectual disabilities. I love the work and can't imagine doing anything else."

"Do you deal with a lot of behavioural issues?" asked Tomas, rubbing the rim of his mug.

"It is rare, but we do have a psychologist, Esmeralda, who is amazing with the kids. She's got a gift to get them back on track with her way of speaking at their level. They don't feel they're being talked down to. Some of the parents don't understand their children and this creates havoc at home. Esmeralda offers free family therapy to those struggling."

"Was Lola struggling with her son?"

Eva hesitated. "Sometimes, with his behaviour. Understandably when he's mute and most likely wants to talk but can't. He gets frustrated and has mild tantrums. But she dotes on her son and loves him with all her heart, which is why I don't understand where she might've taken him. It doesn't make sense."

"I imagine if they don't find the mother then there'll be a custody battle between Andreina and Samuel's father."

Eva huffed. "That man doesn't deserve to care for Samuel. He was abusive to Lola. It was the reason she left him. But I don't believe she ever told the authorities about him, so nothing's on record. It'll make it that much harder to prove he was abusive."

"Was he violent towards Samuel?"

"I tried talking to her once, but she said he wasn't. Though I couldn't tell if she was lying, and I wondered if that might've been the last straw." She focussed past him. "Lola finally found the courage to leave him. But exposure to violence is just as bad as experiencing it yourself."

"No doubt. A lot of mysteries around this case." He cleared his throat. "How well do you know Lola?"

She gave him a quizzical look. "We were close and got to know each other through Samuel and her volunteer work at the school. She'd help with events, read to the students, help those who needed attention. She was a godsend." Eva put a hand over her mouth, her eyes dilated. "I am so stupid. Why am I talking about her in the past tense?"

"It's fine. Only because she's not here, but have hope, Eva." He needed to find out for sure whether they were talking about the same Lola he knew. "Lola sounds familiar to me. Do you know where she might have grown up?"

Eva angled her head. "Lola grew up in Cortes and went to the local high school. I remember her telling me how her father was an alcoholic who wasted his money on drinking. He couldn't keep a job for long. Her mother had to work two jobs to raise her and Andreina. The father wasn't physically abusive, but only verbally, which still does a lot of damage."

Tomas' hands shook, his heart pounding as if it was about to explode in his chest. Eva looked down as if remembering. "I always found it strange how she'd inherited a lot of money from a dead aunt about two years ago, but never bought a new house. The home they lived in was falling apart, and yet she had the money to buy a decent home for her and Samuel. I asked her once, but she changed the subject."

Tomas felt sick to his stomach. "It's possible she needed the money for something more important." He drank down the rest of his coffee, needing to change the subject. He couldn't talk about Lola anymore. He had to reflect. "It's obvious you love your work, but what do you do in your spare time?"

Eva squared her shoulders and pressed her lips together. "I love to read and take slow walks around the centre of Madrid." She exhaled. "Occasionally, I'll take long drives to the Basque countryside. It helps me to come up with story ideas for my book, a work in progress. I love writing."

He was intrigued. "You're a writer?"

"Of sorts. I'm working on my first book. It's a domestic thriller novel where a woman is terrorised by a stalker."

He didn't want to take away her limelight by talking about his love of poetry, and his current works. "Sounds interesting."

"My mother inspired me with books. She would read to me every night as a child. Tell me stories about the small town she lived in when she was young. Interesting and tragic stories, and subconsciously I might have used those tales in my own writing. She tried reading books to my younger sister, Daniela, but she wasn't interested. She's the type that's too high-energy to be still with her thoughts. But I love her dearly."

"Are you two close?"

"We're like best friends."

"And your mother?"

"Up until about a year ago, we lived together, but then I moved out on my own. We're close, too. I don't know where I'd be without her love and support." She averted her misted eyes.

He was curious about her father, but he didn't want to ask too many questions at once. He was hoping they'd see each other again, but how could he ask without pushing her away? She might not have any interest in being friends, as that was all this could be.

CHAPTER 9

Eva sat inside Esmeralda's office, scanning the awards hung beside certificates of her degrees and training in clinical psychology. Esmeralda had come a long way for a woman of only thirty-five years.

Carefully arranged on her desk were two neatly stacked in-trays, a laptop computer with two monitors, and child psychology books, while in one corner stood a filing cabinet, a couch, beanbags, and a toy area. A locked filing cabinet stood behind the desk.

The broad window gave a view of Madrid's downtown skyscrapers, and admitted sunlight that cast a soft glow across her cheeks. Her long, glossy blonde hair nicely framed her petite physique.

"I know you visited Samuel in the hospital a couple of times," Eva began. "How did you find him? Did he give you any clue as to what's going on?"

Esmeralda leaned forward in her ergonomic chair while twirling a pen in her hand. She fixed chestnut brown eyes on Eva's, who noticed an occasional eye twitch. "I wish I could tell you something, but he still refuses to speak. Strange because we have a great relationship. It is obvious he's afraid of something. At this stage, we can't press as it could make him spiral further into his shell. Retraumatise him. We need to give the poor boy time, Eva."

"I understand, and I haven't pressed him at all. Do you think he could return to school anytime soon?"

"Not just yet. I don't believe he is ready."

Eva squeezed her hands. "The nurse did tell me he's wet himself a few times."

Esmeralda nodded. "It's not uncommon for that to occur after a traumatic incident. Lola mentioned how Samuel had wet himself not long after they left his father. Common response to trauma, particularly as a witness to violence. We need to tread carefully with Samuel." Her eyes lit up. "How are *you* doing?"

Eva shrugged. "I'm fine. It's been hard, adjusting to this as it gets me feeling insecure again. I don't want to have those dreams of the past anymore." She had confided in Esmeralda six months earlier about nightmares she was having about her father. Luckily, her colleague had given her strategies to combat the images. Now she meditated in the mornings and grounded herself by noticing her senses: "I can see the chair, I can feel my feet on the floor, I can hear the ticking of the clock, I can smell my perfume," and so on. She even journalled her thoughts.

Esmeralda reached over and took her hand. "I am here for you whenever you need to talk, Eva. Remember those activities we discussed. Keep doing them. It is a process, and I feel that any triggers will be about working with them rather than fighting against them. Validate your experience and you'll be triggered less over time."

Eva's heart warmed. "Thank you so much. I don't know how I would've managed without you these past six months."

"A pleasure."

They heard hurried footsteps and screams from the corridor. Eva stood. "What's going on?"

Esmeralda also rose. "Not sure. Let's go find out."

They stepped out of the office to find a huddle of students and teachers blocking their view of something. As they pushed through the crowd, they saw an EMT crouched over a woman, pressing hard into her chest. "Come on, come on." The man beside him looked familiar. *Tomas?*

When the woman on the floor regained her breath, she realised it was Isabela. But what had happened? Why had she stopped breathing?

Tomas and the other EMT staff member carried her gently to the stretcher and slowly wheeled her away. The crowd parted to let them through.

"I must talk to the principal about what happened. I'll see you later, Eva," Esmeralda said, and hurried away.

"See you, and thanks."

Tomas walked past her with a shy smile. "Hi, Eva. Sorry you had to see that. Walk with us to the ambulance." The other EMT nodded in greeting.

"What happened?" She quickened her pace towards the exit.

He rubbed his hands. "Not sure. We got a call from the principal about a woman in distress. She was having these weird symptoms and was gasping for breath. The hospital will no doubt find out why."

"Of course. I know her. Isabela. She's a mother and volunteers here." As she pushed open the doors, a gust of wind felt as if it penetrated her skin. She moved aside to make room for the EMTs. With an easy shove, they pushed Isabela on the stretcher inside the back of the ambulance. Then the other EMT climbed into the driver's seat.

"Listen, I must go, but I wanted to talk to you about something," Tomas said, leaning out the ambulance's rear door. "Are you free tonight?"

Eva's heart warmed. "I am."

"Great. What's your number so I can text you?" She recited it and he typed into his phone quickly before waving goodbye and closing the door.

What did he want to talk to her about? Was it something about Samuel or his mother?

CHAPTER 10

Tomas swung open the ambulance door and pulled out the stretcher, wheeling Isabela through the doors of the hospital as emergency doctors approached.

"What do we have?" asked a towering female doctor.

Tomas turned to her, frowning. "This is Isabela. She's hypertensive, short of breath, with weakness in her upper limbs. Under control, but it's worth checking out the effects of mercury. There've been too many cases lately."

"Mercury," said the doctor. Tomas nodded while Gonzalo curled a brow. "We'll be the judge of that."

They followed, passing wards and dodging passersby while ignoring the surrounding loud voices and multitude of patients who sat with bored expressions in the waiting area.

"I'll go fill in the report," said Gonzalo and headed towards the ward desks.

Tomas' spine chilled when he spotted two policemen walking inside to approach the nurse in charge at the counter. He scanned and listened but couldn't hear anything. Was it about Samuel? He had briefly spoken to the police about the boy and his ailments, but nothing more had come of why he had disappeared in the first place. Were they still investigating Lola's whereabouts?

The policemen strode past him and stepped into the elevator. Tomas wondered where they were going. Samuel was only twelve and Tomas remembered himself at that age. His father had put him to work in his fruit shop, which barely made a profit. He remembered one time he wanted to attend a popular birthday party, but his father said he had to work most nights and couldn't afford to hire other staff. He'd missed out on many parties and school events, and ended up lonely with hardly any friends. But once he entered high school, he'd started to assert himself, particularly after his father had done the worst possible thing he could do.

Tomas had played on his father's guilt, but he didn't care at the time. He felt he hadn't had a childhood; as if he'd had no voice and wasn't valued as himself. The only time his father had appreciated him was when he'd helped or had done what he wanted. But what about loving him unconditionally? Shouldn't a father love his children without reason or motive?

His gut ached and his legs wobbled beneath him as he heard a voice in the distance. "Tomas. Earth to Tomas," said Gonzalo.

He came out of his reverie. "Sorry?"

"I said are you ready to go?" He nodded. "Where were you just then?"

He shrugged. "Nothing." But when Gonzalo hesitated, he squeezed his shoulder. "Are we going?"

"I might pay Isabela a visit after our shift," his friend said.

Tomas knit a brow. "Why?"

Gonzalo grinned, his eyes lighting up. "She's beautiful and reminds me of my ex-girlfriend. It didn't work out between us, but I haven't had a serious relationship since."

Tomas nodded. "Stop comparing every girl to your ex. You might find the right one."

"Maybe I have." He waved him over. "Let's move."

Once they entered the ambulance, despatch sent them to another incident in Salamanca. "Heading over there now," said Tomas while Gonzalo manoeuvred his way through the centre of Madrid in rush-hour traffic.

Gonzalo chose a quiet highway to Salamanca that allowed them to gaze at towering buildings and monuments while navigating traffic and curves in the road. "Tell me about this woman, Eva. Why do you need to talk to her? Fancy her or something?"

Tomas' cheeks warmed and his parched throat made him hesitate as he swallowed. "No, definitely not. I wanted to talk to her about Lola and see whether she had any idea where she'd be."

Gonzalo faced him briefly. "Isn't that the job of the police? Why are you getting involved, man? What do you hope to accomplish?" He frowned. "It's Lola now?"

Tomas rested back against the seat and briefly closed his eyes to calm his breathing. "I ... I care about the boy. But also ..." He needed to confide in someone about Lola, but was he ready? His gut ached and his hands sweated.

"I get that, but it's not your job to find his mother." He chuckled. "Oh, I understand now. It's only a way for you to get close to Eva, isn't it?"

Tomas shook his head firmly. "Of course not. This is about Samuel and helping him. We might be able to give the police clues." He huffed. "I don't plan to do any investigating. When do we have the time, anyway?" He remembered Lucia leaving him with no warning, no preparation. He had loved her with all his heart, but she hadn't loved him anymore. The breakup had felt like being stabbed, as if she'd twisted the knife deep into his soul.

"She is pretty, though."

"I hadn't noticed," he lied. Who was he kidding? He couldn't get Eva's sparkling visage or glossy hair out of his head. Even the sweet way she looked away when appearing anxious. How would it feel to glide his hands through her hair?

"No harm in seeing someone. Don't you think it's time after ... you know who?"

"I have no intention of having a relationship with anyone, Gonzalo. I'm fine the way I am, and when would I even find the time? Between visiting my mum, catching up with friends, working on my poetry and doing this job, there's hardly any time left in the week."

"Hmm. Whatever you want to tell yourself."

"Let's drop it, please."

Gonzalo took his hand off the steering wheel and motioned across his mouth. "My lips are sealed, man. Sorry." He pursed his lips. "You were going to say something before. About Lola. You seem awfully curious about her. Why?"

The words burst out of him. "I knew her many years ago, Gonzalo."

His friend's shoulders lifted. "That makes sense now. Tell me everything."

***

Eva walked with heavy steps as she thought about Tomas. Why couldn't she get the man out of her mind? His bright blue eyes and beard made him appear rugged. Even the dimples on his cheeks enhanced his looks.

Her thoughts turned to his interest in Lola and Samuel. There had to be more to the story, given his curiosity about Lola. He must have known her, but in what capacity?

Shaking out his image, she passed through the strip of shops to her building. In her first-floor apartment, she found her books, notepads, and laptop where she had left them: on the ash-black couch. She had fallen behind on her thriller novel.

Eva poured herself a glass of water then walked out to her balcony. Resting against the railing, she took in the view of the gardens, nearby apartments, and other buildings. Smells of dust and spices drifted through the air. She loved taking time out to watch people without engaging in the busyness of it all, preferring to stay tucked away in her small apartment that made her feel safe. She trusted few people after what she'd been through, and wasn't about to change her mind so easily about Tomas, despite the sight of him sending tingles all over her body. The only people she trusted had had to earn their way into her heart.

After finishing her drink, she went to her bedroom. Opening her wardrobe, she scanned the few casual outfits she owned. What could she wear for her night out with Tomas? He had texted about meeting her inside the Asian restaurant near her apartment. But now, she huffed, unsure of what to wear.

Rifling through clothes racks, she pulled out a simple black dress. She looked at it, but shook her head. Too dressy. Then she flicked through more dresses, but they all said "I'm interested," which she didn't want. Her outfit had to be understated and casual.

After drawing out five more dresses that lay on her bed and gliding her hands over them, her heart beat fast when she realised the speeding time. She would be late if she didn't hurry and pick an outfit.

With a sigh, she picked up a tan skirt and white cotton t-shirt, dressed, washed her face and put on light, fresh make-up. Staring into the mirror, Eva hated her glass eye despite others telling her she was beautiful and sweet-looking. But she knew with her vision impairment she was restricted, and the glass eye had always aggravated her anxiety.

Eva took a deep, calming breath, squeezed her shaking hands and slowly walked back outside her apartment to meet Tomas. She assumed he wanted to talk to her about Samuel.

Shutting the door behind her, she placed a firm hand on her heart and stepped out of the building to face her anxiety.

CHAPTER 11

Eva stepped onto the cobblestone path down the slope and headed down the few steps towards the restaurant strip. The warm breeze feathered her cheeks and her shaky walk on unsteady legs made her light-headed. Why was she nervous? It wasn't as if this was a date, as no doubt it was about helping Samuel. Nothing more.

She held onto the metal rail down the steps and saw swarms of people sitting at tables outside the restaurant, talking, eating, and drinking. Loud voices rang in her ears as she felt her heart pound. Stomping passersby filled her with trepidation as she thought about Tomas suddenly walking behind her.

As she made her way inside, a male elderly waiter smiled.

"Hi, I've booked a table for two," she said.

"Follow me," the waiter replied.

Her stomach did somersaults as she pushed through tables haphazardly surrounding the space until reaching a table with a view of the greenery and people through the open bay window.

Before she had a chance to catch her breath, footsteps sounded behind her and a light touch on her shoulder gave her goosebumps. No doubt it was Tomas. She turned and grinned, imagining his lips feathering the hollow of her neck as he sat across from her, while she ran a hand through his beard.

"I hope you haven't been waiting long, Eva."

"Just arrived." The awkward silence made her avert her eyes as she scanned the menu, aware of his intense gaze. What was wrong with her? It wasn't like anything could happen between them when they had a little boy to think about.

He picked up the menu. "What's good here? I assume you've been here before."

She nodded. "I have, and I'd recommend the pizzas, nachos, or Pad Thai, but they also have organic meat and fish. If you're a bit exotic, they sell specialty coffee and organic kombucha, too." A part of her wanted to explain how she lived close by, but she barely knew the man. Not that she believed he was a serial killer, but you never knew these days.

A stout waiter with dishevelled hair approached. "Can I take your order?"

Tomas put down his menu and brushed a hand through his stubble. It was sexy. "I'll have the nachos and a strong black coffee, thanks."

"I'll have your Pad Thai and a water," said Eva.

"Of course," said the waiter as he rushed off with a curt nod.

Eva squinted at Tomas. "Was there a particular reason you wanted to have dinner tonight? Do you have news about Lola?"

He shook his head. "Not yet, but my friend in the police force, Leandro, said that he'd give me a heads-up if she's found." His eyes darted. "But the reason I asked you out tonight was ... was to see if *you* could tell me more about Lola. Sometimes having the public help the police can go a long way." He looked at his hands, his eyes briefly appearing distant. "Samuel kind of reminds me of me when I was his age, and I know that feeling of loss. I'd like to help the police if I can, so anything you remember about the day she went missing could be valuable."

Eva hid her disappointment but shook away her attraction towards him. A part of her hoped he'd wanted to see her with no underlying motive. But they were strangers. "You said Lola seemed familiar. Did you know her?"

He hesitated while scrunching up a napkin. "I did know her. We met through mutual friends and went out a few times before she had Samuel. Nothing serious." With eyes averted, his bottom lip quivered. Was something more going on? But it wasn't her place to ask when they barely knew each other.

She pushed aside a tinge of tightness in her stomach. "I remember Lola being worried about Samuel's mutism and tantrums because he couldn't express himself. She wanted to get help but at the time, Esmeralda—our school psychologist, you met her—had a sudden influx of troubled students. Her job is to counsel most of the kids at the school, and she has a limited time to work with them. Lola was looking for something more, so I told her about support groups for carers of special needs kids and gave her referrals. By the time I wanted to ask her about it, she and Samuel went missing. But her behaviour started changing gradually a year ago, when her husband left. It must have been the trauma catching up with her."

"Hmm. Do you think Samuel's father might have kidnapped her?"

Eva angled her head. "I don't think so. He's been gone for at least a year now, so it wouldn't make sense to kidnap her after that."

"You're probably right. It doesn't make sense. Is there any way we can get Samuel to give us signs or ways to communicate? Has he ever spoken to you?"

"No, never in the last couple of years. But Esmeralda was helping him with communication. She's only been on board for the past year, and before that, we had someone who wasn't half as great as Esmeralda. It takes time. I can try with him again, but Esmeralda believes we shouldn't pressure him, or he could regress."

"Makes sense," said Tomas.

Eva felt inspired to see Samuel one-on-one, as the privacy might make him feel less pressured. But would it be best to wait? "It's a waiting game, Tomas."

The waiter arrived with their drinks and food, and set them down. "Enjoy."

"I am not a patient man and hate feeling helpless like this. If only there was a way to speed up the process. Do you think his aunt is good for him?"

"I don't know. She's aloof, but she seems to care for Samuel. Lola never spoke about her sister, so I'm assuming they didn't get along. But it's all the family he has, apart from his father."

"I investigated the aunt's background and found she'd had a complaint made against her by a customer. She's a pharmacist and apparently gave the wrong dosage to this young woman—more than what was safely expected. She won the legal case, but I don't know much more than that."

"Wow. Did she lose her job after that?"

"She did, but I don't know if she's still working in the same industry. I wouldn't mind checking in on Samuel to assess whether she is taking care of him. Care to join?"

Eva's heart palpitated, wondering if they should get involved. It was hard for her to get out of her comfort zone, but Samuel needed special care. They had a right to be concerned about a little boy who was missing his mother, no doubt. "Sure. When did you plan to visit?"

"Oh, let's give it a week for him to settle in."

Eva leaned in. "I hope Lola's okay."

"Samuel did have cuts and bruises over his body, so I'm guessing they ran from something or someone."

Eva's stomach churned. She wished her uneasy feeling to be just that; a feeling without basis in reality. What if something unfathomable had happened to Lola, and how would Samuel cope with another traumatic experience?

CHAPTER 12

I n Chueca a week later, Eva and Tomas strolled along Gran Via until reaching a maroon apartment building with single balconies. Andreina and Samuel were fortunate to live here, as she loved the luxurious and classic neighbourhood with its wide range of restaurants that featured fusion, modern, and avant-garde. A hairdressing salon, jewellers, shoemakers, florists, and restaurants ensured all the essential needs for a resident.

Eva walked through the double timber front doors with Tomas behind, her breath hitching when her shoulder brushed Tomas as he stepped inside the elevator. The quiet between them unnerved her as she waited for the elevator door to open on Andreina's floor.

Before she could knock on the door, it swung open to reveal Samuel, whose eyes lit up. He ushered them inside.

Andreina rushed forward, her lips pressed tight. "Samuel. You should have called me first. You do not let anyone inside the house without my permission."

"Sorry," said Eva. "We didn't mean to invite ourselves in, but he feels comfortable with me. We're glad you've allowed us to visit."

"You are exactly on time," said Andreina as she led them through to the open-plan kitchen and its glossy marble counters topped with layered tea towels, coffee machine and toaster, surrounded by off-white overhead and low cupboards. Samuel sat opposite her. "Would you both like a coffee or something cold?"

"No, I'm fine," said Tomas.

"Me too," said Eva.

"Come on through." Andreina showed them to an apricot three-seater sofa next to two taupe padded armchairs surrounding a SMART TV and cabinet on a plush, flowery rug. A glass-topped coffee table finished the look, and a glass double door gave a view of the cityscape below.

Eva cleared her throat. "We wanted to see how Samuel's doing. How he's settling in."

Andreina pressed softly into his shoulder. "He is doing well, considering, but it was not necessary for you to visit this soon. He is family after all, and I am perfectly capable of attending to his needs." Her eyes darkened as if remembering something. "As for that abusive father and husband. Well, he is a different story and should never be allowed to care for his son."

Tomas turned to Eva for a second then faced Andreina. "Do you have any idea what might have happened to your sister?" Samuel's body stiffened.

Andreina looked at Eva. "Why don't you get Samuel to watch TV in his bedroom? He likes the cartoons."

"Of course." Eva rose and pulled him aside while following him to his room, which contained a double bed with two bedside tables and tube-like white lamps.

Finding the cartoon channel, she raised the volume and watched as his eyes brightened. He moved to his bed, covered by a brown chequered quilt, and picked up a drawing he'd been working on. Dark figures, black trees, mountains and a deep lake. He pressed hard with his crayon as he coloured the sky blue even while his eyes stayed glued to the TV.

Eva didn't want to ruin his good mood, so she returned to the living room and the exchange between Tomas and Andreina, whose veins protruded from her neck. She sat on the sofa beside Tomas, facing Andreina in an armchair opposite.

"My sister's always been a hopeless romantic, and that controlling husband of hers knew how to get her into bed. Before she knew it, she was pregnant with Samuel. That immoral man promised her the world and proposed, but little did she know he was a physical and psychological abuser. I tried to help, of course, but she wouldn't listen and swore he loved her. She said he got mad sometimes because he was under stress. She learned the hard way when she ended up in hospital with a fractured rib and two black eyes. She made up a story about falling downstairs at work and bumping into a table. But I did not believe her story. She claimed to have spoken to the police, but they didn't listen to her, so after that, she gave up telling them again. Not long after, he left suddenly. I found it strange how he easily left that way. He moved to Brazil, where his family lives."

"It sounds like she was lucky to have you as her support system," said Eva.

"Hmm," she said.

"Were you two close?" asked Tomas.

"Not really. We never saw life in the same way. She was the adventurer and not as responsible as she could have been. Too impulsive for my liking."

Eva intervened. "Do you have any children of your own?"

Andreina's eye twitched while a fingernail scraped the inside of her palm. She took deep breaths. "No, never married. But I am grateful to have Samuel living with me. He's like the son I've always wanted."

Eva felt bile in her throat. Was the woman happy her sister was missing so she could have Samuel all to herself? Did she have something to do with Lola's disappearance? Surely not.

Tomas frowned. "You didn't answer me before." He exhaled. "Do you have any idea what might have happened to Lola? Apart from her husband, does she have any enemies you know of?"

Andreina glared. "Who are you? The police? Why are you asking me such questions? If I knew where she was, I'd tell the police, so obviously I don't. That woman made her own choices, and now she has to lie in the bed she made. Whatever happened to her was her own fault. Poor choices. Samuel has always been better off with me. The responsible one and not the reckless one."

Samuel returned to the room and shoved his aunt, shaking his head fiercely.

"What's wrong, Samuel?" asked Eva.

Andreina grabbed his hands. "Behave yourself young man, or I'll take away your crayons. You treat me with respect, Samuel." The boy sneered before stomping back to his bedroom. "He must have heard what I said about his mother, but it was the truth. Now, do you have any more questions? Samuel and I are rather busy."

Eva cleared her throat, realising she'd used the words "*was* the truth." Why was she talking about Lola in the past tense? "Do you think her husband might be responsible for her being missing?"

Andreina laughed. "Her husband's too dumb to plot a kidnapping. She might have made enemies with the husband's family, but who knows. Like I said, I won't lose sleep over her bad choices."

"But aren't you worried about Lola?" said Tomas.

She hesitated. "Of course I am, but what can I do about it? It's the police that need to find her, but I doubt they will."

"Why do you say that?" asked Eva.

"Because she attracts trouble like a magnet and I think this time, she won't be able to get herself out of it."

"How can you be so sure if you don't know what happened to her?" asked Eva.

Andreina put up a hand. "Listen. I do not mean to be rude, but we need to go out, so if you don't mind."

Tomas got up and touched the base of his throat. "We'll be on our way. Thank you for speaking with us."

"Hmm." She rushed to Samuel's bedroom, and he came out. "Say goodbye to our guests, darling."

Eva shook Samuel's hand. "Bye. I do hope to visit you another time." He grinned.

Tomas gave Samuel a high-five, and the boy followed suit. "Bye, little man."

Andreina pursed her lips. "I'll show you the way out." She swaggered towards the door and ushered them out then closed the door quickly behind them.

As Eva walked along Gran Via, she watched Tomas. "What do you think?"

Tomas licked his lips. "I think she hated her sister with a passion." He blew out a breath. "Do you think she knows more than she's telling us?"

"I wish I knew, but I had the same thought." She ignored the stern look of a man who was trying to usher them into his restaurant as they passed by.

"Is Samuel safe with her?"

Eva nodded. "I believe so. I can see how much she cares about Samuel and don't think she'd intentionally hurt him. But she hates her sister. If that was my sister, I would move heaven and earth to find her, and pound on the police station's door every single day. But they obviously weren't close."

Tomas sighed. "Let's hope the police get lucky or find a lead. The longer it is, the harder it'll be to find her."

"I hope you're wrong about that, Tomas. Lola doesn't deserve this if she's in trouble, no matter what her sister says. Anyway, I need to go in that direction."

"If I hear anything, I'll be in touch." Tomas waved to her as Eva wondered whether Andreina had something to do with Lola being missing.

CHAPTER 13

Tomas knocked on his mother Marisol's door, noticing scratches and a loose doorknob. Overlooking the front yard was an unkempt garden with wilting rosebushes, dried bushes and overgrown weeds. It had been too long since he had worked in his mother's garden.

She swung open the door with one hand pressed against her lower back. "Oh, Tomas. So nice to see you. Come in, son. Come in." Her hair was tied in a bun and her short stature made her look weaker than she was. The black lines under her eyes showed she hadn't slept well. He wondered if her back was playing up again.

He leaned in and kissed her on the cheek. "How have you been, Mum?"

She grabbed him by the hand and led him to a back patio as he surveyed the overgrown lawn. "Oh, you know.

I manage, Tomas. But I am trying something new with my health, so we'll see how that works."

He gave her a quizzical look as she followed him inside a shed that was unlocked. He pulled out the lawnmower. "Is it something your doctor suggested?"

She smiled. "Not really. Something more natural."

He decided to talk about it later, after he'd cut the lawn. His mother went back inside, and by the time he'd pushed the mower through the half-metre-high grass, the back of his neck was sweating.

His mother returned with a pitcher of sangria and two glasses on a silver tray. She placed it on the table and poured two glasses, sliding slices of lemon and orange inside the liquid, then stirred it with a spoon.

Tomas sat opposite his mother. A vial of liquid sat on the table before her. "What is this, Mum?"

She picked it up and swallowed a little of the liquid, then wiped her mouth with a napkin. "Oh, I went to the market, and the owner recommended this natural herb for chronic pain. It hasn't kicked in yet, but he said to give it time."

Tomas wasn't a fan of alternative medicine without medical evidence. There were too many charlatans who scammed people out of their money. "How much did it cost, and why would you use something not recommended by your doctor?"

"Oh, Tomas. The painkillers the doctor has prescribed don't seem to work anymore, and I needed to try something else."

He rummaged into the back pocket of his jeans and pulled out his phone. Aiming it towards the bottle, he took a picture. "I am going to research this, Mum. See if there are any positive recommendations or reviews. I don't think you should be trying something without evidence of it working. Don't use anymore until I've checked it out." He reached for the bottle, but his mother beat him to it.

"No, no. I'd like to try it for a while. You don' know how bad my back has been. It's become intolerable. Surely there can be nothing worse than this when nothing else has worked."

He huffed, wondering what he could do for his mother's pain. "I still think you should see a specialist. Surgery might be an option. Think about it, please."

She nodded. "Fine. I will. I'll make a time with the doctor and get a referral." She sipped her drink.

Tomas drank his sangria. Having quenched his thirst, he stood. "I'll start on the door and fix that doorknob. I'll also prune the bushes out front."

"Thank you, darling. Now, what's new with you?"

He took a breath. "This young boy, Samuel, who I treated on the job might be in trouble, Mum." She knit her brows as he explained the whole story.

His mother gave him a reassuring smile. "Oh, darling. I am sure they will find his mother. But this Eva lady sounds just lovely. Is she girlfriend material?"

His heart skipped a beat. "No, Mum. We're only supporting Samuel, that's all. I don't' have the time nor desire to have a girlfriend. Besides, I hardly know her."

"But darling, Lucia wasn't a great woman. Don't let her make you a harsh judge when you might be missing out on the one. Please, darling. Be happy, okay?"

"I'll get started on that door." He drank down the remainder of his drink and walked back into the shed to lock away the lawnmower.

He was tired of his mother trying to marry him off and vowed to never give women another chance. Lucia had hurt him so much that he couldn't breathe.

Eva lay back in her chair at her desk in her office and re-read short stories she'd set for homework. But her mind kept drifting back to Samuel, and when he'd be returning to class. She wondered whether Andreina was being overprotective. Wasn't it better for trauma victims to get back into routine straight away?

She broke out of her reverie when Francisca tapped her on the arm. "Hey, Eva. Did you hear about Isabela after they wheeled her out of here the other day?"

Eva put down her papers. "No. What was wrong with her?"

"I went to see her at the hospital and found out." She shuffled her feet but remained standing.

"Out with it, Francisca. What was wrong?"

"Mercury poisoning. Might have been in something she ate."

Eva tilted her head. "Really. That's horrible. Will she be okay?"

"Yes, but it was a close call. Not enough in her system to kill her, but it gave her symptoms that could have been worse."

Eva crossed her arms, a chill lining her spine. "What is going on at this school? First Lola and Samuel go missing, and now this."

"I don't know, but obviously an accident that shouldn't have happened. How is Loverboy, Tomas?"

"'Loverboy?'"

"Oh, don't give me that 'nothing's going on' crap. I don't buy it. I can practically see the steam oozing out whenever you're near each other. Now don't lie. Don't you like the guy?"

Eva told the partial truth. "He is nice, but I am not attracted to him in the least."

"I am not going to debate this with you for now, but be warned. I will not, and I repeat, will not give up on this. I will keep hounding you."

"Sure, sure," said Eva, chuckling.

"Now let's go for a drink and a quick bite. I want to talk to you about a man I might learn to love. You can at least live vicariously through me, darling."

Eva shook her head, still laughing, knowing that her friend would not let up until she admitted to being attracted to Tomas. But it could never work between them when she had long since lost trust in the entire male species.

Tomas gazed at his computer screen in his apartment, puzzled by the medicine his mother had bought. He could not find it anywhere, no matter what keywords he added. There were no reviews, no recommendations and no manufacturer that produced it. What exactly was in this? He could get it tested, but who would waste their time testing it for no good reason? No, without proof of its value, he needed his mother to stop taking it.

He called his mother, but her phone rang and rang with no answer. He wouldn't think the worst. She might have been in the shower or out in the garden; not that she should be straining her back.

He swallowed and tried her again. "Mum, hi. It's me."

She moaned. "Hello, darling. Is something wrong?"

That didn't sound good. "Mum, what's wrong. Are you in pain?" Silence. "Mum. I was only ringing to talk to you about the medicine you took."

"Oh, that blasted medicine. I threw it away. It's made me feel lethargic, feverish, and my pain's much worse. You were right, Tomas, about not trusting this. I saw my doctor today, and he's referred me to a surgeon. It's time to get serious about my pain. I cannot live like this anymore."

He breathed a sigh of relief. "That's great, Mum. Tell me where you bought this vial. I want to speak to the market owner." She gave him the address. "Thanks. I'll check it out." He pushed a hand against his chest to calm his breathing. "I'm coming over."

"No, darling. I'm going to lie down. The neighbour said she'll check on me later. I don't want you to worry. I love you, my boy."

"I love you too, Mum. But are you sure?"

"Of course, Tomas. With a bit of rest, I'll be good."

He ended the call, his fists clenching at the idea of people selling dangerous alternative medicines. He turned off his computer, grabbed his keys and made his way to the small market on the outskirts of Madrid.

Ten minutes later, he stopped his car by the kerb and made his way to a man selling home-made jewellery. He approached the elderly gentleman who finished serving a young woman.

"Can I help you?"

"Yes, hello. I'm wondering if there's a market stall here selling natural herbs. It was here two weeks ago."

The man's eyes darted. "Yes, I remember. They were only set up over two weekends like a pop-up store, not here for long. But there was this young boy a while back who argued about the prices and wanted to negotiate a cheaper cost. The seller wouldn't budge, so the boy gave up and was about to leave when the seller handed him a flyer. He looked mesmerised by it, but I don't know what it was about."

"Right. Had you ever heard of these herbs before?"

The man shook his head. "No. I only saw them once. I'm guessing they wander around selling those herbs, but who knows how effective they are. It could be a scam."

Tomas nodded. "Thank you." He walked away and pondered whether his mother had bought an illegitimate product. She would have to stay away from it from now on.

CHAPTER 14

Efren carried a small box of lemons to the kitchen and passed a room that was partially open. Voices he knew came through the door, but he didn't recognise any of them. Intrigued after mixed messages he got from both Marco and the community, he stood by the door and listened. One of them sounded like Ana, the leader he rarely saw in the building.

"I can't do this anymore," said the woman whose voice he didn't recognise.

A huff. "Why not?"

"It's not what I thought it was. You lie and deceive people, and I never signed up for that. I want out."

"Listen, what we are doing here is for the greater good. I've dealt with the boy, and he'll treat her with more respect. But you know our mission. I can't control everyone."

Efren waited for more, remembering how Ana had treated the poor girl in the compound. The girl must've done something wrong to deserve such punishment.

"I don't know. My values don't align with the group anymore. I thought the group was different. The other day, Marco ..."

"Marco helps people find their way. Some need more convincing." She cleared her throat. "Think of all the good we are doing in the community, and how we've helped you and your family. Please don't lose sight of that."

"Fine. But how are you punishing this boy? Are you going to report him to the police?"

"Of course. Don't you worry. He won't be a part of our community anymore. Have faith and let's keep spreading the good word."

"If I see that again, I'm not going to be a part of this anymore."

"Understood. You're well within your rights."

Footsteps behind him made him gasp as he rushed through to the kitchen, splashed on a smile and dropped the box of lemons on the table. The three older women gave a curt nod as he helped to prepare fried fish and seafood for dinner.

But what was that conversation about, and what did the boy and Marco do?

"You're doing great, Antonio. Break up the word and sound it out." Eva's heart lifted at the progress her student had shown these past months. She hated the part of her job when students' frustration made them physically lash out. She remembered one student pulling at her hair, and it had taken two other staff members to move him away from her. That incident had reminded her of another time, another place.

The school principal, Ignacio, a sturdy-looking middle-aged man who wore glasses, knocked lightly at the door. She answered while the teacher recited a lesson. "Eva, the police are here and want to question you. They're currently in my office."

What was this about? She remembered that not that long ago the police had questioned her about Lola. Did they have a lead? Was Lola all right, or was it something worse? No, she wouldn't speculate. "Of course." She turned to the teacher who waved her away with a nod.

Slowly making her way down the corridor, she walked alongside Ignacio with an unsettled feeling in her stomach. A tightness in her chest led to tension to the back of her skull. She took deep breaths as she pulled over another chair beside Ignacio near his desk, while two policemen stood and greeted her.

"Hello, I am Officer Sanchez, and this here is Officer Diaz." They shook hands, but the beady eyes of Diaz unnerved her. He sported a greasy beard and stiff posture, towering over her. Officer Sanchez had smiling blue eyes and was clean-shaven. His relaxed posture put her a little at ease.

"What's going on, officers?" she asked.

Officer Sanchez adjusted his pants before shifting in his seat. "We would like to ask you some questions about Lola Martin."

Eva swallowed. "Why? Do you have any leads?"

His expression darkened as he turned to his fellow officer. "Lola Martin was found dead yesterday morning," said officer Diaz.

Eva's eyes blurred, and she pressed a firm hand against her throat, struggling to breathe. She closed her eyes and shook her head. *No, this couldn't be happening. Not to dear Lola. It had to be a mistake.*

A gentle hand squeezed her shoulder and brought her back to the room. "Eva, are you okay? Eva?" said Ignacio. "Can I get you some water?"

Eva shook her head. "No, I'm fine."

Officer Sanchez leaned in with a reassuring expression. "We are so sorry for your loss."

Eva fought back tears as she remembered the bruises and fractures poor Lola had had to endure. She could relate. "We were close. Does Samuel know?"

"Yes," said Sanchez. "The reason we're here is to see if anything strange has happened these past few weeks, or if you remember any small detail you might have forgotten last time."

Eva shed a tear, pushing a hand against her chest to soothe her palpitating heart. "Nothing, Officer."

"Do you know if anyone close might want to hurt her?" She shook her head.

Officer Sanchez turned to Diaz, who added, "How well do you know her sister, Ms Lopez?"

What was going on here? "Not well. Why do you ask?"

"No reason. We are only covering all bases. I know we asked you this before, but have you had time to think about whether Ms Martin had enemies? Did she mention anything that could have got her in trouble?" said Diaz.

"No. She was kind to everyone and had the biggest heart. I can't imagine who could do this to her. Everyone loved Lola. She had a few friends, too, who will be devastated." Eva fought against the clenching in her chest as if enclosed in a vice, struggling to breathe. "How and where did Lola die?" Eva asked.

Officer Sanchez said, "We can't divulge that information, Ms Lopez, but if you think of anything, please let us know. If you can get Samuel to talk about what happened, it would help. He is obviously too scared to give us any signs, but if he divulges anything new, give us a call."

"Of course," said Eva.

The officers got up and said goodbye, then walked out of the office.

Ignacio moved in his seat and touched her on the shoulder. "I am sorry, Eva. If you need time off work, I totally understand. I know how close you two were."

She smiled. "Thanks Ignacio, but I'll be fine. Work is a good distraction." She rubbed more tears from her eyes. "I can't believe she's gone. She didn't deserve this, Ignacio. I need to see Samuel."

"Please give him my best. Give it a week or so, then you could potentially work with him at home, so he doesn't get too far behind in schoolwork."

"Sure. I will talk to Andreina about it and hope she's okay with that."

Ignacio nodded. "Okay then. If you need time off, please holler." He pulled her into his arms and stroked her upper back, comforting her with his support.

She pulled away. "Thank you." She walked through the door as if gliding down into a surreal world that didn't make sense. Her heart went out to dear Samuel. How were he and Andreina coping with the loss?

CHAPTER 15

Tomas stepped outside of his apartment in La Latina and crossed the road. The odour of exhaust fumes mixed with dust permeated the air. Motorcyclists zoomed past him and parked on the footpath, while the sounds of tooting horns, cars skidding, muffled voices of passersby and perching seagulls gave him a headache. He'd had bad news.

The gut-wrenching pain, sense of guilt, and tears wouldn't stop. He had cared for Lola at one time, and she had cared for him. He had to honour her by getting justice and finding out exactly what happened to her. Lola didn't deserve to die that way.

Tourists and locals flocked to La Latina and all the plazas for the array of tapas and Spanish beer which Spaniards and foreigners enjoyed alike, as shown by the year-round congestion of people and traffic. The hustle and bustle of his hometown was not welcome today, but he hoped to comfort Eva who was meeting him at the local bar.

He ambled along the cracked, uneven streets, his heart racing at the idea of seeing Eva. He couldn't stop thinking about the way she pressed her lips together when nervous, or how she rubbed the inside of her palm which seemed to ease her anxiety. Her wit and the way she cared for Samuel endeared her to him even more.

He made his way to a table outside and sat underneath a white umbrella with his elbows resting on the table. Groups of people sat around him as he waited for Eva.

Waiters bustled about until one of them approached, but he waved him away. "Give us a few minutes. I'm waiting for someone."

Tomas assumed the police had spoken to the school about Lola's death. Luckily, his friend in the police force, Leandro, was his contact and occasionally shared information when it didn't compromise their investigation. But Leandro knew about his past with Lola and understood his need for justice.

A tap on his shoulder alerted him. "Hi, Tomas." Eva sat across from him.

Her appearance left him speechless. She wore an off-the-shoulder black t-shirt and tight white skirt. But her sombre expression tugged at his heart. "Hi. Thanks for meeting me."

She waved over a waiter. "A sangria please," she said.

"I'll have the same," said Tomas.

The awkward silence gave way to locked gazes and silence until he broke the ice. "Did you hear about Lola?" She nodded. "Are you all right?"

She shook her head and clasped her hands tightly into fists. Her breathing accelerated, and she bit her lower lip. "I can't believe she's dead, Tomas." He remained silent. "I wish I knew why. It's killing me inside."

Tomas leaned forward and stroked her hand opposite him. "I know, and I am sorry. I can't imagine what you're going through, Eva. I know you were close." His heart burned at the way she turned away, but not before she'd shed a stream of tears.

Eva moved her hand away from his as if ashamed. "It's only been a few days, but I feel like I just heard. I'm still in shock."

"I know. It'll take time, but I'm here if you need to talk. Any time, any day."

"Thanks, but I'll be fine. I know grief all too well."

Was he being too invasive? "If you don't mind me asking, who did you lose?"

She turned to him. "My father."

He shook his head. "How long has it been?"

The waiter set down their glasses of sangria. "Can I get you anything else?"

"No, thank you," said Tomas.

"Okay, then. Enjoy." He walked away with an easy smile.

"It's been a couple of years since he died, but the worst thing is that he was abusive and drank a lot," Eva answered. "We even discovered a lot of family secrets. I was kidnapped around the time of his death, too, but it's a long story so I won't go into it today."

His chest squeezed tight as he realised that Eva had faced more than most. "Have you been able to get closure with your dad?"

She shrugged. "Still a work in progress. He's the reason I have a glass eye." His body stilled. *What the hell.* "All because of low school marks, he threw a glass at me that shattered into my eye. The glass hit my headboard while I was crouching on the bed. It shattered and a shard hit me in the eye. He never apologised for that."

Tomas got up from his seat, pulled her towards him and hugged her tightly while caressing the back of her head. He had no words for what she'd been through. His mind turned to mush at the way his insides flailed.

"Thanks, Tomas." She pulled away, and he returned to his seat, fighting back his own tears. His heart felt like it would explode out of his chest.

"Even if he didn't apologise, his actions showed he was sorry. He stopped drinking and became a better person until ..."

"His death?"

She nodded.

"It's unfair that once he changed he died," Tomas continued. "You haven't had much of a break. I'm guessing Lola's death triggered the pain over your dad."

Eva averted her eyes. "I am sorry. Here I am talking about me when you were close with Lola at one time. How are you, Tomas?"

He steeled himself, ignoring the pain in his heart. "I'm fine. We need to support Samuel. I can't imagine what he's going through."

Eva leaned forward. "Will you come with me to see how he's doing?"

"Of course. If you ring Andreina, we can make a time for tomorrow night. If you're free. I won't be working then."

"Okay." Eva knit her brows. "I take it your friend told you about Lola?"

"Yes. Leandro's a detective with the National Police and will be working her case. Lola seems to have been involved in something dangerous." He sighed. "We need to see if we can get Samuel to talk. He trusts you, so maybe in time."

"I tried, Tomas, but something's truly spooked him. If he knows what happened to his mother, he might not say anything if he's been threatened."

"I don't want you involved in this, Eva. You've been through enough."

She pressed her lips firmly together. "No, that's where you're wrong. I might get anxious at times, but Lola was a friend, and she deserves justice. Besides, I've had a bit of self-defence training. After what happened, I needed to build my confidence." Tomas's stomach somersaulted at the idea she wanted to help. He didn't want anything to happen to her despite her training, because if it did, it would be all his fault. He couldn't let someone down again.

What if he pulled back and let the police solve this? But no, he couldn't stop fighting for justice for Lola and Samuel. He'd been traumatised like that little boy and related to his plight. He had his history with her, too. "I want you to be careful, Eva."

She waved a finger. "Do you know how Lola died? Did she suffer?"

He averted her eyes. "You don't need to know, Eva. Leave it alone."

"Please tell me, Tomas. I need to know if she suffered. Please. I'm a big girl and can take it."

He took a calming breath and pushed the image out of his mind. "Fine." He swallowed. "They shot her before slashing her throat." He clenched a hand. "I'm sorry."

The look in her eyes was much worse than anything he'd seen from her before, and he felt like an idiot. Why couldn't he lie about her death?

Her hands shook. "Overkill isn't it, or ..." Her eyes misted. "She might have still been alive, so they cut her throat, is that it?"

"I'm sorry. Leandro said the medical examiner believes that." He wished he could take her away from all this.

CHAPTER 16

Eva couldn't imagine the terror Lola felt when her enemies had killed her. How she must have worried about leaving Samuel behind without a mother. Too saddening to ponder.

A sense of unease filtered through her pores. Her breathing became shallower, and her throat constricted. Even the way Tomas fixated on her made her feel like a victim.

She didn't want that. She had to maintain her sanity and not cringe at every little thing. Yes, her father had traumatised her, as had her ex-boyfriend, but she didn't have to define herself by it. It was time to move on from her past, but could she?

She drank the remainder of her sangria with quaking hands and perked herself up. Tomas made her feel safe, but she couldn't fall for him. Men appeared nice until you let your guard down, then they'd get you in the worst way possible.

Eva's blood ran cold when she spotted someone in the distance watching her. Someone standing behind a tree, wearing a hoodie and dark glasses. Could she tell the gender?

With a shake of her head, she looked away, knowing she was being paranoid. When she turned back to the tree no one was there. Had it been her imagination? This case about Lola was making her see things.

"How about a cheese and ham board to nibble on?" Tomas asked. She nodded, so he waved to a waiter and ordered the snack. "Let's talk about other things, Eva. I can see you're clearly rattled." She averted her eyes, her heart skipping a beat.

"Of course," she said. "But I told you my story. I haven't heard yours."

His eyes darkened. "Not much to tell."

"Tell me what you do in your spare time. Do you have any interests outside of medicine, or are you a workaholic?"

He chuckled. "Of course." He cleared his throat, his face flushing. Was he nervous talking about himself? "I like to go for runs in the mornings. I enjoy thriller movies, and I ... I ... write poetry."

Eva angled her head. "Poetry? Interesting. Do you have anything published?"

He shook his head. "Only informally in a few magazines, but no book published. That's my next goal, but I do occasional poetry readings in bars."

"Wow. That's amazing. I'd love to read your work sometimes. Do you write with a specific theme or topic in mind?"

He swallowed. "Childhood trauma, love, wars, family life, that sort of thing."

"Sounds deep, but it must be rewarding to do that, even having your work out in magazines. It's an achievement." She stared at his lips, curious about how they'd feel against her own. Was he a slow kisser, or did he devour a woman with his lips? The feel of his mouth against her throat, neck, and ... *Stop.*

He stared at her oddly. "It helps me sort through conflict in my head, lets me express myself, and helps me make sense of this tortured world. Sorry, I'm getting morbid again. How is your writing going?"

She noticed him staring at her lips, but she brushed off the erotic thoughts of him taking her over this table. "I'm trying to do at least a few pages a day and hope to get it published."

"What's the story about?"

"A stalker hell-bent on revenge, with a touch of romance between those who take him down. But I'm only half-way through. It still needs work and who knows how long it'll take." The story was about working through her own inner and outer demons and fighting against injustice. She needed that sense of control.

An elderly waitress smiled at them as she laid out the cheese board. "Enjoy."

"Thank you," said Eva.

"When do you think you'll finish it?"

"Not sure, because it's my first attempt at writing a novel. I've written a few short stories but they're sitting in a drawer, gathering dust."

Tomas picked on a piece of ham and a tiny sliver of it stuck to his lip. "I'd love to read them, dust and all."

"No, I'd rather you not. They're not great. I most likely have to edit those before anyone reads them." She pointed to his mouth, and he wiped it but in the wrong spot. "No, it's over here." She moved forward, touched his upper lip and wiped off the remnant of ham. "All gone."

Tomas gazed at her, not saying a word. He took a breath. "I get that, Eva. I do hope to read them one day as an objective observer. When you've gone through them." She nodded. "No pressure, though."

Eva wondered if they'd still be in touch by the time she finished the story. Once this case was resolved, they'd most likely go their separate ways.

A deep, empty feeling in her stomach made her want to cry her heart out. "I have to finish the story first, but it's been hard to write with everything going on." She placed a piece of cheese onto a dry cracker and bit into it. The way Tomas kept his focus on her mouth gave her palpitations.

"I know." The awkward silence heightened her anxiety levels, especially as their eyes locked while he licked his bottom lip. It was damn sexy.

He angled his head. "Do you have ideas for other stories?"

Eva knit her brows. "Possibly. I have an interest in the psychology of cults, so my next book might be based on that. But first I need to finish this current one."

"Interesting," he said as he placed a hand underneath his chin. "You intrigue me, Ms Lopez. It's as if the more I peel away your layers, the more fascinating I find you."

Her vocal cords froze, and she didn't know what to say. The back of her neck tingled, and she could barely make out the swarms of people rushing around them or hear the revving of engines and beeping of horns. It was as if only the two of them existed in this moment.

Breaking out of her reverie, she grounded herself again. "Anyone can do what I do if they put their mind to it. No big deal, Tomas." She cleared her throat then dove into the nibbles by biting into an olive. It was delicious.

The silence was awkward as they shared the platter until it was time to leave. But the more she got to know Tomas, the more she got herself in trouble with the way he made her feel. She had to stay focussed on finding Lola's killer and helping Samuel.

CHAPTER 17

Tomas wrapped his arms around Samuel. "I am so sorry, man."

"No, noooooo," Samuel said before returning to silence, his body shaking against him in his aunt's living room. Tears dripped down Tomas' neck before Samuel ran over to the corner of the room and cowered, sobbing to himself.

Tomas stared over at Eva, whose eyes dilated while the rest of his body remained rigid. His heart lifted at Samuel's vocalisation. It was progress, despite the sad occasion.

A bookcase in the corner held pregnancy and childcare books that appeared worn at the edges. On a three-seated crème sofa lay plush pillows, three stuffed toys arranged around them. Open bay windows let in soft sunlight which created dark shadows over Andreina's face.

He saw the darkness in Andreina's eyes. But it wasn't grief. It looked like envy. Did she want Samuel only to herself? How did she truly feel about Lola's death?

Eva approached Samuel and lay a gentle hand on his quivering shoulder. "I am sorry, Samuel." The boy shifted then ran off to his room. She faced Andreina. "I am truly sorry."

The woman squinted. "I am not surprised. At least Samuel has a home with me. He's not alone. He'll never be alone."

Tomas and Eva shared a quizzical expression. Did the woman have a heart? He sat alongside Eva on the couch while Andreina sat stiffly in the matching armchair nearby.

"Is that the first time you heard him speak?" asked Eva.

"It is, but I'm not surprised it would take another trauma to extract his sadness. Esmeralda appears to be assisting him," said Andreina.

Tomas took a breath. "If he can tell us what happened to him, it'd be a bonus. Have you tried speaking to him?"

"No, I would rather not re-traumatise him. I am not a psychologist, so I will leave that in Esmeralda's capable hands." Andreina leaned forward. "Would you like a beverage?"

Eva shook her head. "I am fine, but thank you."

Tomas said, "All good." He got up. "I might see how Samuel is doing. Is it all right if I go into his room?"

"If you must, but please don't question him. He is fragile now," said Andreina as she tightened her bun.

"No worries," he said.

As he walked inside the child's room that featured a single bed, bookshelf and armoire, he saw Samuel lying on his stomach near the window as if he needed sunlight on his cheeks. He gazed at the boy when he started to scratch the back of his neck incessantly. "What's wrong, buddy?"

Samuel shook his head and put up a hand as if to say it's nothing. Tomas looked at Eva as she entered the room.

"What's going on?" Eva sat on the edge of the bed, her eyes directed to Samuel.

"He seems to have an itch, and I wouldn't mind looking at his neck. He might've hurt himself," said Tomas.

The door opened further when Andreina made her grand entrance. "Oh, leave it alone. He is fine. Don't you believe I can take care of my own nephew?"

Samuel moved and stood up, sighing as if he was in pain, his hand continuing to scratch.

She huffed. "Fine. If it's okay with Samuel. I am not happy you are invading his personal space, but if you must."

"Is it all right if I check, little man?" Samuel nodded and sat on the other side of the bed as Tomas turned him over across his lap and scanned the back of his neck. The skin was filled with tiny spots and redness. "There's a mark, but I can't see it properly. Do you have a magnifying glass?

"What is it?" Eva asked.

When Andreina stormed off, he said, "I can see only two letters–could be P and H." He whispered in her ear, not wanting to let Samuel hear him. "I think he's been branded or marked. It must have been painful for the little man. Whoever did this, we need to let the police know."

"I cannot believe this."

Samuel stared into the distance as if he was recalling a memory.

Andreina returned and handed him a magnifying glass. "Here you are."

Tomas hovered over Samuel, who readily bent down. He made out tiny letters spelling out "Peace and Harmony" in fine print.

"I'm surprised the hospital didn't pick that up, Tomas," said Eva.

"It's too small. If he didn't scratch himself, we wouldn't have searched there, either." He turned to Andreina. "This must mean something. Do you know what it is?"

"I have no idea. I wouldn't be surprised if Lola put it there. She always had to make a statement." Andreina scoffed.

Tomas had an uneasy feeling in the pit of his stomach.

Tomas, Eva and Samuel sat in a quiet room with Leandro. "Hmm. Interesting, but I'll need confirmation that this is coming from Samuel." He smiled at the boy. "Can I check, Samuel?" He turned to Tomas and Eva with a serious expression.

"Go on," said Tomas. "He is here to help you."

Leandro peered through a magnifying glass, an unreadable expression across his face. "We'll need to look into this." He snapped a photo with his phone.

"Do you think Samuel might have been part of a spiritual group of some kind?" Eva asked.

Leandro placed his thumb and index finger across his chin, pondering. "It's possible, but it could also be a religious group. We'll get our forensic team to investigate." He huffed. "If he was part of a spiritual or religious group, whether it's meditation, yoga, then that's their business. Nothing illegal about that. There are no laws against these groups that wish to help humanity." He hesitated. "Unless we can link it to murder, but at this stage, we have a branding symbol, and nothing else. If Lola was having issues with Samuel, she might have needed a spiritual group to help."

"Did Lola have the same mark?" asked Eva.

Leandro averted his eyes. "As part of an ongoing investigation, I can't disclose that information, Eva."

Tomas got his answer. "You can whisper it to me, friend."

Leandro shook his head. "Not a chance, man."

Eva inched her way forward. "But what about Samuel's fears? That should count for something so you can make this a priority."

"We are exploring all avenues, Ms Lopez. Please leave the police work to us. We'll be in touch if there's anything of value. But there are limits to what I can disclose, so if it is relevant to you both, I will let you know. Otherwise, stay out of this."

Tomas had a bad feeling. He knew there were missing pieces to this puzzle, and that most likely something sinister was involved in Lola's murder and Samuel running away. Could he stay back and do nothing?

CHAPTER 18

N ow Efren, we have chores we expect you to do after our workshops and meetings, but most of all, remember our mission. We look out for each other and abide by the rules."

Efren nodded, curious about two people entering a portable building. He pointed. "Who cleans the place over there?"

Marco waved his hand. "Oh, don't worry about that. We have the regulars clean it." He pointed a finger. "It is out of bounds to you, okay?"

"Sure." Efren's eyes darted around the peaceful space that featured towering trees, low brush, a group of small cabins, weatherboard homes, ugly-looking dormitory-style houses, and a sunken white building. He was curious when an older man and young girl headed inside a cabin on the other side of the sunken building.

Marco looked at him. "He's teaching her self-defence. Specialised classes that work best one-on-one."

"I wouldn't mind learning self-defence. Can he teach me?"

Marco nodded. "Of course, but for now you need to scrub the toilets in this section, fill up the troughs for the washing, and rake the leaves around here. When you've finished, speak to Maria and she'll assign you more tasks. Then tonight, we celebrate with a special feast in the dining room."

He nodded. "Right. What's the occasion?"

He chuckled. "Every day is a blessing, Efren and we celebrate life, love and connection with others. Before you see Maria, complete your assigned tasks, and I shall see you tonight."

The last time he'd seen Maria, she was upset about something but wouldn't explain why.

Eva leaned over the balcony railing outside her second-floor apartment at Plaza de Espana with her friends, Blanca and Kim, and her sister, Daniela. She gazed out at passersby, the multitude of surrounding apartments, the locals and tourists making their way to a strip of shops and restaurants. The warm breeze moved across her cheek as she pondered the plight of Samuel. She hoped his aunt could care for him. She could do with a little more warmth.

Eva headed back inside, and the others followed her to the couch and armchair as they picked up their glasses of prosecco and nibbled from a cheese, ham, and cracker board. "I thought Sofia was coming?"

Daniela scratched her temple. "She had an emergency dance class to take. We wouldn't normally run a dance class on a Sunday, but a few students occasionally need extra tutoring. She sends her regards." She toyed with the gold necklace around her slim neck. "How are you doing, girl?"

"I'm fine, Dani. I don't think the police will do much, though. Too many more important cases to deal with. But I keep thinking about how poor Lola suffered." She explained the branding and cult theory.

Kim, a youth worker and yoga teacher, understood the trauma of youths. "Do not go there, Eva. Take Samuel out and get him relaxed. He might give you some clue if he can let his guard down in a safe space."

"Sounds like a plan. I could do that. But what if I speak to the local church here? Do you think the priest might have heard of this Peace and Harmony group?" Eva threaded a trembling hand through her hair.

"It is a good start," said Blanca, who was a journalist and knew how to investigate. She had endured her own trauma when she had worked for a year in Brazil. "But see what the police come up with first, Eva. This could be dangerous."

"I don't see how talking to a priest can be dangerous. I'll be careful, don't worry."

"The way the world is out there nothing surprises me anymore," said Blanca. "Take one case I'm working on now. A few people in recent times have been hospitalised for mercury poisoning. Some of them have died, too. It's heartbreaking."

Eva gasped. "Why is that happening?"

"Money-making scheme, I'd say. Apparently, it's been bottled to appear like a herbal remedy for chronic pain." She curled a brow. "People want to believe in any magical cure. But it's deadly."

"Jesus," said Daniela.

Eva's phone pinged with a text from Francisca. She got up. "Sorry to break up this morbid topic, but I'm going to heat up the paella, ladies. Francisca is on her way, and I'm sure you're all hungry."

"We'll all help, girl," said Daniela. "I'll get the wine so we can chill."

"I will set the table," said Kim.

Blanca placed her hands across her waist. "What can I do?"

She turned to her. "How about you season the salad?"

Blanca gave her a thumbs up. "Great." She headed over to the kitchen and retrieved the salt, oil, and vinegar. While pouring the oil over the salad, she said, "You and this guy, Tomas, seem close. What's going on there?"

Kim stopped what she was doing? "Oh, leave Eva alone. She is getting to know the man and they have a good cause to work towards: Samuel."

Daniela pulled out the wine from the fridge and winked at her sister. "Right on, Sis. It's about time you get it on with a man. How long's it been since that jerk hurt you? It's time you meet someone you deserve, girl."

Eva sighed. "Oh, come on, ladies. Tomas and I are on a mission. We want justice for Samuel and Lola, so there's absolutely no time to think about anything romantic. Besides, I am done with men. None of them can be trusted."

"What about Tomas? Do you think you can trust him?" said Blanca.

"I don't know. Possibly, but I cannot think about romance now."

"You only need to take it one day at a time," said Kim. "But be careful with this case. Who knows who might have murdered Lola. If it was a particular religious group, you don't know how widespread this can be."

"Would you like me to look into things?" asked Blanca.

Eva's heart warmed at the support and shook her head. The front door opened, and Francisca stepped inside.

"Hi guys. I am sorry I'm late, but let's get this party started."

The girls chuckled, and one by one wrapped their arms around Francisca.

Eva pushed her through to the kitchen. "We can enjoy dinner with a nice glass of wine." Francisca got along with anyone she met, a tad more extroverted than Daniela.

Eva's friends gave her respite from Samuel's plight.

CHAPTER 19

Efren's heart warmed as he drew in the man's wise words, his eyes in a daze as he watched his leader, Cesar. Such heart. Marco stood beside him, equally fixated.

Since living here, he had forgotten about his school suspensions, his mother working three jobs at all hours of the night, barely seeing her, and the tightness in his chest as he remembered the way his father had died. Marco mentioned he'd called his mother and convinced her to let him keep him here for a few months of rehabilitation, which was what he had called it. He had wanted to speak to her, but no phones were allowed while he was on his personal mission. Surely, she would understand.

Efren stared at Cesar, who wore a thick white robe and bowed to his audience with a glint in his eye. "Peace and harmony, my brothers. Repeat after me: peace and harmony." His devoted followers repeated his words like a goose to its flock, Efren included. "Now bow down to the spirit and let him reward us with riches beyond our wildest dreams. Who is your god and leader?"

"You are," said Efren and the loyal spectators of women, children and men who clasped their hands in prayer.

"Yes, we are the only ones you can trust. A new world here with all your blessings. The world out there is cruel, unforgiving, vicious. In here, we will reward you with kindness, love, peace, and wealth. But full obedience is required. Those who don't obey, will be punished. To peace and harmony, my devoted followers. What do you believe in, my devoted people?"

"Peace and harmony," said the people.

"Remember that to obey means your soul will rise back from the ashes and know everlasting tranquillity. All of you here have faced hardship and conflict, but no more. Here you are accepted, loved, and devoted to a higher spiritual self. Transcendence is yours, but only if you obey. What do you believe in?"

"Peace and harmony, our god and saviour."

Cesar waved his hands. "Now this group on my left will be recruiting new followers, selling our products to stall owners around the country. We must continue to sell these herbs to make enough money to sustain us for growing our own crops. Others will start by holding spiritual classes online until they believe and will join us here forever. Those of you who still owe us more funds will be called to us later today if that isn't organised. We will struggle otherwise. That will be all for today." Cesar walked off the stage with Marco following him.

Marco whispered to the leader as he turned to Efren with a curled brow. Were they talking about him? Did they find out he'd entered that building without permission? But surely that woman who was punished had done a lot worse than he thought. Ana wouldn't have hurt her for no reason.

Eva unwrapped her sandwich and took a bite of the salty ham encased in mayonnaise, cheese and tomato in the school staffroom. The tomato dripped on her shirt, and she shook her head at the remnants falling on the table. She dipped part of her napkin in the glass of water and wiped the mess.

Other teachers greeted her with smiles until Isabela stomped inside with her head down in deep thought. "Hi, Isabela. How are you feeling?" Isabela scrubbed her hands clean for a minute but didn't reply. "Isabela?"

She slowly turned after turning off the tap, her hands red-raw after the hard cleaning. Bright red manicured nails stood out. "Sorry?" Isabela's feet shuffled along the ground as her eyes darted past her. The bright designer t-shirt and skirt, with wedged heels made her appear like a top model.

"I am sorry about Lola. Are you all right?"

She forced a smile. "Oh, fine. Thanks." Isabela made her way to the table opposite and lifted her shoulders. "I do miss Lola. We were friends, and she loved helping the kids in class. She was good with them and didn't deserve to die. No one does." Her hands trembled as she threaded her shaky hands through her hair, her eyes skimming past her again. "Something's seriously wrong," she whispered to herself.

"What was that?" Eva's heart went out to her. It was obvious she was taking Lola's death hard, especially seeing as they were so close. Many of the people here had been close to her, including Eva.

"Oh, nothing." Her hands clenched tight as she stared into space in thought. Her breathing quickened as she later bowed her head, tears springing from her eyes.

What was Isabela hiding? "I miss her too and hope that in time Samuel will be okay."

Isabela rubbed her wet eyes. "Samuel is an amazing boy. I wish he would talk about what happened to him. Have you heard anything from the police? Do they know who might've done this, Eva? Are there any leads at all?"

She put up a hand. "Wow. That's a lot of questions. But no, nothing. Esmeralda believes he'll open up in time, and she's working with him. He's too scared to talk. But whatever it was had spooked him enough to stay quiet."

"Sure. Threats don't help, especially when you keep looking over your shoulder to see if they're watching you, listening to you, knowing your every move. Poor Samuel to have to live like that."

What was she talking about? "What do you mean about Samuel having to live like that? Do you know something, Isabela?"

"What?" She unbuttoned her blouse to reveal a redness around her chest.

"Do you know anyone who's being threatened? Or is Samuel in trouble?"

She shrugged. "Why would I, Eva? I only meant his trauma with his father. Nothing else. It's all good, and I'll get over it." Again, tears rolled down her pale cheeks as she wiped them away.

Distraction might help. "Your son's doing well in English. Learning all his words. He wrote an amazing essay the other day." Eva finished the last bite of her sandwich and wiped her mouth with a tissue.

She nodded. "He works hard, but no thanks to my husband. He is hopeless when it comes to his schoolwork. Clueless, in fact. But at least he makes the money. It's one bright thing in our lives." Isabela scratched her temple. "Do you ever realise the stupid mistakes you've made in life, Eva? Wish you could undo those mistakes? Not realising the consequences of your actions until it's too late?"

Eva angled her head, curious. What was going on with her? Did this have something to do with Lola or was it about her family? "Sometimes. Why do you ask? Do you regret something you've done?" Isabela looked over her shoulder but remained silent. "Isabela. I am here for you and don't mind listening. Talk to me."

Isabela leaned forward. "I ... I ..."

Francisca walked into the staffroom and patted her friend on the shoulder. "Hey, ladies. Having lunch without me? But it doesn't look like you're eating, Isabela." She frowned. "Sorry, did I interrupt something? I'll go."

She turned around, about to leave but stopped when Isabella said, "No, don't leave." Isabela touched the base of her throat. "I have to prepare for a class and get my notebooks." She faced Eva. "Thanks for listening."

"We'll talk next time."

Isabela rushed out as if she couldn't get out of there fast enough.

Francisca sat in Isabela's seat. "I'm sorry to come at the wrong time. But is she all right?"

Eva's heart ached. "I don't know. Something's wrong. I feel like she's hiding something. But she's obviously still grieving for Lola."

"Hmm," said Francisca. "I wonder if there's more to that story about the mercury poisoning. She mentioned having a bad piece of fish, but I don't know if I believe her. Something strange is going on, that's for sure."

"But what can we do?" Eva asked. "She needs to come to us. If we force her to speak up, she'll run the other way."

"We could invite her out for lunch one of these days. Get away from the school environment where she might feel more relaxed."

"Could be worth a try," said Eva. An uneasy sense overcame her as she pondered if the mercury poisoning wasn't an accident.

Eva strolled along the path towards Plaza de Espana after work, still thinking about Isabela and her grief. She continued past her apartment above the shopping strip, towards the garden space for her time to write. Following the slope downwards, she made her way past two brown benches opposite more trees and bushes, with nature strips alongside. She loved the small pond-like fountain that featured concrete blocks over it, with a view of the city buildings and multiple monuments that celebrated historical figures.

Making her way to the bench, she rummaged in her satchel and pulled out a notepad. She jotted down notes for chapter and scene outlines, progressing the story from stalker to a risky incident for the female protagonist.

Then the hair on the back of her neck stood up as she again sensed that someone was watching her. Bile in her throat made her wonder if her fictional story was coming to life.

As she closed her eyes and took deep breaths, a middle-aged man sat next to her on the bench. Why was he crowding her space? But she didn't want to be rude and leave abruptly. He might've been lonely, but the man's paunch, worn-out clothing and dishevelled hair made him look homeless.

"Stop getting involved," he said, a creepy smirk plastered across his face.

"Excuse me?" Her heart palpitated and her hands sweated. Small strings of water dripped into her lap.

He turned to her and gripped her arm hard. "Stay the fuck away or people will die." The man looked at passersby with a grin, as if he hadn't just threatened her.

She couldn't breathe. "What are you talking about, and who are you?"

"This is your last warning." The man got up and walked towards the main road as if he didn't have a care in the world.

Eva's thoughts turned surreal as if she wasn't sitting here close to her residence. The man was near her home and most likely knew where she lived. Who the hell was he, and what was she doing to cause a stir? She had only supported Samuel and hadn't done anything she thought would risk anyone's life.

Once she got her composure back, she headed towards the man, who was still in her sight. If she followed him, she might see where he came from, but who the hell was he? Had he been sent by someone else or was he the actual threat? Speeding up, she followed him until reaching the Gran Via, pushing her way through the swirling crowd on the wide footpath. Where was he? She had lost him.

Eva walked back home with heavy steps, trying to stop trembling. What had happened and who was that man? Was it worth reporting to the police?

CHAPTER 20

Eva met Francisca in the corridor outside their classroom, the primary school children outside the room attempting to maintain straight postures. A tall, stocky boy, Diego, wriggled, laughed, and shoved a new student, a meek girl whose name Eva had forgotten. It was Isabel's day to volunteer in their class for the group reading session. But where was she?

"Diego. Stop that. I want postures straight, and quiet please. Or we'll be staying outside here for the whole day and all of lunchtime," said Francisca, who was skilled at disciplining the students. "What do you think, guys?"

A young girl with pigtails and braces giggled. "Sorry, Miss."

Eva spotted Samuel in line just as Diego shoved him towards the boy in front of him. The poor boy whimpered. She was about to say something when Francisca strode towards the culprit. "Diego. I have had enough of your misbehaviour. You are seeing the principal, and if this keeps up, we'll be calling your parents." His eyes widened and his shoulders squared.

Francisca rubbed her hands together. "Do you know if Isabela's coming?"

"I haven't heard otherwise," said Eva. "She might be running late."

Isabela soon scurried towards them, gripping her bag tightly. "Sorry I'm late."

Francisca grinned. "It's fine, Isabela, but would you mind taking Diego to see the principal? He's been shoving other students in line and that will not be tolerated."

Isabela's expression darkened, her hands jittery as she played with her bag strap. She faced Eva with a curious stare. "Of course. Happy to do that." She walked alongside Diego towards Ignacio's office.

"Okay, the rest of you, please walk quietly into class." Francisca turned to Eva,

who shook her head and waited until the last student walked inside and her friend closed the door. "Settle down, please children."

Eva sat beside Samuel and set down her own mathematics book, pens, and notebook. Her shoulders stiffened at seeing his guarded expression, his eyes following others in the room as if he was on guard. Normal for someone who had experienced multiple traumas in his twelve years. "Let's wait for roll call, Samuel."

After all the students responded to roll call, Francisca said, "Today we'll be working again on our multiplication and timetables, so please turn to chapter five in your maths books." She huffed. "Jonay, please take out your book. I will not tell you twice."

A mousey-looking boy with glasses said, "Sorry, Miss Francisca. I forgot the book at home."

"Did you do the homework I asked you to do?"

"I forgot, Miss." The boy cowered.

"All right. Eva will work with you on your timetables after she's done with Samuel and Joaquin. For now, I'd like you to focus as we work through these on the board."

Eva was thankful that Francisca understood the boy's dysfunctional home situation, and that he had found the work challenging. His broken home put him behind in his learning. It was her job to speed things along and she would.

After the general lesson from Francisca, Eva patted Samuel on the back, and rose from her seat. "Great work, Samuel. Do these few exercises and let me help Joaquin for a bit. I will be back soon."

She pulled a chair over to the boy's area and smiled. "Hi Joaquin. Are you ready to start working on this chapter?" She turned to the appropriate section in the book.

"Yes, Miss." He looked over at Samuel and whispered in her ear. "He wet himself in English class, Miss. In another class, too."

She knit her brows. "Who?"

"Samuel, Miss."

She swallowed and realised the trauma obviously caused it. She vowed to discuss this with Esmeralda and brushed the thought aside to focus on Joaquin's work. He gripped the pencil tight as he wrote a story about his soccer win. "How about changing these words so you're not repeating them."

"I have a thesaurus I can use." He flipped through the book while Eva remained curious about his mother, Isabela.

"How is your mother doing?"

Joaquin turned to her. "She cries all the time, especially with her friend on the phone. My mum says it's a friend from her meeting group."

"What meeting group?"

He shrugged as he crossed out his repetitive word and replaced it. "Not sure. I think it's part of a book club. She loves to read."

Eva nodded. "Right." Did she believe it was a book club, or someone giving her trouble? She had to find out.

Standing up, she made her way towards Jonay, working with him until a few minutes before the end of the lesson when Esmeralda walked inside and approached Eva. "I'd like to see Samuel for his session."

"Is it okay if I sit in with him? Only because he asked me to. I think he's a little nervous, not having seen you in a while."

Esmeralda nodded, then rubbed her eyes. "Of course. I'd love to have you."

Making their exit from the classroom, Eva held Samuel's shaky hand. The boy had trembled inside the classroom too, obviously the loss of his mother causing him to regress to bedwetting. She hoped therapy would help.

Eva stepped inside her office. Along with her psychology diploma and Master's certificate, pictures of landscapes and nature gave the room a welcoming ambience.

Eva sat on a chair opposite Esmeralda's desk while the psychologist sat on another chair in the toy space that included sand play, a set of dolls for child therapy, and drawing pads. She had watched Esmeralda at work before and was mesmerised by the way she connected with children and could see right through them.

"Okay, Samuel. Today we're going to work on drawings about how you feel today. You can draw anything you like. It could be about your teacher, Eva or about your aunt, Andreina. Even about the hot weather today."

Samuel nodded, averting his eyes. Eva noticed that he barely looked her in the eye since the death of Lola after the two occasions she'd visited him at home.

While he pressed thick crayons into the sketch pad, Esmeralda turned to her and smiled. "A nice and easy first session."

"That's good," said Eva.

She turned back to Samuel, who was choosing dark colours to represent his images while Esmeralda made notes in her book.

Ten minutes later, he had finished and held out his arm to show Eva. She edged forward and stared at the drawing: a group of dark figures with a cloud hovering over them, and smaller figures surrounding them. What was this about?

"Interesting," said Eva.

"Yes, great work," said Esmeralda, whose eye twitched. "I can see this is about your family. It's you and your parents, right?" Samuel shivered. "It's okay. No pressure. We'll work on something else."

Eva watched the poor boy cower until wetness lined his pants. He had wet himself again. "Oh, Samuel. It's okay. Let's get you changed." She faced Esmeralda. "I can help."

Esmeralda nodded. "You go off with Eva and we'll continue another day."

She waved to the psychologist and grabbed Samuel gently by the hand. "Come on, little man." He was crying. "It's okay, Samuel. I'm here for you." Her heart went out to him. He'd most likely struggle for a long time after the death of his mother, and possible ties to something unknown. She resolved to protect him, no matter what.

CHAPTER 21

Tomas scratched his temple in thought, not having spoken to Eva for the past week. He stood in front of a candy store this Saturday morning, having planned to meet her at Plaza Mayor. He wanted an update on Samuel at school but also wanted an excuse to see her.

Tomas scrolled through his phone as the mild wind feathered his cheeks while hurried footsteps passed him by, as people moved among the cafes and stores. He perused the window display of colourful macaroons, assorted candy, and chocolate balls placed on barrels topped with plastic covers. Tingles along his skin triggered images of Eva's beautiful face.

"Tomas."

He turned to Eva, who looked at him wearily as if something was on her mind. "Let's sit underneath those umbrellas, away from the sun." She nodded glumly and followed him as she kept a metre's distance between them, arms crossed. Goosebumps lined her bare arms despite the heat.

She walked on unsteady legs on the cobblestone ground and would have fallen if he hadn't steadied her by holding on to her arm.

Once they sat, he became oblivious to the surrounding people, his heart breaking at her stern facade. "Eva. Are you all right?"

She sighed. "A lot has been happening, Tomas. Samuel's been wetting himself at school. It's happened a few times, apparently."

Tomas gasped. "I'm sorry to hear that, but he's been through a lot. He's lucky to have the school and his aunt as support." Why did he get the feeling that something more was wrong? "Are you sure there's nothing more bothering you?"

Eva hesitated. "I'm fine, Tomas."

He leaned in. "Eva. If I can help in any way, you need to tell me. Is this about Lola's case or something else? I'm a good listener." She clenched her hands as if debating in her mind. "If there's anything wrong, I can help."

"This homeless-looking man threatened me. Said to stay away or people will die. He told me to stop getting involved."

A coldness penetrated his chest as he reached for her hand. Who would orchestrate all this? "Stay away from what, though?" She shrugged. "Did you report it to the police?"

"It was most likely a hoax."

He swallowed. "Leandro could look into it if you can tell him what this man looks like. It's amazing what they can do with an artist's sketch."

She took a breath. "The police will be busy enough."

"What if someone paid him? If he seemed homeless, he probably needed the money."

"Possibly. He could identify who he spoke to. Do you think it's related to Lola?"

"I don't believe in coincidences. My gut tells me it's related." He explained his mother's involvement with the herbal medicines, the mercury poisoning cases, and now this recent threat.

Eva's shoulders deflated. "A lot has happened. What are we going to do?"

"We start off by reporting the threat to the police."

She nodded. "I will. And I am sorry about your mother. How is her back?"

He sighed. "She got a referral to a specialist, so might need surgery." He paused and thought about those medicines. "I'm starting to think there's a connection between this so-called spiritual group and the herbs."

"Do you think it's a scam?"

He shrugged. "It might be the cheapest way to manufacture the medicine and charge a high price for it. A money-making scam. They probably use it for punishment, too, but what do I know? Conspiracy theory but no real evidence to back it up. I think we need to lie low for a while and not question anyone about this. Someone might be watching, and I want you safe, Eva. Okay?"

"I want you safe, too." Their gaze lingered, and when he edged closer to her, he caressed her chin and trailed his fingers up to her cheeks and around her lips. He loved the smoothness of her skin and the sexy outline of her lips. The moment was broken when she rose. "I have to go now. An urgent appointment."

He put up a hand. "Wait. Listen. I have two tickets to a flamenco show for tonight. My friend, Gonzalo can't make it. Would you like to come?"

She hesitated. "I don't know. I might be busy tonight."

"Don't give me an answer now. Check your schedule and get back to me in a few hours. It doesn't start until later tonight."

"Sure. I'll let you know." Without a backward glance, she rushed off and left him wanting more. What had he done? He promised he wouldn't attach himself to her, and here he was stroking her face and inviting her out to a show. Was he crazy?

CHAPTER 22

E fren took deep breaths while listening to his fellow member, Maria, who was filling in for the yoga instructor. "Tuck your tummy in, Miguel. Yes, you are doing well. Now, breathe in slowly, then exhale. Stretch out those shoulders and place your right leg on the inside of your left leg. Great work, Efren. Remember that the ultimate purpose of yoga is enlightenment and finding your truth. Peace and harmony are our mantra. Say it with me, people. Peace and harmony."

"Peace and harmony," said the group of twenty.

By the end of the session, Efren headed outside with the others, the mild breeze brushing his flushed skin. A queasiness in his stomach made him wonder if more was going on here. But no, there was a reason for everything, and he was feeling better about his life. Soon he'd be able to return to his mother, as he missed her terribly.

Around him, fellow members of teenagers and adults bent over timber supplies as they built a temple for worship. The sounds of men drilling into planks of wood, others sawing timber, and those stacking piles of wood for easy access for part of the roof gave him a sense of community. As per Marco's instruction, he joined in to help.

"What can I do?" asked Efren.

His friend Miguel, who was seventeen, ushered him towards a group of men who were hammering wood to start the frame. "Grab all those boxes of nails and bring them over here."

"Not a problem," he said.

As he wandered around the area, stepping over bits of wood, tape measures, screwdrivers, drills and other supplies, he started picking up the boxes of nails scattered around the building site.

Watching his step, he saw two boys close to one of the cabins whose names he couldn't remember. One shoved the other when Marco rushed towards them. "What is going on here?"

"He kissed Juanita without her permission. She's only eleven." Juanita shivered as she sat on a step, crying.

Marco walked to the girl. He reached for her hand and whispered in her ear. Her eyes widened before heading to a cabin with him. What had he said to the girl, and was he taking her back to her room?

Antonio, a hulk of a man with crooked teeth, hovered over the boy who had started the argument about Juanita. "You disobeyed the rules here, boy. Involving yourself in others' business when we're the ones in charge here. Not you." He inched closer, glaring. "What do you think your punishment should be?"

The boy flinched when a wetness crept through his pants. "I am sorry. It won't happen again. I was worried about Juanita. She's only eleven."

"We'll take care of the boy, don't worry." He pointed a stern finger. "But let me better remind you of your place here." Antonio pounded his fist into the boy's face. Once, twice, three times. He groaned in pain, falling back like a sack of potatoes.

Efren dropped the box of nails with a heaviness in his stomach. *What the hell.* Didn't the boy do the right thing for Juanita? Why punish him and not the other boy?

Antonio gritted his teeth. "Mind your business or there'll be consequences."

Efren' s head throbbed, not wanting to imagine what could happen if the boy didn't follow the rules again.

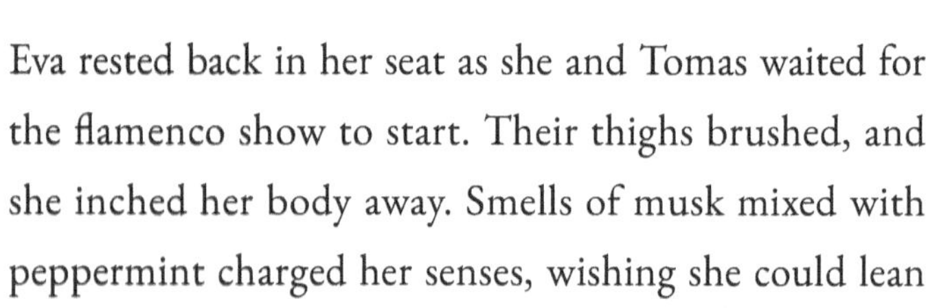

Eva rested back in her seat as she and Tomas waited for the flamenco show to start. Their thighs brushed, and she inched her body away. Smells of musk mixed with peppermint charged her senses, wishing she could lean into more of his scent despite shifting away from it. Guests were seated in front and around them in the darkness of the building and a band set up on stage.

She didn't want his pity after telling him about that threat, but he had insisted. Talking about her fears made them more real, and this threat felt genuine. She appreciated his concern.

"It's about to start," he said.

"Can't wait." Eva faced the stage, mesmerised by a bald man playing the flamenco guitar and a group of three singers beside him. She had the desire to dance and stared even more when two female dancers started clapping to the song. A middle-aged woman in a white dress with flowing sleeves glided around the stage, stomping her feet. The noise resounded in the quiet of the spectators. A younger flamenco dancer swayed her arms as she tapped her feet while lifting her skirt, strutting to the energised Spanish tunes.

Tomas inched closer to her when a slow ballad came on and a different flamenco dancer gyrated to a slow dance with the gentle sway of her arms above her head and expressive emotion. "I would love to dance a slow song with you," he said.

Eva felt her face flush and kept her eyes forward, yearning to reach out to Tomas. It must have been the wine she was drinking, nothing more. She couldn't let him charm his way to her heart when he would most likely hurt her. But one happy night couldn't hurt, could it? It didn't need to mean anything.

Her hand rested along the side of her thigh next to Tomas' hand, and slowly she edged it closer, enjoying the soft sensation. Tomas realised what she was doing and turned to her, but Eva didn't dare look. All she wanted was to feel his touch, his caress, and his soft breathing and scent. The ambience of the smoky atmosphere and soothing music heightened their emotions, too.

At the end of the performance, the guests clapped and moved out of their seats. Eva felt his hand across the small of her back as she moved ahead of him, waiting for those in front of her to head for the exit.

"How about a trip to Retiro Park? It's beautiful at night."

"Sure."

He retrieved his phone. "I'll get us a taxi there, as it's too far to walk. The night is still young."

She could barely breathe from his intense, hungry gaze from earlier. *Get it together, Eva. It's only the romantic vibe here, which won't be long-lasting.*

CHAPTER 23

Tomas and Eva walked side-by-side towards the gates into Retiro Park. She had been quiet during the taxi ride, and the few times Tomas had dared look at her, he'd spotted a car following them. But that was crazy. The driver must've only been doing the same thing as them: going towards the park.

A few steps led to the entrance of the park as he made his way up with Eva, soothed by the warm breeze once they entered. He wanted to hold her hand, but didn't want to push his luck despite their hands touching at the flamenco show. He was feeling things he didn't want to feel but couldn't control. No harm in enjoying each other's company without it meaning anything. Or even a little harmless flirtation.

The lights in the park made reflections down the path as they circled the garden and zig-zagged eventually to the Mediterranean Garden.

"It is beautiful at night, Tomas."

"It sure is," he said, not talking about the garden, but her. She stood against a steel fence before they carried on walking.

"Let me take a photo of you. It'll look amazing in the night." He took out his phone as she nodded and posed. "Thanks." The background view of buildings and hedges gave it a tropical ambience.

They reached a cluster of trees where birds soared. "These trees honour those who died in a terrorist attack in 2004," Eva said.

"I heard about that," said Tomas. "Tired yet?"

"No, we can keep going, but there is no way we can see the whole park on foot. We'd need a tuk tuk guide to get around and see the Crystal Palace, too."

They approached a fountain, and Eva submerged her hand into it. He couldn't help but notice her skirt lifting to reveal the toned outline of her legs and the smooth curves of her hips. His arms reached for her and he pulled her upright. Turning her around, he drew a hair strand out of her eyes, when footsteps and muffled voices sounded behind them.

"We should probably start making a move." He walked off and assumed that Eva was following him. He turned around, but she wasn't behind him. Where did she go? He returned to their original spot at the fountain, but she'd vanished. "Eva. Where are you? Eva?"

No, he wasn't going to worry. This was a big place, and she might have only made a turn away from him. He would find her.

Tomas retrieved his phone and called her, but she didn't pick up. He tried again, with the same result. His heart raced and his legs felt weak as he ran around the park, passing people and cyclists who rounded the corner. *Where are you?*

Tomas walked along hedges and another fountain, peeking around bushes and dried grass. How could she disappear like that when it had only been a few minutes since they last saw each other? *Don't panic. Only lost.*

If he stayed in one spot, she might come to him, so he remained still with his eyes darting everywhere. Passersby stared at him strangely while rushing around him as if he was high on drugs.

When his phone buzzed, he answered. "Eva?" He breathed a sigh of relief.

"Tomas. Can you get me? I'm hidden behind a hedge. I can't move. My ankle's sore and might be twisted. I'm behind the fountain we passed earlier.

"I'm on my way."

Tomas skirted back to the area and behind it in search of a hedge. Where was she? He scratched his head and ran fast, feeling as if hours had passed by. When he finally found her between a bush and a tree, his shoulders relaxed in relief. She had been hidden from the path.

He bent down to her level and scanned her ankle. She winced when he touched it lightly. "Oh, Eva. What happened?"

"I thought I saw someone following me. Before I got a chance to tell you, they were running off. I had to find out who it was, but then I lost sight of them and fell over a boulder without seeing it, obviously, and hurt my ankle. Such a stupid accident."

His skin went cold. Who was following her, and was that driver behind them the culprit? "Did you see what he looked like or what he was wearing?"

She shook her head. "Not clearly. I couldn't tell if it was a man or woman in the dark. But they wore a cap that covered half of the face and one of those COVID masks."

"Was it the homeless man again?"

"I doubt it. This person looked older and bulkier."

"Let's call the police."

She knit her brows as she rubbed her ankle. "And say what, Tomas? I couldn't see the person and there's no evidence of a crime."

"At least you told Leandro about the homeless man. He might get something out of him. Can you get up?" She nodded. "Okay, slowly. I'll get us a taxi at this end of the park, so you don't need to walk much." He called for transport.

Eva rose and held on to his shoulder for balance, but when she walked, she moaned in pain. "I'll be fine walking for a bit. What choice do I have? It's not like you can carry me."

"Oh yes, I can." He flung his arms underneath her legs and walked towards the street. Tomas loved the way her body felt against his own and relished the closeness. What if something worse had happened to her? He hated that feeling of dread.

He put her down on the ground and waited near the gate. "I don't like you being on your own, Eva. If someone's following you, it could be dangerous."

"I'll be fine." Her hands trembled. "I might have been paranoid. It could've been no one."

Tomas had a sinking sense that things would get worse before they got better. First and foremost, he had to protect the woman he cared about.

CHAPTER 24

"**A**re you sure I need to stay at your apartment? I'll be fine at home. My friend, Francisca lives with me, so I won't be on my own." It would be far too intimate for her to stay overnight at his place.

"I'm worried, Eva. Just for one night. Please humour me. I want to take care of you, especially with that ankle."

"It's getting better. I believe it's only bruised."

The taxi finally stopped in La Latina and dropped them off below his apartment. He paid the driver, stepped out and pulled her gently by the hand towards the elevator entrance.

"It's the third floor, so not too far," he said.

As they stepped inside the elevator, they stared awkwardly at each other until reaching his apartment. She kept her arm around him as he opened the door and led her to the couch with fluffy white pillows. A black timber coffee table was beside it, topped with medicine and poetry magazines. A cast iron lamp as tall as her stood in the corner of the wall between landscape paintings.

"I'll get you some ice. We need to ice it every one to two hours." He pulled an ice pack from his fridge and pressed it on her ankle. "Keep it there for twenty minutes. Your ankle's bruised but not fractured. Proper healing will take about one to two weeks."

"Thanks. I'll ask my doctor tomorrow whether I can work."

"Would you like a coffee or tea?" She shook her head. "Okay. I have a spare bedroom and will get you blankets and a pillow."

"I will have a glass of port if you'll have one with me."

"Okay." He rummaged in the pantry inside his small kitchen and pulled out a bottle of port, then poured two glasses. "Here you go." She grabbed the glass and tossed it down. "Wow. Would you like another one?"

"Only one more. It helps with the pain."

"I should be giving you painkillers, not alcohol, but so long as you're not driving." He returned with a fresh glass and gave it to her, but this time, she sipped it slowly.

"Thank you for all this." She scanned the room. "I don't want you to worry. I'm sure it wasn't related, and we haven't done anything to make these people suspicious, other than visiting the police. But we know nothing about this. We're not a threat."

He nodded. "I don't know if I should be worrying about my mum after buying those herbs. What if they involve her in this money-making scam, or worse?"

Her heart ached for him. "Don't think that way. She'll be okay." Eva drew back. "I don't know much about your family, Tomas. Tell me about them."

He tilted his head. "Okay. My mother and I are close." Tomas squeezed his hands and arched brow as if he was struggling to say more. "She divorced my father, who was always chasing the next dream and spending money we never had. Because of him we were poor, and he was never available. My mum kicked him out of the house when I was fifteen and I haven't heard from him since. I'm thirty-two now."

"I am sorry, Tomas. It's hard to live in a broken home. How do you feel about it now without your father being around?"

"A blessing. It was better to have no father than to have one who was always absent and self-absorbed. One who ... Never mind. Better for us this way."

"It would've been hard for your mother as a single parent."

"Somewhat, but she has sisters and friends to help, so it wasn't too bad. Now we're closer than ever." He flashed a smile. "I know she would like you."

Eva gazed past him, her heart missing a beat. "I think we can take this ice off now and go to bed. I mean, for me to go to bed." She felt her face redden and spotted a gleam in his eye. *How embarrassing.*

He picked up the ice pack. "I'll get your room ready." He rushed off, and she pushed herself up, ignoring the pain. Holding on to the edge of the couch, she winced but kept moving towards the kitchen table and held onto that. When Tomas returned, he glared.

"You could've waited for me. Stubborn, aren't you?"

"Sorry, but I hate being helpless."

"I can tell." They made it to the bedroom. "There is an ensuite you can use." He handed her pyjamas. "These are mine you can wear." She grinned. "Goodnight." He made his way out the door and closed it.

Eva washed her face and put on his pyjamas. The scent of soap and lavender filled her senses, and she wondered if it was his scent or the washing powder.

She closed her eyes, with flashes of Tomas entering her mind. The way he gently held the small of her back as he carried her out of Retiro Park. The way he'd rubbed her thigh had aroused her to no end.

Eva tossed and turned at the pain that throbbed, opening her eyes and counting sheep. Images of movement underneath her door made her gasp. Was that Tomas at the door? She waited with bated breath, but when the light turned off and the footsteps drifted away, she hid her disappointment. An emptiness in her chest made her images of him stronger. It would be hard not to dream of this entrancing man.

CHAPTER 25

Last night, Tomas had stood outside Eva's bedroom door with the desire to say a final goodnight. But if he had stepped inside, would they have kept it civil, or would he have indulged in a kiss—or more? Every night and day she was on his mind, curious about the way she tasted or how it would feel if her lips grazed his neck, and lower down.

Shaking off his thoughts, he strolled into the kitchen and prepared a coffee pot for an espresso. He rubbed his eyes after hardly sleeping last night with thoughts of Eva in the next room. A hit of caffeine would wake him up.

While he waited for the coffee to rise in the percolator, light footsteps sounded behind him. "Good morning," said Eva.

He turned to see her hobbling towards him as she made her way to a chair. "How's your ankle?"

"Better, but still sore." She rested her elbows against the table and clasped her hands in thought. "I'd better get home. I'll call a taxi."

He didn't want her to leave. "How about a coffee first? I've got an espresso that's ready." He turned off the gas.

"All right. One cup, then I'll go."

He picked up two small cups from an overhead cupboard and poured the steaming coffee into them. "Sugar?"

"Only one, thanks."

He grabbed a spoon for the sugar, but when he added it into the cup, it spilled all over the counter. Wiping it away, he tried again. Knowing she was behind him made him nervous, and the silence was awkward. "How did you sleep?"

"It was okay, but I woke up a couple of times because my ankle was throbbing. I might take a few days off work."

Tomas sat next to her as he set down the coffee. "Good idea. Would you like breakfast?"

"No, I only have coffee in the morning. Not a breakfast girl, but thanks."

Tomas had had a thought last night about the presumed cult and thought Eva could help. "I was curious about Samuel. Can you tell me how long he's been mute and what the psychologist believes contributed to it?"

Eva sipped her coffee then put it down. "He's had mutism ever since he was ten, according to Lola. He was traumatised when his father gagged him and threatened to choke him if ever he stood up to him about his mother. Esmeralda said that he's associated talking with fear and pain. He chose to stop talking because he feels safer that way. Samuel's working with a speech pathologist too, but for the past two years there hasn't been much progress." She drank down the remainder of her coffee.

"He was obviously hurt wherever he was, so that would've most likely made him regress further, or he could've been threatened."

"No doubt." She took a breath. "Esmeralda believes that if they can treat the trauma he'll begin to talk again. But he still has a lot of fear, which is normal. Not only from his dad but also from wherever he came from. I wonder if the police have any leads."

He looked down at her ankle. "That looks a little swollen. Let me ice it for you." He got up, swung open the freezer door and retrieved an ice pack.

He handed the ice pack to Eva. "Let's sit on the couch so you can rest." With his arm around her waist, he manoeuvred her around the chair but lost his footing. In a split second, he regained his balance when she fell into the nearby chair, with his body accidentally straddling her. Eyes locked, he curved his hand underneath her chin and stroked it gently. The light in her eyes showed need and lust as she caressed the back of his waist, with a light moan. The feel of her pelvis against his own aroused him, heightened when he saw that she leaned towards him and gazed intensely. He licked his lips and edged closer to her until smashing his lips over hers. Her taste was out of his world as he wrapped his arms around her, unable to get close enough to her. He wanted her clothing off, but he took his time circling his tongue inside her mouth. Her gentle moan rewarded him as he explored the roof of her mouth and teeth. With increasing need, he probed deeper into her mouth and hungered for her. *Oh, hell*. He was about to burst out of his pants and wanted to take this to the bedroom, but he knew he shouldn't get in too deep. *Slow down, boy.*

When he finally stopped, she looked away as if embarrassed. "I'm sorry," he said. "Let's get you to the couch." He rose and led her to the couch with his arm around her, an awkward silence arising. Eva sat back while Tomas placed the icepack over her ankle. Why wasn't she saying anything? Her eyes looked anywhere but at him, and he couldn't take it any longer. "I have a few things to do in my study for work, so I'll be back in half an hour."

"I'll get my taxi ready."

"No need. I can drive you home. I don't have to work until later tonight. Unfortunately, I don't always get weekends off."

"It's fine. I prefer a taxi, but thanks anyway."

He swallowed. "If that's what you prefer." He walked to his study, his mind on the kiss and how he wanted and needed more. But why did it feel awkward afterwards? Did she not feel what he felt?

CHAPTER 26

F rancisca pushed her hands together in front of the classroom when Ignacio walked by. She sternly pointed a finger at a student shoving another. "Line up quietly, please class."

Eva stood beside the group and nodded to him. "Ignacio."

The principal held a pile of files in his hands and inched closer to the group, glaring. "I don't want to give anyone detention, so please behave. This is your first and only warning." He smiled at the women, but it didn't reach his eyes. Was he worried about something?

The group of boys and girls straightened up with serious expressions on their faces, obviously fearing the wrath of the school principal. Ignacio knew how to make his presence known and was a strict but fair principal. Sometimes he reminded Eva of her mother, who was nurturing and kind-hearted—the opposite of her father when he drank heavily.

Before the students entered their room, Ignacio walked off with a curt nod.

Francisca recited students' names for attendance before beginning the lesson, her hands flailing with instructions until the group worked on their own. Eva hovered over Samuel, who read over math questions. He gripped his pen tightly with his head bowed down.

Eva was checking his answers ten minutes later when the door opened. Ignacio had returned and entered the classroom. He approached Francisca. "The police are here to talk to Samuel. Can Eva come with him?"

"What's this about?"

"I will tell you in due course, but he can return to class later."

Francisca headed to Samuel and leaned down. "You need to leave with Ms Lopez for a while. Leave your things. You can get them when you return." He nodded, and together with Eva, followed the principal to his office.

She wondered what was going on. Luckily, she had a say in Samuel's well-being as he'd always trusted her. Lola had put her trust in her, too.

Inside the principal's office was the detective, Leandro, who stood beside Samuel's father, a heavy-set man with black wavy, dishevelled hair down to his shoulders, dark, brooding eyes and broad shoulders. Samuel shuddered beside her, holding on to her arm.

"Have you met Samuel's father, Adan?"

Bile rose in her throat. "I have."

"He's recently arrived from overseas and wants to see his son."

Adan shifted towards Samuel, who flinched, shifted his stance and held on to Eva's hand, gripping it tightly. His body and lower lip trembled. "Hi, Samuel," Adan began. "It's okay. I am back and wanted to see how you were doing."

Leandro intervened. "Samuel. Your father would like to take you out tonight on a supervised visit. Esmeralda will be present as you get to know each other again." His eyes darkened. Did he hate this as much as she did? If only Lola had never married the man.

He let go of Eva's hands and clenched his own, cowering into a corner. He turned away and stared up at the ceiling.

"Where's Esmeralda?" asked Eva.

Ignacio knit his brows. "She had an appointment and will be back later this afternoon."

Adan ambled closer to Samuel and touched him on the shoulder, but he shivered further. It was obvious he feared his father. How could this low-life profess to want to care for his son when he was an abuser? "Please, son. Let's talk about you. How is school?"

"He doesn't speak," said Eva.

The man glared. "I can see that, but he's my son and I have the right to talk to him."

She scoffed. "What, after you hurt Lola. Now you expect Samuel to come to you with open arms. He obviously fears you and doesn't trust you."

Leandro put up a hand. "Eva, please. He has rights because there is no record of Lola reporting him for abuse. With no witnesses, it's her word against his."

"No, but she had the bruises and hospitalisation to prove it. It's obvious what he did, and now he expects to come back into Samuel's life. Over my dead body."

Ignacio intervened. He touched Eva on the shoulder. "I understand your position, Eva, but what you said is inappropriate. You have no legal standing here, and there is no evidence that he hurt Lola. Without that, he has the right to fight for custody. He is his father."

"No, he doesn't want Samuel. He only wants someone else to control and overpower. I won't allow it, and I'm sure Andreina won't, either. I'll give her a call."

Leandro's expression changed. "Stay out of this, Eva. It's between the family."

Eva's chest ached. "Fine, but it's not right." Poor Samuel had to deal with his mother's death and now an abusive father. Did he ever catch a break? How much trauma could one boy endure?

CHAPTER 27

O ver a week later, Eva's ankle had healed. She was walking around Plaza de Santa Ana with Tomas alongside her when the buzz of his phone interrupted their quiet.

She leaned back against the wall of a tapas restaurant and spotted motorbikes parked beside a drooping tree, apartments situated above the strip of cafes and restaurants, a green bus dropping off passengers who walked towards her, and towering trees surrounding the buildings. Umbrellas shaded a set of tables for diners eating and drinking in the outdoor space.

Smells of exhaust fumes and dust penetrated her senses while the low, piercing *keow* of seagulls and the muffled voices of patrons around the eateries grounded her. But as she gazed into the distance, a dark, hooded figure caught her eye. The person stood behind a garbage bin close to the eateries before wandering off. Did she know this person, and was she being watched? After everything that had happened, she was becoming hyper-vigilant.

Eva thought about her lunch with Tomas today. He had invited her to Santa Ana after calling her twice during the week, and she had eventually relented. Space to process what was happening between them would be the best thing, but the case of Lola and Samuel kept them glued to each other. It couldn't be more than that.

A tap on the shoulder made her flinch. "Are you ready for lunch?"

"Sure am."

His eyes darkened. "Are you happy to sit outside to eat?"

"Yes. Is everything okay? You look spooked by that phone call."

He cleared his throat and made his way forward towards a stand featuring a displayed menu, staring. "I don't know, Eva. Something weird's going on with my friend, Gonzalo. But I'd rather leave it for now."

He walked over to another stand in between chairs and tables, and glanced at the menu, each area representing a different restaurant. "How about this one with tapas?"

Eva scanned through the menu. "Looks good."

They made their way to chairs and sat around a round rickety table when a lanky waitress smiled and gave them menus. "Would you like anything to drink before you decide?"

"I'll have a sangria," said Eva.

Tomas leaned forward. "Your house wine, thanks."

"I'll be back shortly," said the waitress.

Eva noticed his change of mood since the phone call. She knew Tomas was the type to go all out for those he cared about, but was he looking after himself? A deep sadness sometimes flashed in his eyes, and she knew he carried emotional scars from childhood. But would he open up to her?

The waiter returned with their drinks. They ordered a shared tapas meal comprising meatballs with barbecue sauce, cod, a selection of cheeses, Galician-style cooked octopus, and varied toasted canapes.

Once the food was ready, Tomas dug into his salmon canape. "How's the ankle?"

"It's healed, mostly. At least I can walk and don't limp anymore." She knit her brows while biting into the fish. "Have you heard anything from your detective friend, Leandro?"

He shook his head. "I'll tell you as soon as I know." He wiped his mouth with a napkin, and she couldn't help fixating on his thick, rosy lips, subtle stubble, and piercing eyes. "About the other week, I am sorry. I crossed the line, Eva."

"It's fine."

"I hope we can at least be friends," said Tomas, averting his eyes.

"Of course." Eva's stomach ached and the pressure against her temples was unnerving. It was the right thing to remain friends despite a part of her desiring him.

"Anyway, friend. I'm curious about your relationships. Has someone broken your heart? I can't imagine you'd let anyone get away with anything."

Eva took a breath and wiped crumbs from her cheek. She sipped her sangria, savouring the sweet, refreshing taste. She put down her glass and beamed at a group behind Tomas who were laughing and chattering as if they hadn't seen each other in years. She missed that sense of family from when her father had been alive and sober. "My ex-boyfriend, Agustin, cheated on me with a waitress we knew from a local café." Tomas leaned in and touched her hand, but she pulled it away. "It's fine. It was for the best we broke up."

"Why? Did he do anything else apart from the cheating? Not that cheating isn't bad enough."

The tightness in her chest affected her breathing, but calming breaths helped. She downed her drink. "Yes." She gritted her teeth, with a deep emptiness in the pit of her stomach. "He hit me when I didn't meet his expectations." A flash of his fist pounding into her cheek made her sick. The bruise had remained for weeks. "He hated me talking to male colleagues at work, hated when I put too much salt in his food, and even when I got lost going to a birthday party. All excuses to punch me, pull my hair, and hurl patronising words at me. I'd lost myself by the end of it, but found it hard to leave. He made me think I couldn't cope without him. It's how I felt." She pushed back tears, her throat dry. "The cheating was the last straw. My friend, Francisca, was a great help, and if it wasn't for her, I might have stayed with him."

She could still remember the pain in her legs when he kicked her hard underneath the table. Not to mention the time he yanked her by her hair and dragged her to the room to have his way with her. The bastard had almost raped her. If it wasn't for Francisca ringing the doorbell, she would've been further traumatised. Her friend had convinced her to report him to the police. "The bastard breached the restraining order and did prison time, but not enough in my book."

Tomas' eyes softened as he stood up and wrapped his arms around her. "I am so sorry you went through that, Eva." He sat back down. "I can't imagine what it must've been like for you. That fear, humiliation, pain. No one deserves that, but especially not you, Eva." Were his eyes watering?

"Thanks." Her heart raced as she pressed a hand soothingly against his own.

"The sentencing for domestic violence is never enough. In my opinion, laws should be tougher. Have longer prison sentences," Tomas said as he looked past her, his fists clenched.

"I agree. Once they're released, they go back and hurt the poor victims again."

Tomas tilted his head. "Where is he now?"

Eva's heart palpitated as she thought about his fate. "Once he got released from prison, he contacted me, telling me he had changed. I didn't believe him. I was living with my mother at the time, but thankfully she wasn't home when the house was trashed. The table overturned, slashes on the couch, broken dishes in the kitchen. I called the police, but he ran off. They couldn't find him at his house."

"Is he still on the run?"

Eva swallowed. "Karma got him when I found out he was abusing his waitress girlfriend until her brother found out about his abuse." She took a deep breath. "The brother killed him in self-defence after witnessing what was happening at their home. Agustin threatened him with a knife and her brother retaliated."

"Wow. That's quite the story, but staying in prison for the remainder of his natural life would have been a more fitting punishment."

"At least I don't have to look over my shoulder anymore," she lied. Eva sensed that someone was now watching her, and it had nothing to do with Agustin.

"I am glad you're okay, Eva. If you don't mind me asking, but if you do, tell me to mind my own business."

"What is it?"

"Was your father alive then?"

Eva flinched and remained silent. Speaking about her father made her ill, too.

CHAPTER 28

Tomas looked down into his clasped hands, feeling like a jerk. "I'm sorry. I didn't mean to make you uncomfortable. Please forget I asked." The melancholy in her eyes said it all. The way her shoulders drooped and how the light in her eyes dimmed. He yearned to hold her and never let her go. Tears had formed in her eyes, so he inched forward and wiped her cheeks with quaking fingers. If only he could have protected her then. If only he knew her all those years ago as her support. But no doubt she'd had her friends and family.

"My father was alive, but he'd left us so he wouldn't have known about Agustin. He died about two years ago."

Tomas gave her a reassuring smile. "I'm sorry." He exhaled. "If he was with you, would he have supported you then, considering what he'd done to your eye?"

She shrugged. "I don't know, but possibly when he wasn't drinking. He was a great father when he wasn't drunk."

"I wish I'd been there, Eva, to protect you."

"Me too," she said. "Although it's made me stronger in a way, but more anxious too. I hate confrontations for one and I struggle to sleep at night when I hear about domestic abuse. I have my triggers."

"As do I," said Tomas. He couldn't stop thinking about what his father had done.

"Tell me more about your father, Tomas."

"I know I should've told you earlier, but the timing wasn't right." Eva raised a brow. "I heard more recently that he died too, but my mother's enough family for me."

"I am sorry about your father," she said.

He shrugged. "It's fine. It wasn't like he was father of the year, but I'm not short of support, including friends. I imagine you have lots of amazing people in your life too, including me?"

Eva playfully tapped him on the shoulder. "Do you love yourself much?"

"Well, I am the charmer with women."

"Sure." Eva leaned in. "There is a story there. What happened to the love of your life, Tomas?"

He scoffed. "Lucia was a piece of work. She only cared about herself and loved attention. She was a model, doted on her social media profiles and had even lied about my profession." He chuckled. "She told everyone I was a doctor, and that we were planning to get married."

"You weren't planning?"

"I loved her with all my heart, but I wasn't ready for marriage. Lucia and her parents had different ideas and pressured me. They all treated my mother poorly and looked down on her because she wasn't wealthy like they were. I thought, how can I love and marry a woman who is shallower than the thickness of a pen? She didn't respect my work, my mother, my feelings, nothing. I always wanted to talk to her about deeper life issues, but she preferred talking about her social media posts and making a good impression. She worried about high prices of beauty products. She complained about how she couldn't find the right dress for a party." He shook his head. "Lucia even humiliated my mother in front of patrons when she met her for lunch at a local restaurant. My mum wanted to get to know her."

"What did she do?"

He scoffed. "That woman doesn't even deserve the beautiful name she has. Lucia yelled at my mother about how she needed to lose weight. She complained about a slight tear in my mother's skirt, saying that her old clothing and weight made her look poorer than a homeless woman. My mother started crying." He clenched his hands. "I only found out about this after Lucia left. But at least my mother walked out of that restaurant and left her with the bill. My mum said the look on her face was priceless." He stared into his napkin. "I loved this woman without knowing her true colours, but the part I loved was the side of her she chose to show me. It was a lie, Eva."

"That must have been hard despite her behaviour. You loved her."

"The heart doesn't discriminate, whether they're shallow or deep. Love is blind."

"Do you still love her?"

"No, my feelings for her came and went, thank God. I am free of that woman, but she did have a few good qualities."

"Such as?"

"She cared about children and would donate to charities. I sometimes think her parents had brainwashed her, but she might never change."

"Where is she now?"

"The last I heard she'd married an actual doctor and moved overseas, so she got her wish. I doubt it's true love. Most likely a marriage of convenience."

"I'm sorry you had to experience that pain. It is hard to love someone so much, you don't know where that pain can go. I loved Agustin, despite his dark side. But when he wasn't abusive, he was loving and kind."

"As they all are. We all have a dark side, Eva. We choose to push it down and not let it affect us like others. We control it."

"I wanted to kill Agustin those times he hurt me, but I knew it was wrong. I didn't want my soul darkened because of him. He wasn't worth it, but I've since stopped believing in relationships. They don't work and I seem to be a magnet for abusive men."

Tomas looked away from her. "I hope you find someone to love, Eva. You deserve that and so much more. You're beautiful on the inside and out. You care about people, about children, about justice. You're intelligent and witty, and ..." His face warmed and most likely he had reddened in the cheeks. What was wrong with him? Why couldn't he keep his true feelings to himself?

Eva avoided his eyes and finished the last canape filled with salmon and feta cheese. She chewed and swallowed in an awkward silence. "I think I should go, Tomas. I have work to do at home."

He rose. "Of course. I'll pay the bill."

She touched him on the arm. "No, please let me."

He stroked her cheek as their eyes remained fixed on each other, with heat in his loins. The smoothness of her skin and the warmth of her cheeks made him want to lean in and ravage her mouth. He couldn't get enough of being near her, but he had to get control. "You can pay next time, Eva."

She huffed. "Fine."

Tomas had hoped there'd be a next time as despite their sombre discussion, he enjoyed his time with her, feeling the need to protect her after what she'd been through.

CHAPTER 29

Eva headed towards the road ahead of Tomas, her mind on his words about finding someone to love. She couldn't help but conjure an image of Tomas, as if she could fall in love with him. *Crazy.* How could she think about a man who was unavailable? A man who had stopped believing in love? She had, too.

Dark clouds shadowed the blue skies as she stepped onto the road and turned to see a fast car whizzing towards her. In a flash, two strong arms from behind pulled her out of the speeding car's path. Together, they fell back against the kerb, her neck knocking into Tomas' shoulder. Gasping for breath, she pushed herself off Tomas, who lay beneath her, panting. What in the hell had just happened?

Once she rose, she saw Tomas' legs caught around the drooping tree trunk behind them as he winced in pain and rubbed his back. She approached and helped him up. "Are you all right, Tomas?"

He nodded. "I am fine, but how are *you*? That maniac on the road could have ..."

Eva ignored the looks of those nearby. "I know, and thank you for saving me. It was close." She peered down the road and wondered why someone would drive that fast. But the sense of being watched flickered in her mind. Surely, she hadn't been targeted.

He pulled her back to an empty chair and held her hand. "Eva. Are you sure you're okay? You look frazzled."

"I am fine. Thanks to you, but I'm worried about your back. You need your doctor to check it after falling against that tree."

"I'll be okay, but you're still in shock." He caressed her arm." His piercing eyes soothed her. He shook his head and clenched his hands. "I cannot believe someone would drive that fast around here. If only I got their number plate, but I can remember the car: a white SUV with tinted windows. I couldn't see who was driving because of the windows and how fast it was. Why don't you come over to my place and relax. I'll make you a tea or something stronger. I can't leave you like this."

She shook her head. "Don't be silly. I've got my friend, Francisca at home. I'm not alone, so don't worry. It was a crazy driver in a rush. It's not as if it's likely to happen again."

"Are you sure? I don't mind taking the night off from work."

She waved a hand away. "Stop fussing, please."

He gave her a reassuring smile and walked slowly back across the road. Eva felt safe with Tomas, but she had to feel safe on her own, too.

Back at her apartment, Eva found Francisca on the balcony, gazing at the people walking by. She wrapped her arms around her roommate. The wind brushed her cheek as a chill flowed down her back. She had felt unsettled since almost being run down and wondered if things would get worse before they got better.

Eva told her about the speeding car. The sunlight dimmed when her friend shifted her feet against the railing as if she had something to say.

"Now that I've told you about the near-miss on the road, you seem distracted by something. What is it?"

Francisca curled a brow. "I saw Gonzalo leaving the school after kissing Isabela. She's a married woman."

Eva angled her head. "Wow. Are you sure it was Gonzalo?" She exhaled.

Francisca cleared her throat, then went into the apartment to fetch her wine glass from the coffee table. Returning to the balcony, she said, "It was him. They might love each other."

Eva lifted her shoulders. "I wonder if Tomas knows, but I don't want to get involved. Isabela seems to have other issues, too."

"Right," said Francisca. "It's beginning to sound too weird. But you're not wrong about Isabela. She's been a bit flighty and making mistakes with the students. The other day she kept fumbling her words as she was reading in the group. Something is on her mind."

Eva's heart went out to Isabela. "She must be having marital issues."

"Possibly," said Francisca. "We'll take her out, get her relaxed and hopefully she'll talk. Anyway, let's focus on you. Are you sure you're okay? Should you be going to the police about this speeding car? You mentioned being watched. You don't think …?"

Eva's heart raced. "I don't know. What information do I have? I didn't get the number plate, and many people own a white SUV."

"Still. It could narrow down their choices if they have other information to go on. But why would someone be stalking you?"

Eva shrugged. "I don't know. But that man who warned me must be a sign I'm being watched. I haven't been involved in much of anything."

Francisca stroked the back of her hand. "A warning, perhaps? But I still think you need to go to the police with any minor thing. It could all add up to something."

Eva didn't want to tell the police about this when they had to find Lola's killer and protect Samuel. Why make this more real and anxiety-arousing when it could have been a coincidence and have nothing to do with a stalker? "I don't want to talk about this anymore, Francisca. Let's go inside. It's getting cool out here."

Eva sat on the couch and turned on the TV. She found a comedy show, but her mind wasn't on it.

Her friend joined her. "I wonder how the custody case with Samuel is going."

Eva shrugged. "Let's hope it's resolved quickly. It can't be good for Samuel."

"No, it can't be." She rubbed her hands and raised an eyebrow. "I'd like to know what's happening between you and Tomas."

Eva sighed and averted her eyes. "Nothing. We're friends, but something ..."

Her friend's eyes dilated as if she knew. "Oh my, you guys kissed, didn't you? It happened. I can tell by the redness in your cheeks, and don't damn well deny it, girl. Give me the news."

"Yes, but we shut it down. I'm not looking for a relationship, and neither is he. I've had enough pain with men to last me a lifetime, Francisca. I don't see you being serious with anyone."

She placed her hands on her hips. "We are not talking about me, woman. This is solely about you."

"I have enough on my mind with these suspicious events. I can't cope with anything else. Besides, we have Blanca's wedding next week. Let's focus on that."

"Have you invited Tomas?"

She nodded. "Blanca said it was fine to bring him, but he's coming as a friend."

"Whatever you say."

Eva ignored the fluttery feeling in her stomach. No, she could only see him as a friend, nothing more.

CHAPTER 30

E va climbed the steps inside the St Barbara Parish in Madrid, with its imposing architecture and large courtyard at the entrance. It easily catered to hundreds of guests for any wedding ceremony and had witnessed important royal weddings over the years. Blanca had chosen this church for its rich history and imposing structural presence.

Tomas kept his hand on the small of her back as they climbed the steps, and by the time she made it inside, she was puffing. It was a good workout.

The wedding guests huddled and chatted animatedly until they reached a pew and took their seats behind her friend, Sofia, and Kim's boyfriend, Ricardo. Carlos's best friend, Luiz, Kim, Daniela and her boyfriend, Rafael were part of the bridal party.

"Hi guys," said Eva. "This is my friend, Tomas. These are my friends, Sofia and Ricardo, who is Kim's boyfriend."

"Pleased to meet you both," said Tomas, who wore a well-fitted black suit with a silk shirt, red tie and black patent-leather shoes.

Sofia gave her a cheeky grin and shook his hand. "Oh, the pleasure is mine."

Ricardo pressed his hand firmly into Tomas' hand. "Great to meet a friend of Eva's." He faced her. "I'll be missing Kim tonight, that's for sure."

Eva chuckled. "Don't worry. You have us."

"No doubt," he said as he winked then turned to the front.

Eva waved to Blanca's soon-to-be husband, Carlos, and his groomsmen, as well as Blanca's family scattered around the church. She was nervous for Blanca, who undoubtedly worried about everyone else having a good time rather than herself. If only she could find a love that was as real as theirs, but she didn't see that in her future.

As the small talk continued, Eva felt Tomas's thigh brushing against her own. The pink, long satin dress she wore was tight, with a split on the left side, a low neckline, spaghetti-thin straps, and a pleated waistline. The way Tomas eyed her from head to toe after talking to

Sofia made her blush. Her hands sweated and his woody cologne made her heart flutter. The air conditioner must be malfunctioning.

Tomas leaned in and whispered. "You look beautiful, Eva."

Her chest tightened. "Thanks." She swallowed and felt his hand brush her leg but ignored it, wondering when the ceremony would start. *It is hot in here.*

"I appreciate you inviting me. I love weddings," he said.

She nodded. "I do too, but they can be exhausting. When was the last wedding you attended?" Eva ignored Sofia's wink. She whispered something to Ricardo beside her. *That cheeky girl.*

"An old friend of mine got married in Barcelona. It was a grand wedding with a horse and carriage, a reception in a mansion, and doves flying over the church."

"Sounds beautiful, but expensive."

The wedding march started, and Eva turned with the other guests. Her heart warmed at seeing Blanca at the entrance of the church, linking arms with her father who looked so proud. Blanca wore a Spanish senorita-style wedding dress with tulle gathered at the skirt to the bottom, while the upper part of the dress was fitted with sequins and lace. It was sleeveless with a low back and matching veil.

As she walked inside the church, her eyes were only for Carlos, who shed a tear as he watched her adoringly. Behind her came Daniela, Kim, and one of Blanca's cousins.

When Blanca joined Carlos before the altar, Eva's heart yearned for the kind of love she saw in their eyes. It was mesmerising.

Her heart skipped a beat when Tomas gazed at her.

Then the priest started the ceremony with, "We are gathered here today with Blanca and Carlos, who are joining in holy matrimony. In a moment the bride and groom will say their vows in the presence of all of us and God." He took a breath. "But what is love?"

As she rested back against the pew, Eva felt butterflies in her stomach as the priest spoke of the wisdom of life, and marital love being distinct from other kinds of love. Eva thought her father had loved her in moments when he wasn't violent, abusive or had destroyed her eye. She thought her ex-boyfriend had loved her until he'd become physically violent. It seemed that to the men in her life, love had no meaning, no substance, no real understanding

The clenching in her heart made her avert her eyes from Tomas, who she felt intermittently gazing at her, their arms and legs touching. He appeared to be warm and loving, but was it real, or would he surprise her as others had?

Tomas gently touched her shoulder. She turned to him and forced a smile until seeing something in his eyes that she couldn't put a name to. Was it connection, kinship or something else? But no, she didn't trust her own emotions when she'd created a pattern of misjudgements, suffering, and pain. Did she want to continue to be a victim, or rise above her trauma and take control? How did she do that?

The love she felt for her family and the children she taught was a special kind of emotion that she could trust, but anything other than that, she couldn't.

She broke out of her reverie with the next part of the priest's sermon. "Marriage is not easy, because true love is more than a feeling. It's a choice. It is a covenant or promise to self-sacrifice."

Tomas reached for Eva's hand, and she grinned reassuringly. What was going on between them? She avoided his eyes and focussed back on the priest.

"If you want your marriage to be strong and lasting, you need to choose every day to love the other," the priest continued. "If you choose to do this, your marriage will be one of the most fulfilling, rewarding, and fruitful parts of your entire life."

Eva's heart filled with something she didn't recognise. She found the priest's tone and words comforting and wise. If ever she decided to get married in the distant future, she'd want this priest to perform her wedding ceremony. His words were heartfelt and strong.

After the sermon, Blanca and Carlos recited their vows, and Eva felt tears sting her eyes. Tomas pressed his hand into hers and she wondered if he'd ever let her go. The back of her neck dampened, and her throat felt parched.

The priest said his final words. "You may now kiss the bride."

Carlos leaned in and wrapped Blanca in his arms as they kissed while the guests clapped and whistled.

The guests stood up and applauded again as Blanca and Carlos walked out of the church with the widest of smiles and tears in their eyes. They waved to their loved ones as they stepped outside the church.

Eva approached Blanca, leaned in and hugged her warmly. "Congratulations, beautiful." She kissed her on both cheeks.

"Thanks, Eva." She angled her head. "And this must be Tomas, who you mentioned."

She beamed. "Yes. This is Tomas, a … friend."

He kissed her on both cheeks, too. "Congratulations. Such a beautiful ceremony."

"Thank you, Tomas." Blanca turned to her new husband with a gleam in her eyes.

Carlos wrapped his arms around Eva. "Hi there, gorgeous."

Eva's face warmed. "This is Tomas."

"Congratulations," he said.

Carlos shook his hand firmly. "Thank you, and a pleasure to meet one of Eva's friends. Appreciate you coming."

Eva and Tomas stepped back to make way for other guests, who flocked around them, voices both muffled and deafening as they shouted over each other. She made small talk with her sister, Daniela, Kim and Sofia while Tomas engaged in conversation with Rafael.

But as she laughed at a joke made by Sofia, Eva looked past the people and noticed someone sitting idly in a parked car across the road, watching. She was starting to believe that this was more than paranoia. But it could have been anyone.

CHAPTER 31

E va stepped over glossy outdoor tiles surrounding the wedding reception hall in San Lorenzo de El Escorial, almost an hour away from Madrid. Arriving guests nibbled hors d'oeuvres in the courtyard before sitting down to the prepared meal inside. An array of garden beds and potted tendrils of plants consisting of orchids and greenery, cobblestone fencing, the earthy tones of the stone building, and wide views of the countryside created a rustic ambience.

She was able to breathe in the open air as guests wandered the space while holding glasses of alcohol and snacking on tapas dishes.

After sharing a few snacks in the courtyard while exchanging banter with Tomas, Ricardo, Sofia and Francisca, they stepped inside the reception room that awed Eva. A monumental square fountain dripped water from taps on all sides of a centre post to create a pool.

Separate hedges of assorted shades of green surrounded the monument.

She wandered over to the seating area alongside Tomas, who chatted animatedly with Ricardo about his new business, a popular restaurant in Madrid.

With the formalities finalised and all the guests seated, the food was served. Waiters bustled about the tables serving assortments of croquettes, potato tortilla, and meat platters. Eva leaned into Tomas' scent of wildflowers and cinnamon. She couldn't get enough of the way his eyes looked downward as if in thought, or how his dimples deepened when he smiled. Even the way his eyes lit up as they talked about Samuel. He appeared to be comfortable to show his feelings towards him and children in general. She knew that he was even now remembering his own struggling childhood with his father.

Before they began eating, the master of ceremonies invited the guests to toast the married couple. Eva and the others chose from the variety wines and beer set out on the table. The wine soothed and warmed her parched throat.

She couldn't help but admire the soft lighting that created a romantic and personal ambience, a spacious bar area, a towering chocolate fountain, tall, decorative centrepieces, and a large dance floor. A four-piece band played soft flamenco music in the background, and fancy-looking chandeliers and an interior staircase enhanced the majestic look of the reception area.

Seated with her other side were Francisca, Sofia, work colleagues of Blanca, and Ricardo beside Tomas. She yearned to feel the tautness of his muscles under his tailored suit, and the stubble growing around his chin. She felt something in her heart she couldn't describe and pushed it down as far as she could. This wasn't the time for romance and love. *Love?* Ridiculous. She must have already been drunk.

Francisca touched her arm before reaching out to fork a piece of ham. She chewed it eagerly before speaking. "What are you thinking about, girl?" She had a cheeky grin on her face, which Eva chose to ignore.

"Nothing." She reached out for a croquette and bit into its soft, cheesy texture.

"What did I miss?" asked Sofia.

Francisca turned to her, whispering into her ear when Sofia angled her head. "Hmm. We need to talk alone, young lady. Why don't we go for a walk outside?"

Before she could reply, Francisca pulled her up. "Let's go. I need fresh air."

Rather than make a scene, she obliged and smiled at Tomas, who winked and resumed his conversation with Ricardo. Her heart fluttered.

Eva and the girls headed outside and sat at an inviting bench beside a small pond amidst a cluster of trees and hedges.

The cool breeze feathered her cheeks, and the surrounding nature calmed her mind.

"How's dance teaching, Sofia?"

She took a breath, a dainty hand pressed against her heart. Straightening her posture while her huge chestnut eyes probed into her own, Sofia said, "Loving it, as usual. We've had a huge influx of littlies since Blanca and Rafael did that profile on the school. It's been busy. Daniela's thinking about extending the place, but we'll see how it goes."

Eva leaned in. "Sounds great. Daniela, the entrepreneur." A twig snapped and muffled voices drew close. "Who's that?"

Daniela and Kim arrived in their satin blush pink bridesmaid dresses, which were off-the-shoulder, fitted at the waists, and reached past their ankles. Symbols of elegance.

"I hear you, Sis. I am the entrepreneur and we're doing big things." Daniela lay a hand underneath her chin. Kim smiled and stood demurely beside her.

"That you are," said Sofia. "I was saying how we've had more recruits. Do you still want to hire another dance teacher?"

Daniela nodded. "Oh, yeah. I'm looking at my networks and seeing who might be looking for work. Otherwise, I'll advertise."

Eva beamed. "That's great news. I know you're an astute businesswoman, Daniela. I wouldn't expect anything else."

"Thanks, Darl," said Daniela.

Eva faced Sofia. "Would Reina be interested in dance?"

Sofia shook her head. "No, my daughter prefers acting and drama. I'm looking into classes, but they're not cheap. You never know. She might change her mind in a few years."

Daniela shifted in her seat as she gazed around her in the quiet. "I cannot imagine how you do it on your own, Sofia. You need to find yourself a rich man but still work for me as my dance teacher."

She nodded. "Not many older, nice ones left. I've given up on men and have enough to keep me occupied with Reina, all of you wonderful people and my job, of course."

Kim intervened. "I would be happy to babysit, Sofia. Any time."

"Thanks, Kim, but I'm sure you're plenty busy with Ricardo."

Kim pursed her lips and straightened her posture. "I always have time for my friends. Give me a call anytime."

Sofia smiled. "I'll keep that in mind. Thanks." She turned to Eva. "About Tomas, girl. How much do you like the guy?"

Eva brushed a hand away. "Oh, stop it. Nothing is going on. We're only friends."

"He is plenty sexy," said Daniela.

"Please, Dani." Eva's heart skipped a beat when she noticed Tomas and Ricardo approaching. But when his phone buzzed, he turned around and walked in the opposite direction to take the call. She hid her disappointment, wondering who would ring him this late at night.

Tomas locked eyes with Eva as he walked towards her, yearning to hold her in his arms and slow dance with her. The night was still young.

But when his phone rang, he stepped away and found a quiet space to take his call. It was Leandro. "Hey, man. What's up?"

"I got the results back from the lab. The herb your mother was taking."

He gasped. "What did you find?"

"The vial contained lavender, passionflower, rhodiola and some chamomile. But it also contained purified mercury. Luckily not enough to cause too much damage."

"Jesus, Leandro. Mercury? This is happening way too often considering the other victims we've treated. Do you have any leads at all?"

"Now, come on, Tomas. I can't tell you everything."

"I appreciate it, but you know me. If I can help, I'd like to. If something strange is going on in my community, I need to help them. You know what I've been through and how I can't let others be taken advantage of like that."

"Like you were with your father?"

"Exactly. But are you sure there's nothing else you can tell me?" He took a breath. "Besides. I know you've helped your friend, Rafael, in the past, too."

"Oh, I did forget about that man who threatened Eva. She was right. He is homeless and someone paid him to give her a script. He's not involved and couldn't identify the person who spoke to him. After arranging a meeting with the man, he felt someone blindfold him from behind and bark orders. He never saw the guy."

"That's a shame. Hopefully he might remember something else," said Tomas. "Is there anything more about the sale of these herbs?"

Leandro huffed. "All I can say is that witnesses have mentioned a group: a suspected cult using part of their community to travel around Spain. They sell these herbs for quick cash. They move around quickly with their own stalls, but they've been known to distribute to other market stalls. This is rare, as it means they communicate with more people and leave witnesses behind. They flood that area with as many herbs as they can get before moving on to the next suburb."

"Do you know where this cult might be?"

"Not yet, but stay out of this, Tomas. Leave it to us."

"Thanks, Leandro."

"I have to go, Tomas. Have a good night."

He ended the call and made his way back to the quiet outside space, but the group had left. He returned to the reception area and sat back in his seat while many couples danced to a slow ballad. Eva sat on her own, sipping on a glass of water and rubbing the back of her neck. He yearned to glide his hand across her skin and trail his lips over it.

"Hi Eva. They've abandoned you."

She nodded. "Dancing, as you can see."

He cleared his throat and held out his hand. "Care to dance?"

Eva's face held a fleeting dark expression before smiling. "Okay."

As she rose, he placed his hand on the small of her back and led her to the dance floor, beaming at the couples already there: Blanca and Carlos, Daniela and Rafael, Kim and Ricardo, and Sofia with a man she didn't recognise.

Tomas put his hands around her waist while Eva placed her hands over his shoulders, not caring how intimate they might appear. He couldn't deny that he needed to be close to her tonight, needed to feel her hard against him, needed to trail his hands over her smooth skin, and needed to feel her heart beating against his. Why couldn't he get her out of his mind when every night he thought about her? Then throughout sleep, he dreamed about her, only to wake up with Eva on his mind. She haunted his mind day and night, but what could he do about it? He had no control of his brain, his feelings.

CHAPTER 32

Eva closed her eyes briefly as her weak legs moved to the slow song, the warmth of Tomas' hands against her back. His lime scent drew her further into his chin and their lips were close enough to dare kiss. But as if they could do that in public. What would others think of them dancing together? She didn't care in this moment as her body felt like it was floating on a cloud where only she and Tomas existed.

Tomas inched his way closer until his lips grazed the side of her neck. He lingered as he moaned quietly, his breath accelerating and his hands tightening against her waist. His hand threaded through the back of her hair, massaging it until wispy strands fell out from her bun. What was this man doing to her? She was highly aroused by the feeling of his warm skin across his neck and her heart fluttering over his scent.

When the music stopped, a new slow song played. Tomas angled his face towards her and lingered with the look of hunger in his eyes. "You look beautiful tonight, Eva. So beautiful. I ... I ..." She became speechless and breathless. "Never mind."

Eva licked her lips. "Thanks, Tomas. You look nice, too." When someone's hip knocked into hers, she remembered they were in public. "Hey, Daniela."

She leaned in with Rafael in her arms. "Blanca's about to change into her going-away outfit." Daniela winked in her direction.

"Nice," she said.

Eva moved away from Tomas ten minutes later when the music stopped and the crowd dispersed. The master of ceremonies announced the couple's imminent departure, requesting the guests form a circle.

Tomas held her hand, his eyes on her. She felt as if he was peering into her soul and intermittently gazed at him, too.

When Blanca and Carlos joined the crowd, with huge smiles splashed over their faces, they made their rounds of the guests, including their parents who would most likely be the last they'd greet.

When Blanca wrapped Eva in her arms, she whispered, "You two look amazing together."

She ignored the comment. "Have a beautiful honeymoon, Blanca."

"Thanks, Eva." Blanca made her way around the circle of guests until Carlos came up and hugged her. "You two make a beautiful couple," said Carlos.

"We're not a couple, Carlos. Have a great time and look after my friend."

He beamed as he pulled away. "For life."

Once the married couple made their way towards the exit, the guests yelled and clapped until it became quiet, and the ceremony ended.

Eva said goodbye to family and friends before Daniela pulled her aside while grabbing her bag from the chair.

"My goodness, Eva. You and Tomas looked as if you were about to make love right there on the dance floor. Both oblivious to the crowd."

"Oh, come on Daniela. We were only dancing."

"Hmm. If you say so, but he has it bad for you. So bad. What are you going to do about it, girl?"

She shook her head. "Nothing. We're only friends."

Daniela softened and hugged her. "It's okay to love, Eva. He's a great guy, so don't let him get away. Love is worth it."

Eva wanted to believe her, but she had to protect her heart. "I'm leaving. But I'll see you soon."

Daniela blew her a kiss. "See you, gorgeous."

Tomas watched her with hunger in his eyes. Did he have erotic thoughts about her or was it only her imagination? "Are you all right?"

He nodded. "All good. Ready?"

"Yes, let's go. I've said goodbye to everyone." She remembered his phone call earlier. "If you don't mind me asking, was that the police on the phone? It seemed serious."

"Let's not spoil tonight, Eva. I'll explain tomorrow."

She didn't push it, but her mind ran rampant over worst-case scenarios. But if someone was hurt, he would tell her.

Eva stepped into his car and swung the passenger door closed. "It was a beautiful wedding."

"It was. The bride and bridesmaids were beautiful. It reminds you of the beauty in the world and not only the darkness."

She angled her head. "It sure does."

"I loved dancing with you, Eva. So much."

Eva's throat dried up and she didn't know how to control her heart flips. She kept her eyes focussed through the side window as trees and bushland passed her by. She didn't want this night to end. But soon she'd be in her own apartment, and he'd be in his and who knew when she'd see him again.

Tomas rested a hand on her bare knee and caressed it. Her breathing stopped and her eyes closed to relish the feel of his muscular hands against her leg. She felt safe with Tomas, but another part told her he could hurt her as others had. She wanted him more than she'd ever wanted any man, but her mind got in the way. Could she abandon her logical thoughts for one night, or should she do the right thing?

CHAPTER 33

The quiet of the night instilled an inner peace as Tomas walked alongside her in silence. His head lowered as she made her way to the elevator accessing her apartment.

"I'll say goodbye here. Thanks for the lift and for coming to the wedding."

Tomas had his hands in his pockets, his eyes scanning the area. "My pleasure. Anytime."

Eva was about to turn, but Tomas took her shoulders and turned her body towards him. He leaned forward, but rather than kiss her, he held her gaze and brushed a hand over her brow before trailing it down to her parted lips. She wrapped her tongue around his index finger, gently nibbling and licking with her tongue as she closed her eyes. Tomas moaned and moved his hand to her chin. His lips grazed hers, tasting like dry wine and spices. Hungrily, he explored her mouth deeply as if starved for food. His hand caressed one breast, and she leaned into it, ready for more.

He shifted from her lips and planted tender kisses around her neck. "Oh, Eva. You make me crazy,"

Eva gave him easy access until a group of youths behind them screamed and laughed as they passed, breaking the spell. "I'd better go."

Tomas's eyes darkened. "I understand."

Eva pushed the button for the elevator and headed upstairs.

When she entered her apartment, she saw tired eyes staring back at her. Francisca approached. "Hey there. I only just got back myself. Ricardo drove me home. Why is your hair all messed up?"

Eva finger-brushed her hair, then sat on the couch beside her roommate. "It's been a long night, that's why."

"Right. So, the man I spotted downstairs wasn't Tomas? Are my eyes deceiving me?"

She shrugged. "He dropped me off."

"Really. But why did it take you this long to get back inside? Were you talking?" She raised an eyebrow, mocking her.

"Oh, cut it out, Francisca. Yes, we kissed for the second time, but then a group walked by so I realised I shouldn't have done that."

"Why not? Don't you deserve love?"

"Because of all the things that could go wrong. He is a paramedic and does shift work, so I'd rarely see the man. He's got his issues with trust, and I can't fully trust he won't break my heart. He seems different to my ex-boyfriends, but how do I truly know that? How do I know he doesn't have another side, a darker side, without knowing him well?"

"You know him well enough."

"What? A few months compared to a lifetime with my friends, my family. I can't risk being hurt again. It's too much. Besides, not to be a broken record, but we need to find out what happened to Samuel. His safety and well-being are a priority. It's my focus now. I don't have time to be thinking about a man who no doubt mistrusts women, too, after his ex-girlfriend hurt him. No, it's easier to stay friends."

"Why did you kiss him?"

"I don't know. We were having a tender moment, and it felt right. But now I realise it was all wrong."

"Love is not logical and not wrong. You followed your heart, girl."

"Love? Who's talking about love? I am attracted to the man, but that's it. Nothing more."

"Right. Okay then." She crossed her legs on the couch. "Any leads on the case?"

"No, but I am worried about Samuel. What if he's still in danger? Nothing has happened so far, and I know his father's back, but is he safe? I still wonder where he escaped from."

"You mentioned he might've been part of a religious or spiritual group with the branding on the back of his neck. Could this group be dangerous?"

Eva swallowed. "I hope not, but I've got an uneasy feeling about this. Something doesn't add up. If they weren't dangerous, why would Samuel have cuts and bruises on his body? Someone had to have done it to him."

"It could have been from running around the bush and getting scraped by the trees or falling into rocks."

"No, the police seem to think they weren't from accidents. They were intentional cuts and bruises. How can anyone do that to a small and vulnerable twelve-year-old?"

"I know, but worse things have happened, Eva. Keep yourself safe and don't get involved."

"How can I not when Samuel's my student? I love him like he's my own, and Andreina could do with more warmth."

"But is she looking after him well?"

She nodded. "I believe so, but she hated Lola and seemed to be jealous of her."

"You don't think…"

"Who knows? A few people could be involved. We'll have to wait for the police to catch her murderer."

"Just be on your guard." She sighed. "I know you always are with your security needs, but be careful."

"I will." She rose. "I'm off to bed. Goodnight."

"Goodnight, Eva. Don't dream of Tomas."

Eva huffed as she closed her bedroom door and readied for bed, but in her mind's eye, she saw Tomas kissing and caressing her. She had never felt such a strong attraction before, but love? No, definitely not.

CHAPTER 34

"He's hyperventilating. Give me the oxygen mask, Gonzalo."

Tomas handed it over. "Here you go." After Samuel's breathing calmed, he wrapped the boy in his arms and lay him back on the bed.

Andreina's eyes widened, and she scratched her neck, leaving red marks. Samuel tugged at the mask, and Gonzalo pulled it off. "He's going to be fine. Only minor bruising and a bit of anxiety. He doesn't need to go to the hospital."

Andreina shed a tear. "I don't know what happened. He ... he screamed. He made a sound, so he must have been scared. I rushed inside his room and saw that his window was open. Someone had to have come in, but I didn't see who left."

"Have you called the police?" asked Gonzalo.

"Yes. They are on their way, but who could have come in here and attacked Samuel? How can they encroach on our private space this way?"

"Can I get you a glass of water, Andreina?" asked Tomas.

She sat on the edge of a chair while Tomas got up. "Not me, but for Samuel."

"On it," said Tomas, who went to the kitchen and filled a glass. His chest burned at the idea someone would break in only to hurt a poor, innocent boy. Why?

On his way back to the bedroom, he heard doors slamming closed outside. Then the doorbell rang. It was five o'clock in the morning.

Tomas swung open the door to see police cars and a forensics van. He greeted Leandro and two other officers.

"Hi Tomas. We got a call about an attack on Samuel. We have the forensics team."

"Come in. We've been treating him." He ushered them towards the bedroom and watched the forensics staff take their kits and supplies from the van. He greeted them as they walked inside and prepared to investigate the bedroom.

Officer Sanchez stood opposite Andreina. She shuffled her feet and fidgeted with her hands. Her whole body quaked. The police took her to a quiet corner in the living room and took her statement while Tomas and Gonzalo put away their medical supplies. Samuel rested on the sofa, staring up at the ceiling while the forensics team got to work.

Tomas joined Leandro in the living area. "What are you thinking?"

Leandro put on gloves and slowly wandered around the living room to inspect windows and dust furniture for fingerprints while jotting down notes. "I wonder if whoever came wanted to take him, but his screams stopped them." He pressed a finger to his temple. "I won't speculate until we've gathered enough evidence and can get information from Samuel."

"Do you think it's a cult member wanting to take him back?"

"I don't know, but his father has recently arrived. Though I don't believe he would try to jeopardise the custody case by kidnapping his own son."

Tomas said, "Samuel has been traumatised enough."

"He sure has. If we can get him to speak, it'll help. But it has to be in his own time." One of the forensics men began dusting the window for fingerprints. "Did you see anything strange when you first arrived, or any unusual person hanging around outside?"

"No, nothing," said Tomas. "It was all quiet in the street."

"I'll get the officers to canvas the street to see if anyone witnessed an intruder. I'll also check for CCTV footage. But we may get nothing, depending on the angle of cameras."

Leandro scribbled further notes, then approached Samuel on the couch. "Hi, Samuel. Do you remember me?" Samuel nodded. "I am here to investigate what happened. How are you feeling?" He stared past the detective. "I was wondering. Do you like drawing?" Samuel nodded again. "Great. Do you think you could draw exactly what happened, especially the person who hurt you? It would help us with our investigation."

Samuel knit his brows and nodded. He bowed down, picked up a pencil and drew an outline of a man picking him up out of bed, and Samuel kicking him in the face. The man who climbed through the window had a bulky build, with shoulder-length wavy hair.

"Did the man try to kidnap you?" Samuel nodded. "Do you know this man?" He shook his head. "Okay, thank you, Samuel. This is very helpful." Leandro winked.

Some time later, the forensics team packed up their equipment and took everyone's fingerprints to eliminate them from the investigation.

Andreina placed coffee cups on the table for the police officers and Leandro. She sat at the table and lifted her own coffee cup to her trembling lips. "I think it's Adan." She turned to Samuel. "Was it your father in disguise?" Samuel shook his head.

"Okay, we can rule him out, but he could have hired someone. I would not put it past that creep. It's not like he didn't traumatise Samuel when he was living with them."

"We'll interview him to rule him out." Leandro sighed. "Can you think of anyone who might have a grudge against you, Andreina?"

"No, not for a long time since my work incident, as you know."

Leandro handed her his card. "If you think of anything, no matter how trivial, please give me a call. We'll have a police car patrol this street tonight."

"Thank you, Detective. I do appreciate that."

Tomas and Gonzalo headed back inside their paramedic van after waving goodbye to everyone.

"I cannot believe that happened. Poor guy," said Tomas.

"Exactly. I wish I knew what was going on. First that boy, Efren, goes missing and now Samuel is attacked. Someone has a grudge against children." Gonzalo gripped the steering wheel and banged his fist against it.

"Are you all right?"

"I am scared for this community, Tomas." He knit his brows. "Scared of innocent people being poisoned with mercury. What in the hell is going on with this mercury business and hurting kids?"

"I wish I knew, but the police will find out. Leandro's a top-notch detective, so he'll get to the truth."

"I don't know anymore," said Gonzalo.

Why was his friend acting this way? He'd never let victims get to him this way before. He had been behaving strangely for weeks now. "Is there something you're not telling me, friend?"

He shrugged his shoulders. "Nothing." His phone buzzed, and he stared at the display, arching his brow, hesitating.

"Why don't you answer it?"

"No, it's not important."

Tomas knew he was lying but wouldn't push it for now. Surely, he didn't know more about Samuel's situation than he was letting on. No, impossible. He trusted his friend. Gonzalo would tell him if something was wrong.

CHAPTER 35

Later that afternoon, Eva rested on an ergonomic chair in Esmeralda's office, her chest on fire. What was Samuel's father, Adan, trying to do? Re-traumatise Samuel? She had an uneasy feeling about the man and wondered whether he had anything to do with Lola's death. It wouldn't surprise her in the slightest after having met the man while he was still married to Lola. The man was a deviant, and she had to make her case with Esmeralda.

Esmeralda leaned forward in her seat as she tossed a pen between her hands, her eye twitching a few times. She scrutinised Eva while resting back against her chair. Her eyes softened. "Listen, Eva. I will be there on supervised visits with Adan once this situation with Lola is resolved."

"If only the police had believed her and put the abuse on record. She tried but they didn't listen. But there is proof of her injuries in the hospital when she was beaten by that shark. Isn't that enough?"

She rested back against her chair and lifted a document. "There was no evidence that Adan hurt her. But I have written a support letter in favour of Samuel remaining with Andreina, which should help. I understand Samuel's not close with his father and was a witness to the abuse." Esmeralda huffed. "I do not doubt for one second that she was abused, but my hands are tied when it comes to law enforcement."

"But Lola is dead, and she cannot report him now, can she? What if he killed her?"

Esmeralda hesitated as if having the same idea. "It's possible, but again, without evidence, it's pointless. As his father, he has rights." She leaned forward. "Things will work out. Why don't we change the subject. How are you sleeping lately? Still having nightmares?"

Eva shook her head. "No, not as often, and that's thanks to you. I don't know what I would've done if it wasn't for you, Esmeralda."

The psychologist reached for her hand and patted it with a grin. "It was all you." Esmeralda's shoulders squared and a light in her eyes soothed Eva. "This is why I love my job, Eva. It's worth the sacrifices I make to be there for the staff and students. It's a challenge when I wish I could split myself in half and help everyone. Some can't be helped, yet others can. Giving them a better life, a better future, and self-respect." She smiled. "I've spoken to Ignacio about more funding to help those in need, and he's agreed. He's considering recruiting another psychologist alongside me."

Eva nodded. "That's good news."

"It is, but it'll take time before that happens."

"It's a good first step. I know how hard you work with all these students. But you need to take care of yourself, too." She rose.

"I am, Eva. Don't you worry about that."

"How is that boyfriend of yours?"

Esmeralda waved a hand away. "Oh, we've decided to call it quits. I don't trust him because every time he says he'll do something, he does the opposite. But he does have a big chunk of money that goes to good causes at times." She huffed. "Still, it reminds me of bad past relationships. Bullies, abusers. I'm better off on my own. I love the freedom and control to do what I like without having to answer to anyone."

Eva nodded. "I get that. It's not easy to trust people. I should know." She rose. "I'd better go. See you soon." She swung open the door and ambled down the corridor. Spotting Isabella, she waved hello, but the woman stared straight ahead and ignored her. Eva turned around and called from behind. "Isabella, hello."

Stopping in her tracks, the woman waved back. "Sorry. I had other things on my mind and didn't see you there, Eva. I'm going. See you tomorrow."

Eva stepped closer and placed a comforting hand on Isabela's shoulder. "What's going on? You seem upset about something."

Isabela's breathing quickened as she scratched the centre of her chest. Her feet shuffled and she attempted a smile that didn't reach her eyes. "Oh, you know. Family stuff with my boy, my husband. Not getting enough sleep." Her eyes misted. "But I have a plan to change things, to make sure things work out. You'll see."

Eva had an uneasy feeling and could tell she was lying. Something else was going on. "Listen. Let's leave this place and have a coffee. We can have a nice chat."

Isabela fixated on her but then shook her head. "No, too busy. I have somewhere I need to be. I'll see you tomorrow."

Eva knit her brows. "Are you sure?" Isabela nodded. "Okay then."

She got a sick feeling? Should she have tried harder to have that long chat? What was Isabela's hurry? Did she have a big secret?

Tomas stood outside Gonzalo's apartment after not hearing from him for a few days. He had been acting strangely, missing days of work at different times, not sleeping, and receiving phone calls from a mystery caller.

He leaned in to ring the doorbell when a lanky woman stepped out with a beaming expression. "Bye Gonzalo." She flinched at seeing Tomas. "Aah ... hello. I needed to talk to Gonzalo about a medical issue." Quickly she scurried to her car parked by the curb.

Gonzalo averted his eyes and stared at the ground. "What are you doing here?"

"Seriously?" Tomas put his hands on his hips and shook his head. "Isn't Isabela married? What the hell are you doing with a married woman?"

He shrugged. "I care about her and she's thinking about leaving her husband."

Tomas scoffed. "That's what they all say, but sneaking around with her isn't right. I thought something was wrong with you, but here I find out you're having an affair. Does the husband know?"

"No, of course not. Why would he?"

Tomas inched closer. "Well, if she wants to leave him, she'd have to give him a reason. This is a complex situation, Gonzalo."

"I don't know what she'll tell him. Jesus, man. I can't stop seeing her. We have fun and I might be falling for her. Please don't give me grief." He scoffed. "Do you want to come inside, or are you planning to stand outside to give me a hard time?"

"I am sorry, Gonzalo. I hope you're not going to get hurt, that's all." He stepped inside the house with an uneasy feeling. Affairs usually didn't end well, and who knew if he could trust Isabela to do right by his friend.

CHAPTER 36

E va sat on a hard timber chair, her feet resting on matte floorboards. She savoured the view of potted artificial plants against colonial windows, a set of stools leaning against the bar counter, and suspended round lamps that gave the space a tropical yet cosy ambience.

"I wonder how Blanca and Carlos are doing in the Basque Country," said Eva.

The gleam in Daniela's eyes brightened. She had always been the free spirit, the party girl. "I wish I was there with them, but Rafael and I are planning to go there soon."

"After what happened the last time, Daniela, are you sure you want to go back?" asked Sofia, whose dainty baby-blue fingernails scraped her cheek. She was always the rational one in the group.

Daniela nodded. "Hell, yes. I'm not going to let my past dictate my joy in life. No way." She rubbed her hands together with a gleam in her eye. "We should all make a trip of it."

"I hear what Daniela's saying and what you're saying, but we can compromise. We could travel to France's Basque region. That way we're close but not in the middle of it," said Kim, who liked to mediate as the peacemaker of the friendship group.

Daniela shrugged. "I could easily do two trips: one with Rafael and another with you guys."

Eva laughed. "Any excuse for you to have fun and get away from real life, ha sister? But not everyone has the flexibility you do with your business."

"Not true, Sis. I work damn hard, but I like to enjoy the fruits of my labour," she added. She had suffered a lot two years ago because of family secrets, but at least now everything was out in the open.

Francisca put a hand on Daniela's shoulder. "You deserve to take as many trips as you like, provided you look after yourself and don't burn out. Even holidaying constantly can be exhausting. You need balance." Francisca loved to nurture others, but it sometimes bordered on over-protectiveness.

A towering waitress set down their sangrias and cocktails with tapas dishes that included croquettes, ham, a range of cheeses, bread, chorizo sausage, assorted pastries, and fish bites.

Daniela was the first to dig into the cheese and bread. "I try." She faced Eva. "So, Sis. What's happening with the murder case? Any leads?"

Eva shook her head. "Not that I know of, but I read in the news about a young boy who's been missing for a couple of months. His name's Efren. Apparently, he was last seen at one of those markets selling herbs."

Sofia's eyes widened. "Is that a coincidence, or do you think it has something to do with Samuel and this special group?"

"The article mentioned that detectives are investigating a possible connection, and that they believe a cult is involved. What if that poor boy's been recruited into this group? So scary. Even Samuel got attacked by an intruder. He's okay but still not talking. Something's scared him." She explained the remainder of the story.

"Samuel has been through a lot. I would not wish it on my worst enemy." Kim threaded a hand through her jet-black hair, having also endured trauma.

"I hope he'll talk one day. He needs to trust it's safe enough to talk," said Eva.

"He might not feel that way." Francisca touched her gently on the shoulder. She gestured for Eva to dig into the food.

Eva bit into a chorizo sausage, then sipped on the sangria. "I know, but I wonder how long this is going to take. Tomas was telling me he's had a few victims of mercury poisoning, which is a frightening thing to be happening in our community."

Daniela angled her head as she threw a croquette into her mouth. "Talk to Blanca when she gets back from her honeymoon. Or you could talk to Rafael now. I know they're working on a story about mercury and the effects. They might be linking it to the cult, too."

Eva nodded. "Interesting. Blanca should be back within a week, right?" Daniela nodded. "Or I might speak to Rafael. The sooner the better."

Francisca put up a hand. "Be careful. If you're being watched, take extra care. Don't forget those few incidents."

Daniela, Kim and Sofia all stared at her wide-eyed, and Eva realised she had not told them anything about possibly being followed at Retiro Park, almost run down on the road, and threatened by a homeless man who'd been paid off. She summarised the story.

"I'm sorry. I didn't say anything, but I didn't want you guys to worry. Francisca lives with me, so she knows when something's wrong. But nothing has happened since then. The stalking has stopped."

"You don't think there's a connection with this police case?" asked Kim.

"I spoke to one of Tomas' friends and police contact, Leandro. He's looking into it."

Daniela waved a hand. "Leandro's friends with Rafael, too. I didn't know he knew Tomas, Eva. It's a small world."

Sofia leaned forward to reach for her cocktail, skolling the remainder of it down. The bangles around her wrist jangled. "Have you visited churches or spoken to the religious community about cults? If they're connected to religion, it might be worth exploring."

"I did plan to do that and might consider it. Thanks for reminding me, Sofia."

Daniela rested a hand underneath her chin. "Enough negative talk. I want to know about Loverboy. How is he?"

Eva shook her head. "Oh, stop it. We are only friends." Her face warmed.

"Right," said Sofia. "Does the fact that you kissed him not mean anything?"

Eva shrugged. "Well, maybe it was twice but … you know … it was shut down. I mean, the second time we were interrupted. But I need to leave it at that."

Daniela gave her a cheeky grin. "I say, go for it. Enjoy him, at least."

"Typical of you to say that," said Francisca. "Her heart is involved, so let her tread carefully and at her own pace."

Kim nodded. "I agree. Why create conflict within herself if she is not sure? Better to take it nice and slow." She frowned. "When was the last time you saw Tomas?"

Eva hid her disappointment. "Not since Blanca's wedding a week ago. But he has texted a couple of times to check in." She wondered why they hadn't got together and missed him. She couldn't get his kisses out of her mind.

"Too long," said Daniela.

"I might have been abrupt with him after a group of youths interrupted us. My logical mind got in the way. He might be upset."

Sofia intervened. "You need to explain how you feel, Eva."

Eva drank the remainder of her drink. Since seeing Tomas, she hadn't been able to sleep or eat properly. Her thoughts broke when her phone buzzed with a notification. Retrieving it from the table, she clicked on Isabela's text. *Can I meet with you? It's important.*

CHAPTER 37

Tomas flashed back to his kiss with Eva. His heart had sung until she had brushed him off and walked hurriedly into her apartment. He hadn't seen her for over a week and admitted to avoiding her. But Eva could have contacted him after their second kiss. She was either doubtful or didn't have strong feelings the way he did.

He didn't know how he could keep his hands to himself when he was with her. He feared he was falling for her. What could he do with these intense feelings? He couldn't shut them off, but he couldn't commit to anything more than a fling. Would it be wrong to have sex with the woman he was attracted to? Did it have to come with strings?

He lounged back against his sofa on this lazy Sunday, and hovered over his phone, scrolling to his contacts list and finding Eva's number. His poetry reading was coming up, and they had discussed getting together for that. At least he'd have an excuse, and she would most likely agree, given they were both writers.

Clicking on her number, Tomas waited. "Hi Eva. It's me." Silence. "Eva?"

She cleared her throat. "Hi, Tomas. It's been a while. How are you?"

"Fine. You?"

"All good here. I assume you heard about Samuel's father returning?"

"I heard from Leandro about that, yes. Have you heard about what happened to Samuel at his house?"

"Yes, from school. Samuel doesn't get a break."

"There's still no clue about his attacker though." His heart squeezed tight at the idea that Samuel might be in danger.

"At least the police are watching the house for now."

Tomas took a calming breath, relishing the sound of her voice. "Sure, but there is a limit to their resources. They need to find his attacker."

"Of course." Silence again. "I am thinking of visiting a few churches to put feelers out about any known groups calling themselves *Peace and Harmony.*"

His heart raced. "Why would you do that? Put yourself at risk?"

"I live close to a church, so it'll seem like I'm religious, that's all."

He knew he wouldn't change her mind. "At least let me go with you. We can work as a team."

"I would prefer doing it on my own. Besides, I'm sure you're busy with work and ... women."

He laughed, thinking that no one could ever measure up to Eva. She was unique. "No women, but I am busy with work and catching up with friends. Life, as we know it. But I have ... I have ... missed you."

"Tomas, let's forget what happened. It was a mistake and ... I don't need more complications right now. My sense of security's been shaken with this whole murder case, and I can't focus on anything else right now. Are we still friends?"

Tomas felt a stabbing pain in his stomach and took a deep breath. She obviously didn't feel as strongly towards him as he did her. Best to know now. "Of course. Friends." He pushed aside the burning ache in his chest. "I was calling about my poetry reading. Would you like to join? It's scheduled to happen next Saturday."

"Sounds good. Text me the details and I'll be there."

"No worries. Talk then." He ended the call, thinking he'd struggle to wait to see her for another six days, but he had no choice. It wasn't as if his home in La Latina was walking distance to her place in Plaza de Espana.

He worried about Samuel and how he'd been attacked, bringing out more of his protective instinct. Whoever had hurt a vulnerable twelve-year-old would have to pay. He had to do his own research. Even this boy, Efren, who was announced in the news was possibly connected to this case.

Tomas reached for his laptop, and did a search on news articles about missing people over the last year. His eyes widened at seeing the thousands of people in Spain alone who went missing each year. He narrowed his search to Madrid. An article mentioned that recently Spain had seen an increase in the number of missing person cases. The missing people were not limited to any age group, and they left grief-stricken families behind without closure.

As he rubbed the back of his neck, he typed in *mercury poisoning in Spain* but couldn't find anything, apart from environmental pollution in Brazil. When he typed in the words, *cults in Spain*, the findings were myriad, including dangerous cults that controlled women and children through religion. An *El Pais* newspaper article reported that sects in Spain often named themselves as meditation or yoga groups to lure people of all backgrounds, even professionals.

Tomas scrolled down the article which went on to report that some cults recruited through the internet, while others spoke to people on the street. Some might put up signs and offer spiritual or religious classes. Occasionally, people would be introduced by a friend or acquaintance to the cult or group.

Tomas remembered reading about Lola's murder and how she'd inherited money from an aunt two years earlier. Did the cult know about this and somehow lure her into it? No doubt she may have been vulnerable, and struggling to raise Samuel on her own. The cult might have helped her to feel heard and promised a cure for his mutism.

CHAPTER 38

Eva's hands lay on a soft cotton tablecloth over a round table in a corner café at Plaza de Espana with Isabela gripping a steaming espresso, her hands shaking. Isabela's eyes glazed over as if she hadn't slept and appeared ungroomed. The woman jumped at every footstep that passed by as if she was constantly on guard.

They sat on high white stools with a view of the glass doors, open to invite patrons in. The smell of tapas and assorted herbs and seasonings whet her appetite. Isabela mentioned not having an appetite so opted for only a hot espresso.

She wore her hair in a bun and a scarf around her neck, with dangly gold earrings, a choker and bangles giving her an aloof wealthy appearance. On the inside, something was going on with her and Eva was determined to find out what.

"How are you doing, Isabela?"

The woman shrugged as she tightened the scarf around her neck as if her hands needed to move. Her eyes flitted back to the door whenever a customer walked in. She placed a finger to her temple when a loud group entered the café. "I'm okay. Busy with family and the school volunteer work. Nothing more to do but spend my husband's money, too."

Eva nodded. "Joaquin is doing remarkably well, especially in maths. But the other day he was doodling on his pad. He drew a woman crying. I asked him where it came from, and he said that he'd seen you crying at home. I hope I'm not overstepping, but I care, and I like the way you contribute to the school. I worry about you, Isabela, and I'm here to listen to whatever's going on." She sighed when Isabela's head shifted back to the door, her feet jittery. "I know you miss Lola, but I get the feeling there's something more. If I can help, please let me."

Isabela touched the bottom of her jaw, curling a brow. "Can we move over to that corner table? It's a bit more private."

Eva got up from the stool. "Of course." She followed her to the corner table and cushioned chairs further away from the door. "Okay. What did you want to tell me? I'm all ears."

Isabela's lower lip quivered. "Before I start, I hope you don't judge me." She stretched out her fingers and rubbed her palm. "When I decided to get involved, I didn't know the truth. I didn't know what was going on. I would never put my son, husband or …"

Eva angled her head. "Or who?"

She exhaled and bowed her head. "I'd never want to put my family in danger, or friends. The thing is …" Her phone buzzed in her bag. She rummaged for it and when she looked at the display, her face drooped. She quickly turned away. Eva waited but she grabbed her bag from the chair beside her, her eyes darkening. "I have to go. I remembered an urgent meeting. Please excuse me."

Eva placed a gentle arm on Isabela. "Please tell me what's going on. I can help, and if you need the police, we can go to them. Who called you?" She stared past her. "Let me know you're safe. Are you?"

She laughed. "Of course I am. Don't worry, Eva. I appreciate your concern, but I'm fine. It's nothing a bit of problem-solving won't fix." Scurrying to the exit, she waved. "Bye."

Eva stared after her, then slumped. She picked up her phone from her bag and called the police station. "Yes, hello. My name is Eva Lopez. I need to speak to Detective Leandro."

The officer responded, "I'm sorry. He's out now. Can I take a message?"

"Yes, please. Get him to call Eva Lopez. I believe it might be urgent. It's important he gets this message. Otherwise, I'll come down to the station."

"I will relay the message, Miss. Thank you for the call."

She ended the conversation and gazed towards the exit, thinking about what Isabela had been about to say before rushing off. It had to have been the message on her phone. She had been about to tell her something important, but someone stopped her. Who could it be, and what spooked her enough to leave? Was someone watching them?

She wondered if the police would get involved without probable cause to monitor Isabela's movements or search her phone. She needed evidence and thought about following her the next time she was at school. Attending the nearby church might offer her clues.

CHAPTER 39

E fren turned to Maria. "I think I saw Marco going inside that cabin with a young girl." Last week, he was sure he'd seen him enter the cabin with a different girl, a teenager who appeared to be new in the group. He had questioned Marco about it, but he had brushed it off, saying that he was offering her counselling sessions. Efren felt uneasy because his arm had been around the scared girl. Maria stared past him, silent. "Maria?"

The stocky woman in her thirties reminded him of his mother. Even with her strict attitude, she had kind eyes. Sometimes he wondered if she had a family of her own. Sadness filled her eyes sometimes. "Do not defy me, Efren. I suggest you mind your business before you disturb anyone. If Marco is there, don't let him know you're there. He'll get upset."

He nodded, curious as to why he couldn't question things in his new community. "Is he offering counselling sessions, Maria?"

The woman angled her head with a blank look. "What?"

He waved a hand away. "Never mind."

Despite this area being out of bounds for most members, Efren headed to the cabin quietly and turned the doorknob. *Locked.* Curious, he walked to the back to where he spotted a small window, its curtain partly drawn. Inside, he spotted the teenage girl. Marco stood beside her with his arms on her shoulders.

"But sir. Can I please finish these chores?" she said meekly, with her dainty hands threading through her bob-style brown waves.

"I think you know what you need to do, young lady."

A tear streamed down her cheek as he yanked her by the arm. He pushed her down to the couch when he unzipped his pants, prodding her head between his legs. "Get on with it, and don't stop until I tell you to."

Efren's heart raced, feeling nauseous. *What the hell!*

Inspired by Sofia to explore religious spaces to find anyone who knew about cults, Eva walked to St Anne's Catholic church after work the next day. To allay suspicion, she had decided to say she was doing research for her book. The church was near her apartment, and she was only taking an evening stroll. Nothing wrong with that.

Stepping inside, she took in the empty church. A sign on a concrete post announced religious events, the night's Mass, and other daily matters. Fans mounted on the posts lining the church helped relieve the heat.

Eva sat in a pew and breathed in the quiet space of the church, a coldness penetrating the air. She closed her eyes and waited to attend evening Mass, curious about whether church members here knew anything about spiritual or religious groups that were a front for a cult.

She broke out of her reverie when the priest, a sturdy-looking man, began preparing for evening mass. He spread a clean white cloth over the holy table at the altar, then clasped his hands in prayer as he scanned through the bible.

Swarms of people soon entered the church, moving to the rows of pews, some of them stoic while others sat with relaxed postures. Music in the background put her in a religious and tranquil mood. She picked up a brochure on the pew beside her and skimmed through it.

After the mass an hour later, Eva made her way to the priest. She squeezed her hands together while the priest smiled in greeting.

"How can I help you, young lady?" He put down the Bible, put his hands together and waited. His blue eyes fixed on hers as he unclasped his hands and rubbed his bald patch.

Eva steadied herself. "I'm an author, and I was wondering if ... if you could answer a few questions for research purposes."

"Go on."

"I am writing about sects or cults, and was curious to know if you have any ideas about communities that might be operating as spiritual or religious groups in the area. Particularly those with a mission or mantra promoting peace and harmony. Or those groups who sell refined mercury and herbal medicine of sorts. Any that you might know in the countryside of Spain?"

He frowned. "Okay. That is heavy, indeed." He ushered her over to a front pew. "I've heard many stories over the years about nuns leaving their convents due to being part of a suspected cult. Even the Pope has spoken out about the Christian Palmerian church disguised as a cult, but none that I know of more recently. It has spread over the news for many years. I have no personal experience of any groups that exist today or those professing those words, 'peace and harmony'. I am sorry I cannot tell you more."

"Do you know of any spiritual groups that might discuss their expertise through yoga or meditation practices, or any New Age Catholic groups you might know of?"

He smiled. "My dear child. I have no knowledge of such groups, but we do run many programs for the local community. However, these programs are a part of the church and not anything related to spirituality or alternative health approaches. You could enquire with some of the fellow parishioners who might have joined spiritual groups. I know there are several here who engage in such groups." He rose from his seat. "This isn't about research, is it?"

Eva swallowed. "No, I am worried about a friend who might have got caught up in this type of group."

"This is the job of the police, so tread carefully," he said.

"Thank you for your time, Father."

She made her way outside the church and was hit by a cool gust of air. Did she have the energy to enquire with other churches, when most likely they wouldn't say anything to a stranger even if they did have knowledge? What if they were involved, which could put her in more danger?

Footsteps behind her made her turn, and the priest put up a hand. "I do remember something." His eyes darkened. "A man attended Mass here, but he appeared out of place. In passing, he spoke to a few fellow parishioners about offering spiritual enlightenment classes and yoga."

Eva's shoulders lifted and her body felt light. "Can you describe this man?"

He nodded. "Vaguely. He wore a cap and glasses so I couldn't see his face properly. The thing that stood out was him touching his leg as if he was in pain. That's all I remember."

"Had he been to mass another time?" He shook his head. "Do you know if anyone took him up on his offer?"

The priest shrugged. "I don't know, but the man handed out these flyers before he left. I assume he was advertising the group, but it had nothing to do with us."

Interesting. "Did you offer to pin up the flyers on your board out front?"

"I did, but he said it wasn't necessary. He preferred talking to people about it."

"It's helpful. Thank you."

She made her way to the street to hail a taxi, but bumped into Tomas on her way, who was headed towards her. His tight black pants and white fitted-t-shirt accentuated his toned physique, causing tingles through her body.

"I was hoping to see you, worried that you might put yourself at risk by talking to church members. Let me at least come with you."

"I spoke to the priest. He told me about this parishioner who spoke to a few people about spiritual classes and yoga. But who knows if we're just clutching at straws. Not everything is connected, surely."

"Hmm. Interesting, but who knows. It might be worth talking to Leandro about this."

"Possibly." She shifted. "This man might be a local."

"It does sound suspicious."

She took a breath. "I have a meeting planned with Daniela's boyfriend, Rafael, about his research into mercury poisoning. I need to go."

"I would love to go with you," said Tomas.

She swallowed and ignored his searing eyes as if they weren't burning a hole in her chest. Oh, how she yearned for this man. "Okay then. Let's go."

CHAPTER 40

E va rang the doorbell to Rafael's house, knowing Daniela would be home having recently moved in with him.

Rafael opened the door and ushered them inside. "Great to see you both."

"Hey there, guys," said Daniela who wrapped her arms around her and Tomas. She wore a skin-tight leotard with a loose linen top over it, her hair a little dishevelled, no doubt from her late dance class.

"I'll get us snacks, and we can get started," said Rafael, walking away.

Eva scanned the landscaped back garden. A nectarine and a lemon tree, low brush and ferns framed an immaculate-looking green lawn. Her shoulders brushed Tomas' as they made their way to the patio, where Rafael set down a tray of chorizo sausage, herb crackers, hard cheeses, and ham. A radio played music softly in the background.

Daniela carried a tray of glasses and a jug of sangria, setting them down on the rickety slatted timber table. "Home-made sangria," she said.

Rafael sat opposite them. "The lawn you guys are looking at is not my doing. I wish it was, but I pay a gardener to maintain it at least once a fortnight."

Tomas nodded. "Great work. I might need his number."

"Of course," he said. "Who has time to weed and garden these days? My work takes me everywhere and I sometimes get late-night calls. I'm lucky Daniela understands how career-minded I am."

"It's why I love you, Raf. Your ambition, your dedication to the community, and your big heart." She inched closer to him when Rafael pulled her by the chin and devoured her with his lips.

Eva's face reddened, especially when Tomas's eyes dilated at the sexy way Rafael's tongue continued to dive deep into her sister's mouth. She wanted to say something but knew they'd stop. She yearned for the deep and abiding love they shared. It was as if they couldn't get enough of each other.

Daniela pulled away from Rafael then poured the sangria into four glasses, acting as if they hadn't just shared an erotic display of affection.

She and Tomas looked out over the vista. Their thighs touched and a tingle down her spine made her gasp. Why couldn't she get these arousing thoughts about this man out of her head?

Daniela's lips pursed. "How are things, Eva? And be honest. The stalking?"

Eva took a breath. "It seems to have stopped, so I'm fine. I'm a big girl and can take care of myself. I don't want you guys to worry."

Daniela gripped the glass. "Well excuse me for caring as a sister should. Hell, you should have told me the instant it happened and not weeks later."

Rafael caressed the side of her neck. "Honey. She told you. It doesn't matter when. If the tables were turned, would you have told your sister?" Daniela remained silent. "I didn't think so. You guys love each other and want to protect each other. So long as we know what's happening, we'll keep our guard up. Leandro's on our side. If anything seems suspicious, we need to let him know straight away."

"No doubt," said Tomas. "Have you heard anything from him recently?"

"Nothing," said Rafael. "But these things take time and if you rush it, lives can be at stake. Don't do too many things at once, and if you need something, let me know." He opened his laptop and clicked on keys as if searching. A manila folder of papers lay beside him.

Eva nodded. "Thanks, Rafael. Will do."

"I hope they find this teenager, Efren," said Daniela. "But he might just be a runaway and not a part of this cult."

Tomas leaned forward. "Any chance you'd know where his mother lives? If we understand Efren's background, it could give us clues about a possible connection."

Rafael typed into his computer then rummaged into his pocket for a miniature notepad. He reached for a pen on the table and jotted something down. "Here is Efren's mother's address."

Tomas tilted his head. "How did you find it so quickly?"

He laughed. "I have my ways. If I tell you, I'll need to kill you, so mum's the word. Do we have a deal?"

Daniela punched him in the arm. "Oh, Raf. You make me laugh, but I do love your ingenuity and resourcefulness."

"Same here," said Eva.

Tomas' swallowed and threaded a shaky hand through his hair. "Has Leandro got any leads on Efren?" Rafael shook his head. "I'll speak to his mother."

"Make sure no one follows you," said Rafael.

Eva's shoulders shook as if a cold piece of ice dripped across them. "I'll come with you. Make sure you stay in line."

Tomas frowned. "Let me do this on my own, Eva. I don't want you involved anymore."

"I'm not taking no for an answer. Lola was my friend and I'm sure that whoever kidnapped Efren is connected to her."

"Hmm," said Rafael, placing an index finger against his chin. "Be careful, Eva. This sounds bigger than all of us."

"I will be careful, Rafael." Eva bowed her head, wanting this nightmare to be over. She hated being on shaky ground and not living her life freely.

Rafael glided a hand through his ash-black hair, his rich brown eyes fixed on her with concern. "I have found out some things which I left out of my recent news articles. My friend and boss, Fernando, doesn't want me rocking the boat too much." He reached for the manila folder and caused a pile of printed documents to scatter over the table. Picking up a piece of cheese, he swallowed it whole.

Eva scanned through the documents. "I do appreciate this, Rafael."

Rafael flicked through a page. "There have been stories about groups using mercury to weaken people, so they don't leave the community. It's about using a substance to control, but long-term use leads to cognitive impairment."

"Lola had mercury in her system when she might have been trying to get away. How could she escape if that was the case?" Eva's hands turned numb as if she was feeling her old friend's pain. How could anyone be so cruel as to kill her, most likely in front of her son?

Rafael leaned forward. "It affects everyone differently, but my guess is she might have not had much in her system. If we could get Samuel to talk, it would help, but he's obviously too scared." He clicked on keys on his laptop. "I have special access to specific sites that allow me to cross-check mercury victims in the last five years to those who either had chronic pain or were wealthy. I believe they target those who have intolerable physical pain, so they can sell them these herbs at market stalls and try to recruit at the same time. Not only that, but they must do their research on those who have the means to give them large donations."

Tomas cleared his throat. "Lola was a single parent, Rafael. Do you think she was targeted because of her inheritance?"

"It's possible she gave the group her inheritance. But also because Samuel was having behavioural problems at the time they went missing. They might have seen her as someone vulnerable, someone who needed help. I am guessing she escaped because she realised, they weren't the spiritual group who prioritised their well-being."

Eva's spine chilled as the realisation hit her like a stack of bricks. It made sense. "My goodness, Rafael. I was telling Tomas that she lived in an old, decrepit house and never bothered to buy a new one when she had the means. It sounds as if she might have given the group her inheritance."

"That would be my guess," said Rafael.

Eva huffed. "Do you think they disguise themselves as a spiritual group?"

"No doubt." Rafael turned to Tomas. "Leandro's been helping me with my current news stories about mercury connected to spiritual groups. As an investigative journalist, I usually get priority with important breakthroughs in a case when it's safe for me to publish the news."

Eva had an uneasy sense about all this and hoped that speaking to Efren's mother might give them clues about Samuel and Lola.

CHAPTER 41

Tomas shifted his shoulders as he slammed his car door. He walked alongside Eva until they reached the shops close to where Efren's mother lived.

Eva faced him. "Do you know if she's home?"

He nodded. "I spoke to her on the phone." He turned his broad shoulders sideways to pass through the crowds, almost choking on the dusty air that smelled of gasoline fumes.

Passersby nudged into him and Eva as they manoeuvred their way through the city of El Rastro, engines humming, and scents of dirt and dust in the air. The tree-lined street featured a narrow path they walked along. A strip of cafes and flea markets bustled with patrons outside the apartments.

Tomas stepped over the curb towards the apartment building where the warm wind brushed his cheek as they headed up a lane and inside the building. After being buzzed inside, he looked over his shoulder to make sure no one was following them. He didn't see any suspicious activity and doubted they were being watched after they'd kept a low profile for weeks.

A short, stocky woman with a round face and tight bun swung open the door. She wore loose pants and a t-shirt. "Tomas?"

"That's me," he said. "This is my friend, Eva. This is Carmen, Efren's mother."

Her face was pallid with dark circles around her eyes. "Nice to meet you both. Please come inside."

She led them towards an open living room that was cosy with a chestnut brown sofa, three brown footstools, a small TV resting on a low cabinet, and an array of religious paintings hanging on the wall. Indoor plants surrounded the space. "Can I get you an espresso or something else?"

"An espresso for me," said Tomas.

"I'll have a tea, thank you, Carmen," said Eva, sitting down on the sofa beside Tomas, careful to maintain her distance.

"Are you all right?" Eva asked.

"All good," he lied. Why couldn't he tell her how he felt when all he got from her was 'don't touch me' vibes. He knew she was attracted to him, but he wasn't aware of the depth of her feelings. All he knew was they were on a mission and had to remain focussed.

Carmen returned with a tray of hot beverages and set them on the table. "Here you go." She sat on an armchair opposite without taking a beverage herself, her fingers running over her thighs. "Please tell me you have news about Efren. Please." Her eyes pleaded as if they could bring her son back.

Eva spoke first. "No, sorry, Carmen. But we'd like to help find him if you can explain exactly what happened the day he went missing."

Carmen fidgeted then touched the base of her throat, tears running down her cheeks. Tomas hated doing this to her, but anything she might have noticed could give them a lead. "My Efren has a gentle spirit, but his behaviour got worse over the years." She slowed down her erratic breathing. "The day he went missing, Efren said he was visiting a friend. They were meeting close to the market near Plaza Mayor. I knew that day he wasn't in the best of moods, so I thought him catching up with his best friend would help. After his father died two years ago, he was never the same. Always angry, confused, and sad." She fought back tears. "Then he started getting bullied at school. I reported it but nothing much changed. Lately, I'd been thinking about changing schools, but..."

"But what?" asked Eva.

She huffed, fiddling with the centre of her throat, redness staining her cheeks. "It didn't matter where he went. The fact of the matter was that his father's suicide would always cast a dark shadow in our lives. Kids eventually find out the truth."

Tomas' felt a lump in his throat, speechless. That poor boy lost his father to suicide? He couldn't imagine the unanswered questions and guilt Carmen must've had. "I am sorry, Carmen. Children can be cruel at the best of times. Did you consider counselling?"

Carmen nodded. "He went a few times, but it wasn't for him. I know I'm at fault, too, because I work multiple jobs to keep food on the table." She rubbed away tears. "If I'd spent more time with him, things would have been different. If I'd had financial help from family, this might never have happened. He might never have run off or—"

"Don't blame yourself, Carmen." Eva gave her a reassuring smile. "Do you think he might've been kidnapped?" Tomas suspected the same.

"I don't know, Eva. Possibly. My Efren would have come back. He didn't have much money on him unless he's become a thief. A part of me wants him to have run off because I don't want to think the worst."

"I assume you told the police all this and spoke to his friend," said Eva.

"I did. That's how I found out he hadn't met him that day. He must have got caught in something. He was having nightmares, too."

"What kind of nightmares?" asked Tomas.

Carmen shook her head. "Someone chasing him down a narrow street and catching him. It was always the same dream." She shifted in her seat and smoothed her pants while Tomas sipped his espresso, appreciating the mixture of bitterness and sweetness. "He came home once with a flyer that advertised a spiritual workshop about day-to-day problems. About relaxation and meditation. I suggested he attend, but he had no interest."

"Would he have changed his mind about attending?" asked Eva. The lady shrugged.

"Do you have the flyer with you?" Tomas leaned in and sipped the remainder of his coffee.

"He must've taken it with him because I haven't found anything in his room." Carmen rubbed her damp eye. "Do *you* think he's been taken?"

Tomas frowned. "I wish I knew."

Carmen's bottom lip shivered as she leaned forward with tears running down her cheeks. "Please find him."

Eva got up from her seat and crouched down to her size. "It's okay, Carmen." She squeezed her shoulder. "We will find Efren. He'll be okay. Trust that we'll help, and the police will, too. Do not lose hope."

She rubbed her eyes and looked up. "The police? They don't care about my boy. All they care about is getting their bonuses and pretending to help people as they patrol the streets. They have not had one lead yet." Carmen headed to the kitchen. She returned and forced a smile. "I'm sorry."

"Will you be all right?" said Tomas.

"I will be. Thank you for wanting to help Efren."

Tomas feared for the boy's life and worried for his mother. What if Efren had been targeted for the group? Had they recruited him into this cult?

Eva and Tomas sat on his couch at his apartment, watching a TV news program. The sense of security she had around Tomas made her feel connected to him, and it bothered her. She couldn't get attached.

She inched forward. "I'm curious, Tomas. Why so much interest in Lola's case? I know you mentioned dating her, but I get the feeling there's more."

Tomas' body froze. His hands flailed as her pursed his lips. "Guilt, Eva. Lots of it." He bowed his head. "I cared about Lola, but I didn't love her. She wanted a future. I told her I wanted to break up. She reacted by being angry and sad at the same time. Lola stormed out of my home and ran down the stairs. I went after her, trying to stop her, but she fell on her stomach and hit her head. Luckily, she had no head injury, but …"

"But what?"

He pushed back tears. "Lola was pregnant, and she lost the child. It was my fault we lost our baby. I was only eighteen and Lola was nineteen. I wasn't ready for marriage, but if I'd known about the baby, I would have supported her." He sighed. "If I'd known, I would never have broken up with her."

Jesus. Why didn't he tell her sooner? The guilt must have stopped him.

"It wasn't your fault, Tomas. She should have told you. You couldn't have known." She couldn't imagine the pain he felt over losing a child.

"You're right, but I still feel guilty. Like I should have run after her faster, or stayed with her longer to see if we could make it work with a baby."

"I am sorry about your baby, Tomas. But staying in a relationship for the sake of a child doesn't work." His eyes misted, and she held his hand, wishing she could take away his guilt.

CHAPTER 42

The following Saturday, Tomas squeezed a sweaty fist tight as he stepped inside the bar, the smell of spices and beer filling the air. In his right hand, he held a piece of paper, a poem to read aloud tonight.

He sat at the bar, his bottom slipping on the stool as he shifted his position. "Can I have a beer, please?"

"Sure thing," said the stocky bartender who was short with dishevelled hair. "You doing the poetry reading tonight?"

Tomas nodded before handing him cash. "I am a bit nervous. It's my first time at this bar."

The man pushed his beer across the counter, moisture glistening on the glass. "You'll be fine. The patrons here are friendly and love these readings. They tend to draw a crowd."

He moved to other customers while Tomas waited for Eva to show up. He hadn't seen her since meeting with Carmen a few days earlier and missed her like crazy.

Tomas had met with Leandro at the police station, but it turned out they'd already gathered the same information from Carmen, so it wasn't news to them. He mentioned they had leads, but as civilians there was only so much he could tell them. Leandro had ordered him to stand down and to not take the law into his own hands because of the dangers. Tomas would lie low and focus on tonight. He was busy enough with life in general. He didn't need to make more trouble for Eva. He wanted to keep her safe.

His phone rang in his pocket. He saw Eva's name on the display. Oh no, she wasn't cancelling out on him, was she? "Hi Eva. Are you coming?"

"Of course, but I'm running about ten minutes late. When do you go on?"

"In about half an hour, so there's still time."

"Great. See you soon." He ended the call just before it buzzed again. "Gonzalo. What's up, man?" Silence. "Gonzalo?"

"Sorry, I hope I'm not bothering you, but I had to vent." He hadn't mentioned his poetry reading to any of his friends, as they weren't interested in literature. But he knew Eva was. "Isabela broke up with me."

Wasn't he only having a fling? "I didn't know you guys were serious, but I'm sorry."

"We were starting to get serious, and she was going to leave her husband for me."

Tomas winced. "Again, I'm sorry, Gonzalo."

"I know you don't like the fact she's married, but they're separated, Tomas. They sleep in separate bedrooms. I feel like crap. I cared about her a lot and thought she might be the one. I think she might have lied about their separate lives."

"It's probably for the best. It could get messy. What was the reason?"

"I don't know the reason, but it hurts like hell. The funny thing is that she did it by text. I haven't even seen her for the past few days."

"You should at least have a conversation with her. She can't break up over text."

"You're right. I'll go see her tomorrow night," Gonzalo mentioned.

"Why not tonight?"

"My parents have invited me over for dinner, so I'm about to leave."

"Okay. If you need to talk tomorrow, let me know. I'm here for you, Gonzalo."

"Thanks, man."

Tomas ended the call with a heavy heart, thinking about how cruel it was to break up over a text message. Didn't anyone connect with people anymore? Why did mobile phones change the course of true connection?

The manager of the bar approached and slapped him on the back. "Ready for the reading, Tomas?"

He nodded. "Ready as I'll ever be." In his mind, he reviewed the story he had recounted to Eva about the baby he'd lost. Part of his poetry expressed that loss and guilt over Lola. He wanted to honour her in this poem and help her find justice.

"We'll call you up in about ten minutes. Finish that beer of yours." He swaggered away when Eva walked into the bar.

His vocal cords failed him at the beauty before him. She wore a silky red dress with a long split on the side and had enough cleavage revealed to make him burn with desire. Her lips were ruby red, her eyes tinged with a smoky eye shadow. Even her hair thrown into a bun with wispy strands falling over her temples aroused him. *Wow!*

Eva approached him at the bar, leaned forward and kissed him on the cheek. "Hello."

He pulled away from her. "You look ... amazing."

She blushed. "Thanks. How do you feel?"

Rose and orange scents surrounded her as she stood awkwardly by his side, while men around the bar glued their eyes on her. Even a few women stared in her direction as if jealous that their partners were ogling her. Despite her being somewhat overdressed, he was besotted.

When Tomas was called over to the stage, his heart pounded. He grinned at Eva, who touched him gently on the shoulder. "You'll be fine. Deep breath."

Five minutes later, he walked onto the stage, tightly gripping the paper. At the microphone, he shifted his stance. Why wouldn't his heart stop racing as if he was about to have a heart attack? Eva reassured him with a wink from the table.

Steeling himself, he took a calming breath. "Hello, everyone. I'm Tomas De Leon, and what I'm about to read is a poem about how love finds you even when you don't want it. It's an excerpt from a collection of poems I plan to publish independently in the next few months. Thanks for being here today."

His eyes lingered on Eva, whose expression appeared neutral despite her gaze being fixed on him. He bowed his head, scanned the sheet and started to read. The silence in the room gave him a sense of control, but he wondered what people thought.

Reading out his last line, he breathed a sigh of relief at the round of applause accompanied by whistles and screams. Eva rubbed her eyes. Had she been crying?

The manager entered the stage beside Tomas, squeezing his shoulder as he leaned into the microphone. "That was touching, Tomas. Touching. No doubt you have a lot of talent. Good luck with the work." Tomas smiled. "Next up, we have Marisol on the stage with her poem. Give her a round of applause."

Tomas approached Eva, who had sat at a nearby table in the corner of the bar, a glass of wine in front of her.

"That was beautiful, Tomas. So beautiful."

"Thanks. It was nerve-racking, but I got there in the end." He sat beside her as they listened to a few more poetry readings and had more drinks.

"Care for some dinner now that the readings are done?" She nodded. "Great. I'll grab us menus and we can order."

CHAPTER 43

L oud, yet indecipherable conversations around the bar deafened Eva. She watched Tomas eat his potato omelette while she chewed on a piece of juicy steak served with thin chips. Smells of herbs blended with oven-baked meats whet her appetite. At least twenty people were seated around them at spaced-out tables and chairs on sticky linoleum flooring. Waiters bustled about, carrying trays of alcohol and food while the bartender shook a cocktail container for a group of rowdy women.

"I know we haven't spoken much about what Carmen said, but there seems to be a connection between the mercury poisoning and these spiritual groups disguised as cults. What do you think?" asked Eva.

"It appears that way," said Tomas. "Leandro mentioned they have leads to chase up, but he won't tell me anything. I've crossed the boundary limit of my privileges."

"I can understand that," said Eva, sipping her Prosecco wine. "He has to protect you when you're not trained to fight these evil people."

He angled his head. "Who says I'm not?"

"You're a paramedic, Tomas, not a policeman."

Tomas forked his food and chewed thoughtfully. He put down the fork and looked at her with a hand underneath his chin. "As a paramedic, I've been through my share of violence and trauma. I once had a man pull a knife on me. I was treating his wife, who said she'd fallen down the stairs, but I knew she was lying. When I questioned her one too many times, the man threatened me."

Eva flinched, her heart feeling like it was exploding. She couldn't imagine anything occurring to Tomas. "What happened? Were you hurt?"

He chuckled. "I kicked the knife out of his hand and pounded into him. I restrained him until the police arrived. So, you see, I've had self-defence training, because in this line of work you don't know who you'll get. Gonzalo and I need to be safe."

"What about Gonzalo? Is he trained?"

He nodded. "We attended classes together, so we can defend ourselves and others we love and care about."

When their eyes lingered for a minute too long, Eva averted hers and cleared her throat. Her body shivered.

"But still. Leandro is your friend and has the right to be worried. You're not in that field, so he wouldn't be a friend if he didn't worry about your safety."

"Would you be worried about my safety, Eva?"

She hesitated. "That's a silly question, Tomas. Of course. We're friends."

He knit his brows and swallowed his food while a few patrons left the bar. Others patted him on the back, including a skinny blonde. "Great work on the poem. Good luck, Tomas." She inched her breasts closer towards him. "How about I give you my number?"

Tomas looked at Eva who shrugged. "Not this time. I'm taken."

The woman licked her lips and winked. "Your loss." She strutted towards the exit and whispered to the group of people she had arrived with.

Eva gasped, hating her jealousy. He had a right to see whoever he wanted. "Why did you turn her down?"

He scratched his brow. "I am curious, Eva. Are we just friends?"

Eva's chest tingled. "What do you mean?"

"Just that. Are we friends or more than that?"

"Tomas, please. Don't we have enough to focus on now, with this case? Let's leave things the way they are, okay."

"What if this situation goes on for years or never gets resolved? They might never find her murderer, do you realise that?"

She decided to ignore his question. "Have you had any other traumatic experiences in the field?"

His eyes darkened. "Too many to count, but I survived them all because I'm a fighter. I always have been and always will be. I never give up on anything, Eva. I'm stubborn that way."

"Good to know," she said. "I'm a fighter too, and I never give up. If I believe in something, I believe in it. With experience behind me, I can generally predict what will happen."

"Crazy, Eva. No one can predict the future. Don't you see? Circumstances change and people grow. If you keep believing the same things you don't grow on a personal level and always stay stuck in the past."

"And you're not stuck in the past?"

He nodded. "Yes, but I'm a work in progress and like to take risks. I believe I can work through it with the right people by my side. I'm resilient that way."

Eva wasn't sure what they were talking about, hating to talk in riddles. If he cared about her, why didn't he admit it? Why was he being vague and using generalities to make his point? She couldn't believe he had dealt with his past when he couldn't be honest about his feelings. Saying he possibly wanted to be more than friends didn't mean he was admitting his true feelings. But then again, did she want that?

His eyes met with hers. "Do you feel like dancing?" She nodded. "How about we get out of here?" A little harmless fun couldn't hurt.

Tomas lifted his head and gazed at the multiple levels in the nightclub. Women ogled him and men stared at Eva as they pushed through the congested group of people. Lights flashed, and the thumping sounds of bass and Latin beats brought out his fun side.

Smoke spread around the DJ to create an effect as he spun funky music with his headphones on. People clapped and waved to the beat, singing to the lyrics of a Gloria Estefan song until he changed the tempo of the music to a ballad that sounded like a Luiz Miguel tune.

"Let's dance," Tomas said as he prodded her to the dance floor.

"Okay," she said.

Tomas breathed in her floral scent as he placed his hands around her waist and Eva rested her arms over his shoulders. He closed his eyes as they danced to the slow Luis Miguel ballad, his heart racing. The smoothness of her skin and sexy outline of her angular neck made him yearn for her. He struggled to not run his hands over her whole body.

He loved the way her eyes lowered when she felt nervous and anxious. Even the way she rubbed the base of her throat when embarrassed. Her glossy hair felt warm against his skin, and he needed to get closer to her. He couldn't sleep or go through his time awake without a picture of her in his mind day and night.

Tomas turned her chin with a gentle finger. "Are you enjoying yourself?"

"I am. You?"

"I'm in good company, so of course. But it's a bit loud in here. How about a coffee at my place?"

Eva winced as she ignored the men around her watching. He held on to hope as she pondered. Surely visiting as a friend didn't need to mean anything. Only a cup of coffee and she would leave. "Okay."

"Great. Let's get out of here." He held her hand and pulled her through the crowds. Some of the other dancers shoved back. With a shake of his head, he ignored men winking at Eva and calling out "Beautiful." As long as they got out of there, he wouldn't start a fight with men who knew she was otherwise occupied with him. Why still flirt with her?

Having a coffee at his place didn't have to mean anything, and he wanted to spend more time with her. No harm in that.

CHAPTER 44

Efren snuck around the kitchen, searching for a phone. He desperately wanted to call his mother to tell her he'd made the wrong decision coming here. He'd lost faith in the group after what he'd seen. His chest burned, his mind flashing to images of that young girl doing the unthinkable to Marco. He couldn't unsee it.

This wasn't a place that helped people but rather exploited and used them for their own gain. Asking people for money, slave labour, and child abuse. No, he wanted out, and had to help those who were forced to be here.

There were two groups here: those who had the funds to donate, and those who worked hard to sell herbs and other goods, as well as recruit. So far, he had had only had to sell products, but no doubt they'd get him to recruit, too.

He remembered Antonio hurting the boy who'd stood up for Juanita. What about the boy who kissed her? As far as he knew, nothing had happened to him. Even Ana had punished that girl for rejecting Armando's advances. It was her right. But he wondered if Marco had been testing him, and would he see him as having failed?

Bending down over a low chair, he spotted a mobile phone in a basket. *This is it.* His moment to call his mother to save him. There was no way he could escape on his own. He thought about Samuel's mother after she'd escaped with her son. Was that why Marco was checking on Samuel at the hospital? To see if he'd speak up? But obviously he hadn't, or the police would've been here in a heartbeat.

Efren reached for the phone and hid it in the clasp of his hands, knowing he had to find a safe space to make the call.

"What are you doing, Efren?"

Chills ran down his spine as he slowly turned around. "Marco. What's going on?"

His glare made him shiver. "I could ask you the same thing."

Ignoring the strong beat of his heart and wobbly legs, he angled his head and faked a smile. "I'm about to plant more herbs and was looking for seeds but I couldn't find any here."

Marco inched closer. "Hmm. What do you have in your hands?"

He hesitated. "Nothing."

Marco leaned in and yanked the phone out of his hands. "I thought you knew the rules, Efren. No phone calls."

He swallowed, his throat dry. "I ... I miss my mum and wanted to see how she is. Can I make a quick call? Just for a minute."

Marco hesitated, his eyes darkening. "I've been hearing news around the place, Efren. Apparently, you've been going to areas you should be avoiding. Asking questions about our true mission here. Have you lost your way again?"

He shrugged as a coldness penetrated his shoulders. If he didn't lie, would they punish him or worse? "I'm curious, that's all. But I'm happy to do what you ask, Marco. I haven't lost my way, and I believe in the mission."

"Right. Well, your actions say otherwise. I think punishment for going against the rules is in order, Efren." He chuckled. "I don't believe you wanted to ring your mother for a friendly chat. Come with me."

Efren's vision blurred as Marco dragged him out of the kitchen and held firmly on his arm, no doubt leaving a bruise. What the hell had he done? Did he just sign his death warrant?

Tomas spilled sugar on his kitchen counter while Eva glanced around his apartment. She flicked through a book on a bookshelf, the back of her legs underneath that short dress triggering his desire. *Hell*. He needed to get a grip and make the espresso.

"You've got a variety of books," she said. "Not only about paramedicine, but also poetry and literature. I wouldn't have guessed you liked the classics."

Tomas carried the tray of coffee to the table in his living room and Eva sat on the couch. He handed her the cup. "I hope it's not too strong for you." He grabbed his own and sat beside her, the steam curling around his nose.

She sipped. "It's good. Thanks, Tomas."

The awkward silence made his body tense. *Say something.* "In answer to your statement before, my mother loved reading literary fiction. It was her escape from my father's ways. I found a few cheap books at a market one day and bought them for her. She's been reading them ever since. She loves my poetry, too."

"It's touching, Tomas." She averted her eyes and stared at the bare wall. "I am sure your book will sell well once you publish it."

"Thanks. I hope so. What about you? How's your writing going?"

She shrugged. "I'm still working on the first draft, but it's slowly coming along. I don't have as much time as I'd like, but writing a little most days helps."

"I'm guessing if you love writing thrillers, you love reading them, too?" He couldn't stop staring at her cleavage as he imagined his tongue gliding across the centre of her chest and making her moan. He wanted to trail his lips over her throat and thread his hands around her waist and lower. *Stop it.*

"I love psychological thrillers, but not so much horror. Usually they don't end well."

"There's a fine line between thriller and horror, isn't there?"

"True, but one of them has a lot more gore than the other. Do you like that genre, too?"

He nodded. "I am like you. Not a fan of the blood, but prefer the suspense and intrigue you get from guessing who the killer is. Like you said, with horror, you don't always get the resolution at the end. It's irritating. I hate things that are unfinished or not resolved." He turned to her as she rested back against the couch with one leg draped over the other, her bare thighs undoing him. He looked away. "I'm guessing you like literary films and books, too?"

"Oh, yes. I love the drawn-out slow-burn romance. Not so much the forbidden, unrequited, or even tragic love you find in a few of them."

"Like *Romeo and Juliet*, the tragedy, or *Gone with the Wind*, the unrequited love?"

"Yes, they are classics, but I prefer the happily-ever-after. There's enough negativity in this world without having to read about it, too. Don't you think we need the escape?"

Tomas put down his cup and inched closer towards her, noticing she didn't shift. Their thighs brushed. "I agree. If you can get that escape in fantasy or realism, it's a bonus in life. I think we've both had enough pain in our pasts to last a lifetime, Eva. You deserve the world and more."

"Thanks for saying that. So do you. I'm glad you've got your mother."

"I imagine you and your mother are close?" She nodded. "That's good. Family's important when they're there for you. I like your sister. She is the life of the party, isn't she?"

Eva chuckled, her eyes lighting up. "Don't get me started. But she's my friend, too, and we've been through a lot together. Daniela's suffered, but now she's doing well with Rafael. She deserves that kind of absorbing love."

He squeezed her shoulder. "So do you, Eva." Slowly she faced him, her eyes darkening with something akin to desire. His finger caressed her cheek as he trailed it down to her lips and leaned in. Her head moved in as the world around them closed in and only her lips were in his sights. The hitching of her breath, the shake of her shoulders and the soft lick of her bottom lip made him hunger for her. Gently, he pulled her chin towards him and smashed his lips across hers, gliding his tongue tenderly inside hers, tasting coffee and herbs in her mouth. When his tongue dove deeper into hers, she reciprocated and pushed her body closer to his.

He pulled away and rose without saying a word. Eva got up too and followed him to his bedroom.

As he entered the room, he reached for her back and unzipped her dress, letting it flow below her. He gasped at the sight of her slim, curvaceous body, brown lacy underwear and matching lacy bra. The floral and spicy scents aroused him as he yearned for her. Wanted her, needed her.

She hugged her body as if shivering, so he wrapped his own arms around her and led her to his bed. She lay back while Tomas pulled off his own shirt and pants, then lay on top of her. *What a gorgeous sight. Will I ever get enough of her beauty?* His mouth plunged into hers again as he glided his hands around her hair, yearning for her as his hands trailed between her thighs and over her underwear, her body shifting forward to put pressure on his hands.

The sight of her closing her eyes and moaning heightened his desire for her.

Eva touched his manhood and caressed it in a slow motion up and down while he planted kisses across her chest and cleavage. He delved into the inside of her bra and smoothed his fingers over a nipple. Needing more, he unclipped her bra and threw it to the floor. He bowed into her chest and sucked on a nipple, aroused by her guttural sounds.

"Oh, Tomas."

He inched up, looking at her. "So beautiful, beautiful." He circled his tongue around her areola and nipple, then moved on to the right breast while his fingers plunged inside her mound underneath her underwear.

"Oh, yes," said Eva. "Right there."

He held back his own arousal and pulled off her underwear as she lifted her legs and moved out of them. He removed his own underpants and then, flesh to flesh, he savoured the feel of her vulva against his penis and licked across her breast. Stopping the action, he leapt quickly off the bed and found a condom inside his top drawer.

Back in bed, he probed two fingers inside her. She writhed and wriggled as if she wanted more. The pace of his hand increased when her breath accelerated, and he pushed deeper inside her until she climaxed.

The arousal in her eyes was beautiful to watch, but he needed to be inside her. Putting on his condom, he slowly entered her. She guided him gently deeper with her hands. Tomas buried himself to the hilt and let out a strong moan, like nothing he'd ever experienced before. Eva climaxed a second time and the sound couldn't have been more beautiful. This amazing woman was both his curse and his blessing.

CHAPTER 45

The next morning, Tomas woke up and watched Eva sleep. He could gaze at her for hours in her peaceful, blissful state as if her eyes smiled back at him. The sheet was draped over a toned leg. A hand covered one breast, leaving the other on display. He slowly traced its outline while getting hard again. *Hell.* He needed her now, but she remained asleep. Was it crazy that he wanted to wake her up for sex again?

Naked, he reached over for his phone on the bedside table and switched it on. Several phone calls from Gonzalo startled him. Why was he ringing so early in the morning? It was only seven o'clock on a Sunday, and he knew they weren't on shift today. He was hoping to spend the day with Eva, but now he wasn't sure.

Quickly moving out of bed, he put on clothes and headed to the bathroom so he wouldn't wake Eva, and called his friend. "Gonzalo. Is something wrong? You've called me three times this morning. What's up? Do we have an emergency shift?"

"Tomas. I might be in trouble."

His heart churned. "Why? Spill, man."

"It's Isabela." He sounded out of breath.

He wondered if the husband found out about them or if she'd hurt him again. But he didn't sound good. "Is it her husband?" Silence. "Gonzalo. Tell me."

"She's dead, Tomas. Dead."

Tomas flinched, speechless. *What the hell.* "Are you home?"

"No, I'm at her apartment. Her husband's away and the police are here. I'll give you the address." He recited it, realising it wasn't far from Carmen's place in El Rastro.

"I'm on my way, man." He ended the call and headed back to the bedroom, shoving his arms and legs into his clothes as Eva slowly roused from sleep and rubbed her eyes.

"What's wrong?"

He hated leaving her, but he had to be there for his friend. "I'm sorry, I have to go."

She shifted up in bed. "Why?"

"It's Gonzalo. Isabela's dead."

Eyes wide, she got out of bed and picked up her dress from the floor. "I'll come with you."

He shook his head. "No, I'd better find out what's happened. I'll call you later." He hated leaving her, but he had no choice.

"All right." She headed to the bathroom and returned a few minutes later. As they walked out of his apartment, she waved goodbye.

"I can drive you if you like."

She shook her head. "No, you go be with your friend. I'll find my own way." As they separated, he hoped he hadn't been cold towards her. But right now, he had only his friend and poor Isabela on his mind.

Tomas sat on a chair near Leandro and Gonzalo. The detective jotted in a notebook as Gonzalo gave his statement, his expression gaunt.

"I told you that I came in the door with my spare key, then I found her like this."

Tomas couldn't help noticing the blood-stained kitchen floor and a tarp over the body. He hadn't seen Isabela, but he could only imagine what she looked like with her throat slashed. A hand lay outside the tarp until a uniformed officer tucked it back under. "What were you doing at her apartment? Are you two friends?"

"We were lovers." He sighed. "Isabela's husband was renting this place out, but it had been empty for the last month until they could find a new tenant. This was our meeting place."

"Right. Were you still together?"

"She broke up with me by text, but I called her and asked to meet face to face. She agreed, but I don't know what happened in the space of two hours."

Leandro nodded. "Do you think her husband could have done this?"

Tomas waved a hand. "Come on, Leandro. Give the guy a break. He's grieving. Hasn't he had enough of your questions?"

Leandro's eyes darkened. "It won't be too much longer, Tomas. I have to do my job. Why don't you go outside and meet us there."

"No, I'll wait," he said as he patted his friend's shoulder.

"I don't know, detective, but lately she'd been preoccupied about something; wouldn't tell me what was wrong," Gonzalo said. "Something had changed between us. A few times she came close to telling me, so maybe something spooked her. I think she planned on telling me the truth today, but ..." His eyes misted.

"When do you think her demeanour changed?"

"It's been a few weeks. I know it was more than her worrying about her husband." Gonzalo rubbed another tear from his cheek. His face had paled, and his body looked small. How could he be embroiled in this?

Two male paramedics came inside and lifted the body onto a stretcher, while a forensics team started dusting for fingerprints.

Leandro looked at Tomas. "Let's head outside and we'll finish up there." They exited the building and made their way to a small garden strip.

Gonzalo hunched over a fountain overlooked by an angel statue, and stared at the flowing water, deep in his own thoughts.

Leandro gave him the time to reflect and approached Tomas. "How well did you know Isabela?"

Tomas's heart broke for his friend. "I didn't know the lady at all. I only met her once after her hospital admission for mercury poisoning."

"Right," said Leandro. "When you met her that one time, did she say anything about anyone at the school she didn't like or argued with?"

"Nothing like that," said Tomas. "We brought her into the hospital and once I knew she was stable I left. But

Gonzalo stayed back. I could tell he cared about her even then."

After a few more questions, Leandro moved to Gonzalo. "Are you all right to continue?" The EMT nodded. "Is there anything else you can think of that might give us an insight into her change of behaviour? Even trivial matters can mean something, Gonzalo."

His breath hitched as he scratched the centre of his palm. "She seemed worried when I was running late for one of our dates. She bit my head off, angry that I hadn't called her to let her know. But I was in traffic and don't like ringing while I'm driving. We had an argument about me being more responsible and then ... then ... she stormed out when I got to her apartment." He palmed his face and shook his head. "I should have protected her, Leandro. I should have asked harder about what was wrong. She must have been worried that someone hurt me, but why would she think that?"

"That's what we're going to find out. We'll be questioning her husband, close family and friends. Also, we'll check any security cameras that might catch someone in the area or entering her apartment."

Tomas approached them. "Do you think she was killed in the apartment?"

He shrugged. "That's for the medical examiner to determine. Right now I can't give you any definitive answers. But stay away from this, Tomas."

Tomas put his hands on his hips. "Too many coincidences for this not to be linked, especially after Efren went missing."

Leandro ignored him and turned back to Gonzalo. "How well did Isabela know Lola?" He turned to Tomas. "I am not speculating about any links here. Just gathering facts. I suggest you not make any assumptions about her murder, Tomas."

"They were acquainted, but I don't believe they were close. I never met any of her friends, but I knew her husband gave her free rein with them. As far as I knew he wasn't controlling, but who knows if he found out about the affair."

Leandro closed his notebook. "Thanks, guys. Go home." He turned to a policeman who was walking around the garden. "Canvas for witnesses. Talk to neighbours on either side in the building, and see whether they've seen anyone suspicious lurking around or entering the home."

The sturdy-looking policeman nodded. "Right away, sir."

Tomas quailed at the idea that this could be linked to Lola's death, especially when Isabela had first been poisoned with mercury. At the time, they might have been weakening her defences and giving her a warning, a scare tactic. But did she go too far this time? Far enough to get herself killed?

CHAPTER 46

E va's heart warmed while her eyes darted towards Ignacio and Esmeralda in the school staff room as they hugged other staff members who were close to Isabela.

Esmeralda threaded a hand through her hair. Her eyes were like tiny dots, as if she hadn't slept much these past two nights. Her blouse looked barely ironed and her deflated posture showed her despair. Had she been close to Isabela, or was she grieving on behalf of those who were?

"My office door is always open, so please don't hesitate if you're struggling. It will take time yet to work through this." Esmeralda rubbed her eye, which twitched again, before patting the female sports teacher on the shoulder. She wandered to another group.

Eva clasped her hands in her lap as she stared at her cold cup of coffee on the table, while Francisca remained silent.

Something was on her mind, but before she could ask, Ignacio approached.

"How are you both doing?" Ignacio asked.

Eva gave up on her drink. "It is sad, but I didn't know her that well. She did great work for the school, and it'll be a huge loss, Ignacio."

He pursed his lips. "Hmm. Indeed. I feel especially sorry for her husband and son, who will need to deal with this tragic loss. How do you get over the murder of a loved one?"

"It'll be tough for a while," said Eva. She turned to Francisca, who remained frozen in place and quiet.

"She was there for the children and treated them all like her own. I'll need to find her replacement in the classroom. It won't be easy." Ignacio also glanced at Francisca. "Do you know of anyone who might take her place?"

Francisca's eyes turned hard. "She's hardly been dead a minute and you're already thinking about replacing her? What's wrong with you?"

Ignacio flinched, something unreadable in his eyes. "You are right, of course, but school business doesn't stop, and we need as much help as we can get for the children. They are my top priority."

Francisca stood up. "You are right. I'm sorry, Ignacio. I need to prepare for the next class. I'll see you both later."

She scurried out of the room as if she couldn't get away fast enough.

Ignacio raised a brow. "Is she all right?"

"I don't know. She didn't know Isabela that well, so I'm wondering why it's affected her this much. Unless something else is going on."

"Find out and let me know. I care about my staff and want to make sure she's coping in the job. There are enough stressors in this work."

"But that's life, right, Ignacio?" Eva asked.

He nodded. "It sure is." He fiddled with his Rolex watch then looked at the time. "Isabela's husband has requested time off for his son, which is understandable, so he won't be in class for at least the next week."

"No worries." She rose. "Before I go, I wanted to let you know that the speech you gave at assembly was heartfelt and beautiful. I could see a lot of tears in the group."

"Thank you, Eva." He waved. "I will see you later." His eyes moistened before he moved and sorted piles of papers on the table.

Strange. Was Ignacio affected by Isabela's death more than he was letting on? Of course, as the principal he had to maintain a strong presence and be a sounding board and support for others, too.

She made her way to class with heavy steps. It felt as if the atmosphere had turned grey.

After school that day, Eva tried to relax while having dinner with Francisca, who was shuffling the chicken stir-fry around her plate in silence. Her eyes drifted past her and the constant sighs made her wonder what was on her mind.

"Are you all right?"

"Fine."

Eva angled her head. "No, it's not fine. I can tell. Come on. What's going on?"

She forced a smile. "What happened between you and Tomas? I noticed you didn't come home a few nights ago. Did you ..."

Eva blushed. "I will tell you if you explain what is on your mind. Do not distract me, young lady."

She huffed and put down her fork. "I saw Isabela in the corridor the day before she died. I asked her what was wrong, and she said something weird." Francisca looked away. "Isabela said that looks can be deceiving, and she'd been deceived. Forced to do something she didn't want to do. When I asked her specifically what she meant, she ran off into the wind. I ran after her but she left before I could stop her."

Eva bowed her head, a sinking sensation in her stomach. "Don't feel bad. Remember I tried talking to her not that long ago." Her friend nodded. "But someone messaged her, so I think she was being watched." She took a deep breath. "We both tried to get her to talk, but she refused. It's not your fault or mine. She made her own choices."

Francisca shook her head. "I don't know, but I should have convinced her to tell me, Eva. If I'd pushed harder. This could have prevented her ..."

Eva squeezed her shoulder. "Don't blame yourself, Francisca. I'm sure you tried your hardest, but you can't force someone to tell you anything. You could not have known this would happen. You might as well blame me for not forcing her to talk. She must've been too afraid."

"You're probably right, but still, I feel like I should have done more for the poor woman. Whatever she was going through might have been serious enough to get her killed." Francisca slid a hand through her tangled hair.

"Possibly, but it's up to the police now to find her killer." She chewed her remaining rice and sipped on water.

"I wonder if it was someone she knew." Eva's mind veered towards Isabela's husband. Her friend had drifted off, as if there was more to her story. "You know something, don't you? Come on, spill."

"Nothing."

"Do not nothing me, Francisca. What do you know that I don't?"

"Isabela was having an affair with Tomas' friend, Gonzalo."

Eva gasped in surprise. "Oh, no. Do you think the husband found out about it and killed her?"

"I don't know, but we can't assume anything." Francisca exhaled and squeezed her hands tight. "What the hell is going on here, Eva? I am genuinely scared and think there are too many connections."

"When I met with Isabela, I called the police, but I don't know if Leandro followed up. He might've, but they would've needed probable cause to question her further. Although I am curious about that mysterious message she received."

Francisca frowned. "The police can check her phone and find out." Her eyes shifted. "But what could she know? She couldn't have been involved, could she?"

Eva crossed her arms and dug her nails into her elbows, a chill enveloping her entire body. "I am starting to think there are too many things happening. We have Isabela's mercury poisoning, Samuel's attack, and others going to hospital for mercury poisoning. Then there's the selling of these herbs for chronic pain, and this young boy, Efren, missing. Too many to be coincidences."

Francisca's pupils dilated and she put up a hand. "Hold up. I have no idea what you are talking about. Who's Efren?"

Eva explained all that had happened, and how Tomas liaised with Leandro about Lola's murder. But now were they treating Isabela's murder as possibly linked to Lola's murder or was it the husband who had found out about her affair with Gonzalo? She couldn't believe Gonzalo was involved, or was he? She didn't know the man well enough, but she trusted in Tomas and his friendship with the man.

CHAPTER 47

Tomas leaned forward and lit a candle on the table. A vase of fresh flowers in the centre set off two plates bearing napkins folded like envelopes. The dark ambience gave the kitchen a romantic vibe, and he couldn't wait for Eva to arrive. He had missed her over the past week, after the first time they had made love. He couldn't stop thinking about that night. They had spoken over the phone a few times, particularly about Isabela's death, which still made him reel.

He wanted to forget about the horrid events that had been happening lately and focus on Eva. He wanted them to enjoy one another, as if they hadn't had a care in the world.

Tomas checked the oven where a chicken and chorizo was baking. He opened the oven door and pricked it with a fork. It was almost ready.

He rubbed the back of his neck with sweaty hands, then opened the fridge to check on his drinks. Taking out the chilled cava wine, he placed it on the counter to allow it to breathe a little. Now he waited for Eva. She should arrive any minute now, but why was he nervous? It wasn't as if they were strangers and hadn't shared intimacy before. They had kissed twice before making love, which was like nothing he'd experienced. It was like floating in heaven since sharing their deep affection for each other. That was all it was, wasn't it? Not love. He couldn't think about that now when they were having fun and still getting to know each other.

His reverie broke when the doorbell rang. On unsteady legs, he opened the door and gasped at the beauty before him. She wore an open pink shirt with a black camisole underneath and a tight-fitted white linen skirt that fell below the knees. Her full lips looked good enough to suck on. *Stop it.*

"Hi Eva. Come in."

"Tomas. Thanks for this dinner," she said, standing awkwardly. She came to the kitchen.

"Would you like some cava wine?" he asked. Eva nodded. He poured two glasses. "Here you go." Their hands brushed and his heart did a little dance. *Hell.* It was as if they hadn't made love with all his jittery nerves.

Eva scanned the kitchen. "This looks great. I love the ambience and the amazing smell. What did you make?" She sat down at the table.

"Nothing but the best Spanish chicken and chorizo bake. I hope you like it."

She nodded. "I love it. My mum makes the best, but I'm sure yours will be just as great. I didn't know you knew how to cook."

"My mum taught me when I was about ten. She didn't worry about gender roles. My dad was different though, thinking I shouldn't have been in the kitchen. But she ignored his stupid thoughts without him knowing."

Eva chuckled. "Your mum sounds great. How is she doing with her chronic pain?"

Tomas angled his head. "Much better now that she's seen the orthopaedic surgeon. I paid for her to see a private specialist, so it didn't take long. She's due to have surgery in two weeks, which should help."

"That's great. I guess you'll be playing nursemaid."

"No, luckily my aunt's coming down from the north, so she'll look after my mum while she's recovering. Of course, I'll be around, too. My aunt'll need her breaks."

Eva sipped her wine. "It sounds organised."

Tomas got up and pulled the baked dish out of the oven. With a large spatula, he scooped up the contents of the dish into two plates with its chicken thighs, spicy sausage, mixed peppers, olives, and cherry tomatoes, the wafting smells of thyme, garlic, and vinegar permeating his senses. It aroused his hunger.

He set a plate down in front of Eva. "Here you go. Enjoy."

Eva's eyes widened. "Oh, this smells great."

Tomas sat down and dug into his dish, forking the chorizo and chewing it while Eva did the same. When she licked her lips and closed her eyes to savour the taste, he became hard underneath the table. *Control yourself, Tomas.* If it was up to him, he'd make love with her right on this table and skip dinner. "Oh, I forgot the tomato bread." He retrieved the tray of bread and placed it on a chopping board. He cut a piece for Eva and handed it to her.

"Yum. I love this type of bread. It goes well with the dish." She bit into the hard bread and chewed it delicately. "I can taste the garlic. Nice. Is this sea salt?"

"Only the best sea salt to make it nice and salty."

Eva laughed. "The first time I tried to make it I didn't realise I added a few rotten tomatoes on the bread. When my parents chewed on it, you should have seen their faces. Their eyes dulled, but they pretended it was okay until they couldn't hide it anymore."

"So, they didn't finish it?" asked Tomas.

She shook her head. "No, they said it could make us all sick and took out some other bread they had in the freezer. I haven't made it since. Too traumatic."

"How old were you?"

"Only twelve."

"Wow. That's a long time for you not to make it. Surely, you're over the trauma and don't need counselling anymore."

"Ha ha," said Eva. "I usually only make garlic bread without the tomatoes. I do like to mix in hard Vienna bread with fresh pieces of tomato, seasoned with salt and olive oil. It's a nice mix."

"You should make it for me one day."

Eva hesitated. "I will. Easy to make."

Tomas chewed on his chicken while Eva devoured a piece of pepper. Seeing her tongue move in her mouth made him desire her again. If only they could rush their dinner—but no, he had to be a gentleman. "How is teaching going?"

"Great. The kids are so enthusiastic to learn, and I feel blessed to have the greatest job in the world." Tomas loved seeing the light in her eyes. "But sometimes it's hard to please those parents who put too much pressure on their children. Those stressful times make me crave to be a writer full-time. But at least I get to do it as a side hustle."

"I get it," said Tomas. "With any job, you can't have it rosy all the time. I admire your tenacity for writing."

Eva smiled. "Thanks. How about you? How's paramedicine?"

Tomas shifted his posture. "Amazing when we can save lives, but obviously not great when we can't. I do wish I was God sometimes."

Eva leaned in. "But it's pretty rare though, isn't it?"

"It is. Most of the time people know when to call for help so we rarely get any deaths. But I remember one time, someone came close. It was a family of a particular culture who didn't believe in blood transfusions. They didn't call for help until their son was close to dying. Another few minutes, it would've been too late to save him. But their daughter finally convinced the parents."

Eva touched the base of her neck. "That is scary to think that people's culture gets in the way of saving lives. There's a fine line between doing what's right and having these fixed beliefs."

"I agree, but some people will never change their beliefs in spite of what happens."

When they finished their meal, Tomas rose again and placed a box of churros on the table with a side dish of milk chocolate. "I must admit, I bought these from the bakery. I don't know how to make homemade churros."

"Oh, I beat you there. I do."

He chuckled. "This isn't a competition, you know."

She angled her head. "Isn't it?" A cheeky grin splashed across her beautiful face, causing him to desire her again.

"You have to make them for me. No doubt about that."

She beamed. "I would love to. Now do we get to dig in?"

"Of course. But let me show you how to eat them the right way."

Eva knit her brows. "Oh, and what way is that?"

He grinned. "Like this." He picked up a churro, dipped it in the chocolate then leaned forward and inserted the end of it partly in her mouth. She chewed and moaned at the taste while some of the chocolate dripped down her chin. He wiped it from around her lips and licked his finger. "Tasty."

Eva stopped chewing, her breath slowing down. He continued to feed her with the churro as he moved to sit beside her. This time, the drip of chocolate around her mouth was coveted by his mouth and so he licked it from her mouth.

Tomas pulled way and grabbed a napkin, then wiped her lips. Time had stopped as their eyes locked. *Christ.* He needed her now.

CHAPTER 48

Efren's body shivered as he hugged himself when entering a small barn alongside Marco. He sniffed at the musty pig smells and body odour. Dead pigs hung from hooks, and sacks of flour lined the dirty floor. Containers of salt and other supplies were packed on shelves. In one corner stood his friend, Miguel, shirtless. Efren's breath caught and his heart went out to Miguel. His hands were tied to a steel pole beside an empty one. Was that his spot?

Marco turned to Efren. "This is what happens to those who don't abide by the rules."

"But what did Miguel do? Why is he here?" His friend looked at him with groggy eyes, and shook his head as if to warn him.

Marco cleared his throat. "You'll know soon enough." His eyes drifted to the entrance when Ana stepped inside the barn. "Hey, Ana. I thought you'd do the honours with Miguel after I secure Efren."

Her eyes gleamed as she shook her glossy hair from her face. Under different circumstances, he'd say she was beautiful. "With pleasure, Marco."

Marco shoved Efren towards the pole. He lifted his arms, secured handcuffs around his wrists and then hung him by his wrists on a chain secured to the empty post. Efren winced at the coldness of the metal. Was he going to die here?

Ana shook her head. "I heard you were spying on me, Efren."

"I'm sorry," he said. "I didn't mean to. I was only curious."

"You will be sorry," Ana said.

Marco heaved. "I want you to punish Miguel. He's refused to get Juanita pregnant." He sneered at the boy. "This is your last chance."

Miguel's head drooped. "But she's only eleven. Just a child."

Ana spat in his face. "You piece of shit. If you understood the mission, you would know that procreation is how we survive and thrive. Age doesn't matter when we have a purpose. A bigger vision." She rummaged through a cupboard and retrieved a long whip, then slid her hands over the handle with a creepy smile.

Marco turned Miguel around, and then Ana swung the whip high above her head and brought it down with all her strength on the boy's back. Efren trembled and closed his eyes, not daring to see the pain in his friend's eyes. He felt cold and dead inside as he lost count of the strokes of the whip.

Miguel begged. "No more, please. I promise to obey you. Please."

She laughed. "I don't think you've learned yet." Marco nodded in assent and squared his shoulders while gazing at Efren.

Swinging out her arm again, she flogged him and left red welts all the way down his back. Her satisfied smile made Efren sick.

"I think he's had enough," said Marco.

Ana shook her head. "No, he deserves nine more."

Marco grabbed the whip from her. "Get over your antipathy towards teenage boys. It's Efren's turn now, but I'll do it."

Efren's heart pounded as he braced for pain.

Tomas and Eva devoured each other's lips as he guided her towards the couch. He didn't want to wait until they got to the bedroom, so he pulled away from her and lay her on top of him on the couch.

His gentle hands removed her pink shirt, and then he pulled the straps of her camisole down and lifted it over her head. A white lacy bra lay underneath. His finger trailed the centre of her chest until reaching an aroused nipple, playing with it from inside her bra.

Tomas changed positions and lay her down underneath him while he unzipped her skirt, letting it slip slowly down her legs. After taking off his own shirt, he pulled down her underwear and slipped it off her body as he stared at the smoothness of her flawless skin. "I need to taste you." Eva nodded. "So badly."

He sat her up on the couch with her legs spread open while he leaned in close and delved into the juncture of her thighs, kissing and licking. Taking a breath, he inserted two fingers while reaching with his lips and kissing her sweet spot. She gasped and moaned as she held his head gently towards her. Tomas looked up to see her blushed skin and closed eyes, savouring the moment. He couldn't help getting aroused even more, especially when he planted his tongue inside her and dug in deep to taste her. She panted and brought her body closer to his mouth. "Oh, Tomas."

He stopped and looked up at her. "So beautiful."

After pulling away, he lay her back on the couch and took off the remainder of his clothes, moved up to her lips and kissed her hard while manoeuvring his manhood over her. He pushed himself inside, circling his hips. Their kiss became deeper, their mouths hungry for each other as they kept on writhing and grinding into each other until they screamed in climactic bliss.

When they were both spent, he spooned himself against her on the couch and played with the strands of her hair. "You are amazing, Eva."

She grinned. "So are you."

"Will you stay the night? I don't have work until tomorrow night."

"I'd like that."

The silence between them was comfortable as he stroked the side of her cheek and trailed his hand down the centre of her throat. He loved touching her and could never get close enough. Was this love?

"What are you thinking about?"

Eva sat up on the couch. "About Isabela. Have you heard anything more from Leandro?" She picked up her clothing and put it on.

"No, but Leandro did mention they were looking into organisations which could be considered spiritual groups.

Nothing's panned out yet. I told him I want to be there when they find the right place, and he said it's probably a good idea as an EMT. If anyone's hurt they'll need medical assistance. But he's warned me to not veer away from him and to only do my job."

Eva shook her head. "He's right. It's too dangerous, and I wouldn't want you to go. It's suicide, Tomas. But you could go as an EMT so long as you stay away from trouble."

Tomas put his shirt back on. "The police and detectives will instruct us. I'd be there to help. Besides, I can take care of myself."

She cleared her throat. "I would want to come, too. We can help each other."

A burning ache in his chest made him stop what he was doing. "There is no way I would let you go."

She glared at him. "Hold on." Eva put up a hand. "I don't care that you have training, but I'm not some helpless female. I can protect myself."

Tomas winced. "I would not put you in that position because I ... well ... I just wouldn't. End of discussion."

Eva scoffed. "End of discussion? Are you serious right now? Do you know how patriarchal that sounds? If you didn't know, we live in the twenty-first century and not in the damn Middle Ages. You can't be serious."

He put his arms across his chest. "I am serious, Eva. After all that you've been through—your father's violence, your ex-boyfriend, and the kidnapping you experienced. I can't let you go through something like that again."

"Damn it, Tomas. I am a big girl and don't need your protection. Stop mollycoddling me. I'm a strong, independent woman and I do not need you telling me what to do, so accept that."

Tomas inched his way towards her as she slipped on her skirt. "Damn you, Eva. I won't watch you get hurt."

Eva pressed her lips together and let go of her unzipped skirt. "You're a pain, Tomas."

Tomas knit his brows, his mouth close to hers, her breath short and eyes locked with his. "No, you're a damn pain, Eva."

"You know I'm—" Tomas couldn't resist her strong, sexy side so kissed her hard. He pulled away. "—right."

Before they said anything more, Tomas ripped off her skirt and panties, then pushed her against his kitchen wall, devouring her again. His lips trailed her breasts underneath her bra as his fingers probed in between her thighs again. She was so damn hot, he couldn't get enough of her.

As their clothes came off again, they made love with more hunger and need. Hell, he wanted her in every possible way, and that scared him.

CHAPTER 49

Eva sank her feet into the soft, squishy sand of the Valencia beach. The colourful buildings behind her cast shadows over the shore as the scorching sun bathed her sweaty skin. But she felt comfortable in a long sarong over her bathing suit as a blazing gust of wind brushed her flushed cheeks.

Tomas draped an arm over her shoulder. He wore a loose grey shirt over a skin-tight white top. His eyes wandered to find a spot they could lie on, but he seemed preoccupied by something. Was he thinking about his friend, the distressed Gonzalo, or was he thinking about Efren, who was still missing and most likely a part of the cult now?

Tomas settled on a spot and lay down a towel and beach bag while Eva did the same. She sat up and held her legs while Tomas grinned in her direction.

"You've never been to Valencia?"

Eva shook her head. "First time. It's beautiful. It gives me the feeling of the Amalfi Coast on flat ground."

He intertwined her fingers with his and looked around. "The three-and-a-half-hour drive was worth this place, don't you think?"

"Oh, definitely. It is a shame we don't have beaches in Madrid. Not that I'm a great swimmer, but it's a nice vibe to be around water, to relax and sunbathe." An image flashed before her. "I remember the time my dad had one of his good days when he was sober. He brought us to a swimming pool near our place and pretended it was the beach. He'd make me swim between his legs and would throw me high into the water. It was fun, and ... and ... I miss him." She held back tears, and Tomas gave her a reassuring smile as he squeezed her hand. She wanted this man more and more by the minute. "My mum packed a picnic, and we ate at the gardens in Plaza de Espana like we were at the beach. It was the next best thing."

His eyes lit up. "That sounds like a great memory. Any others?"

Eva cast her mind back as young children walked by, flicking sand over her legs. She wiped the grains away. Other beachgoers lay underneath umbrellas or played ball in the water while men chased after children at the shallow end of the beach. "I remember when my dad would pick me up from work near the bus stop. I was working late at a retail store while still going to school. He would always bring me dinner. It was the best hamburger I'd ever had. He knew I liked them, so he made it our weekly routine to get me the same food every Friday night. I loved him for those bonding moments we shared. He was a different person, a real father who loved his daughter. But not when he wasn't himself. He had this dark side, so it took me a long time to trust people, men in particular. I still struggle with trust, Tomas. It's like it's been cast into my very soul, a part of me. Like something I can't shake. I lived in this whirlwind where I didn't know what I'd get. Would I get the good dad or the monster dad? Life became so unpredictable to the point that I was anxious all the time, even when there was no need to be."

"That's what anxiety is, Eva," he said while stroking his hand over her hair, which she found soothing. "But I hope you can trust me."

"I hope so, too."

"It can't have been easy living that way, not knowing what would happen, as if you were walking on eggshells. I get it. I lived that way too, but with my dad it was the opposite." He grasped her hands. "It must have been hard not knowing whether he'd love you from one day to the next. But at least you knew your mother loved you. That had to make up for what your dad did to you, right?"

Eva shrugged, not agreeing with his assessment. "Not totally, but she has helped to give me that security I needed. It was hard at school when I was put down by girls who didn't understand my condition. Even the boys bullied me. Not to mention my ex-boyfriend, always pointing out I was cross-eyed, weird, and not of this world. It's not like I wanted to have a glass eye, Tomas. I had no control over that."

"I know, and kids can be cruel. Even boyfriends." He leaned forward and kissed her tenderly on the cheek. "You are amazing, and I for one, cannot tell any difference. I don't see your glass eye. I just see you." He turned to face her and drew a hand across her cheek while licking his lips, almost oblivious to the noises, splashes of seawater, and children's laughter in the water. "Let's go for a swim."

Eva rose, pulled off her sarong, lay it on her towel then joined him in the water as he splashed her instantly in the face. "Oh, come on." She shivered in the water, despite its warm temperature.

Tomas swam a distance away, kicking his legs while the water splashed into her eyes. She rubbed them and slid underneath the waves to swim in his direction and reach him. He floated on the water closer to her, then wrapped his arms around her body, squeezing her bottom. "Oh, cute and sexy."

Eva laughed. "Cut it out. We're in public, so keep your hands to yourself."

Inching closer, he kissed her hard as she reciprocated and squeezed his lower back, not worrying that others were all around them. He pulled away and caressed her lips. "I cannot get enough of you, Eva. I love spending time with you."

Her heart warmed. "I do too, Tomas."

After swimming their separate ways for five minutes, Eva made her way back to her towel and lay back with her eyes closed while Tomas kept swimming. The sticky water dried quickly under the hot, glaring sun. This was the life, she thought. No problems, no murders, but just plain old fun with the man she ... she loved? Was she in love with Tomas? No, she couldn't be. It was a deep affection, that was all.

As if she'd drifted off to sleep, she woke up to the sound of a thump beside her. Slowly rousing, she spotted Tomas playing ball with a group of young men.

Sitting up, she noticed something on the towel beside her. A small bottle of liquid with a string attached around it. A tag hung down. She reached for the tag, her chest pulsating. *What the hell.*

Eva gasped and her eyes watered in fear. Her skull squeezed tight with tension. This had to be a joke. Was her stalker back, and had he just sent her a message?

Tomas stomped back to Eva, whose face twisted at an awkward angle, her head shaking as if she couldn't control it. Something had happened.

Salty water dripped from his body as he rushed to her side, his heart racing a mile a minute. He would do anything to protect her. "What happened?"

She swallowed then gave him the bottle, his pulse thundering as he instantly looked around for any suspicious person. What if the stalker was here? Was it the man on the phone who looked at him strangely, or was it the woman pretending to be a mother to the young girl beside them? No, he was getting paranoid. This person was long gone by now. "We'll talk to the police."

She shook her head stiffly. "Who is playing with us?" She pursed her lips. "I thought the stalker had all but forgotten me, if this is the same person. This message, 'peace and harmony' written on the tag, and what's in the bottle? Is it mercury?" Her breath quickened. "Maybe getting involved in this wasn't such a great idea. I'm scared, Tomas. Have we gone too far with our questions to Carmen, Rafael, the priest at the church? Did someone see all that even when we didn't think we'd been followed?"

His eyes darkened as he shifted forward and wrapped his arms around her, his hands stroking the back of her head. "I will make sure nothing happens to you, Eva. You are safe with me. Always."

"Thanks, Tomas."

He got up, shook out his towel and put it around his shoulders. "Let's go straight to Leandro. I'll give him a call."

When Leandro answered, Tomas explained the message.

"Okay, I'll have police circle her apartment for a few days." Leandro promised. "Wrap up the bottle carefully and bring it here. We'll check it for prints."

"Okay, thanks, Leandro." He turned to Eva. "We'll visit the police."

As they walked to his car parked a few minutes away on the side of the road, goosebumps covered his skin despite the sun burning it raw.

Tomas stepped inside his car and waited until Eva was buckled up before starting the motor. He headed out of Valencia and drove back towards Madrid, savouring his special time with Eva, knowing she'd be safe with him. "Are you all right?"

Eva peered through the window without turning to him. "Fine."

His hand gripped the steering wheel tight as if he could imagine squeezing the life out of this stalker. "The police will catch who is doing this."

Tomas wanted to feel more positive than he was, but he couldn't express that to Eva. He was anxious enough for the both of them, her hands fidgeting in her lap and feet shuffling every few minutes. "I know they are close, Eva. If you don't have faith in the police system, have faith in Leandro. He's a brilliant detective and he's on our side. He'll get to the truth. Please believe that."

"I hope you're right."

The silence for the remainder of the trip, apart from the soft music playing on the radio, was comforting for Tomas.

If only he believed this situation would get better before it got worse. It was an uneasy feeling he had.

CHAPTER 50

E fren winced at Maria. He hated being stuck inside this dirty barn, strung up like a rag doll. His arms were aching, and he was thirsty. Were they going to kill him?

Miguel looked at Efren. "It's going to be all right, man. Have faith."

"I'm sorry," Maria said.

Behind her, two people walked inside: Marco with Luna, an older girl of about seventeen with whom he'd gathered berries.

Marco glared and unchained him from the post. He fell and rubbed his wrists. which were raw and red. "You're fulfilling your mission today. If you don't follow the rules, you'll be punished in the worst way."

"Leave him alone," said Miguel.

Marco scoffed. "Like you've got control now. You shut your mouth Miguel, or I'll literally sew it shut."

Maria watched him with sadness. "Marco, wait. Can't he be punished another way? I'll get him to do chores around the kitchen. Please. Not this way."

Marco pressed his lips together, inching forward as he grabbed her by the neck and squeezed her windpipe, her eyes widening in terror. "Your job is not to question our mission, or you'll be next. Understand?" He let her go.

Maria took deep breaths and rubbed her throat. "Of course."

Marco shoved Efren forward until they arrived at the small cabin. Luna's shoulders fell flat, and Maria walked away with drooping shoulders.

The three of them entered the room that contained a king-sized bed, a two-seater sofa, and an open lounge area. It was bare except for the chains, handcuffs and whips strewn around. He turned his nose up at the tangy smell of blood. Other smells of sweat and body odour nauseated him. What happened recently in this room?

"Go on, Luna," said Marco, who lay back lazily on the sofa.

Luna pulled off her cardigan and the camisole underneath. Scars lined her chest, and what looked like cigarette burns dotted her abdomen. "I want you to play your part, Luna, or I'll hurt your brother. I know where he lives," Marco continued.

Luna wept, but she wiped the tears away. She closed her eyes while licking her lips and touched the centre of her chest.

Efren felt sick. "No, I can't do this, Marco. Please. I'm ... I'm a virgin."

He scoffed. "The act of procreation is part of our mission. The more believers we have, the stronger we'll become as a community. It's part of God's plan, Efren."

His blood boiled and his chest burned with anger. "But she's too young." Efren shook his head and headed towards the door. "I can't do this. I'm sorry."

Marco leaned forward. "Get on with it or someone's going to get hurt. Badly. If you don't do this, I'll kill either you or your mother. Play by our rules or suffer the consequences."

Luna inched towards Efren and caressed his bottom lip. His body shook. "It's okay."

"But I don't know what to do." His bottom lip trembled, and tears cascaded down his gaunt cheeks.

Luna touched his arm. "It will be quick, and I will do everything."

"Get on with it. I don't have all day," Marco said as the creep licked his lips, his hands crossed behind his head. He smiled. The pervert.

Efren stared at him with contempt, then turned to Luna. What choice did he have if he threatened to hurt his mother?

Luna took off the rest of her clothes with sadness in her eyes. His hand reached out to her, wiping away her tears.

Tomas gently held Eva's hand as they walked towards the market stalls in Plaza de Espana, not far from Gran Via. She wondered if she was still being followed. Whoever had left them that bottle in Valencia was lying low.

Eva faced him. "How did you find out about this market stall?"

His gut tightened. "Earlier, when we saw Leandro after Valencia, I overheard two policemen talking on my way to the men's room. They mentioned how one of the cult members might be selling herbs at this Plaza event. One of the guys said that because they're chasing up other leads, they didn't think it was a solid one. They also didn't have the manpower to check it out."

"Understandable when they have limited time and resources," said Eva. "But is it wise? It could be dangerous."

Tomas shook his head. "Plenty of people here, and you'll be safe with me."

Shadows crossed the concrete path as they passed bushes, towering trees, and rich flower beds. The whir of motors and speeding cars alongside the path grounded her.

They passed green lawns. Timber benches and tables with central umbrellas gave a swarm of locals and tourists places to eat, drink, and scroll through their phones. A row of market stalls displayed bags and accessories, ice-cream shops, cafes, millinery, stuffed toys, and jewellery. Neon festival signage and the rhythm of Latin sounds gave the park a funky and active vibe. Crowds flocked around.

Eva made her way around a large dome-like sculpture, and behind it found another market stall underneath a marquee. Was this the place?

Tomas approached a man who appeared to be in his fifties, sitting beside a teenage boy of about fifteen. The boy sat like a stone. His light green eyes and tall, lanky stature strongly contrasted with the man's stocky build and greasy dark hair.

Tomas picked up a plastic sealed bag, and inside it was a bottle, labelled with a strange name that Eva couldn't pronounce. "What is this?" he asked.

"Oh, it's for any ailments you might have," the dark-haired man replied. "Back, neck, sleep issues, mental health issues. You name it, this is natural stuff. Best of its kind." He winked towards the boy whose eyes looked tired. "Isn't it?" The boy nodded and stared at Tomas. Coming closer, Eva saw that his scrawny body looked malnourished.

She swallowed, an uneasy sense running down her spine. The man appeared sleazy, and the way he stared at the boy was concerning. Were these members of the cult? "Have you done trials on these medications?"

"Of course," said the man. "Got the reports to prove it." He pulled a stack of documents from underneath the counter and handed them to her. She gripped the piece of paper that recited statistics and a list of exorbitant prices. Another document cited the results of medication trials, but anyone could fake this. "Here's our flyer about courses we run." She took that, too.

The flyer discussed spiritual groups: *Welcome to our spiritual space. Our group is about spiritual connection, enlightenment, healing of self and others, and personal development. Develop your intuition and fulfil your dreams by connecting with a higher power.*

We hold workshops and activities about spiritual/psychic development classes, connecting with spiritual realms and your higher self. There are meditation and yoga demonstrations, the exploration of karma, trance, energetic healing and the journey to higher consciousness. Meet a special community in a safe space at one of our regular meetings.

The man's greasy hands showed her other products as he distributed more sealed bags. "These two are great for peace and harmony, with a hint of lavender and other special herbs. They can be a great introduction to what we offer in our groups. My little friend here is a fan of our yoga classes, and he's come a long way. Haven't you, boy?"

"Hmm," he said, his eyebrows raised and his hands fidgeting.

"We even sell creams over on the far left here."

He took a tester from under the counter and started rubbing ointment on the boy's wrist. But the way his hand tenderly stroked the boy, whose hands shuddered, made Eva sick to the stomach. He continued to caress the boy's hand while the boy cowered, his eyes watering. The creepy man drooled as he topped the bottle of ointment and returned it to the spot underneath the counter.

The glare in Tomas' eyes unnerved her. "No," he said to himself.

When the man turned away, the boy whispered, "Help."

Eva's heart palpitated as she turned to Tomas. He lurched forward, his eyes blazing with fury, hands clenched and teeth grinding as if he was on a manhunt. Before she could say anything, he stormed over to the man, grabbed him by the collar of his shirt and threw him to the ground. He kneeled over the man and punched him over and over again. The boy ran to Eva, and she wrapped her arms around him.

Eva's heart kept pounding. "Stop, Tomas. Stop. He's had enough. Please."

But Tomas was oblivious to her words. He threw one punch after another. The man's eyes were bloody, and his cheeks bruised as he no longer moved. Was he dead?

Eva let go of the boy, rushed towards Tomas, slapped him and pushed him hard. He stared at his hands as if having woken up. She quickly called 112. "Yes, hello. I need an ambulance and police." Reciting the address, she watched Tomas cower then cover his face as if ashamed. A deep sadness in her chest made her want to wrap her arms around him, but another part of her wanted to scream. It was the violence. The violence. *Not this again.*

Eva stood a few metres from Tomas, who sat on the ground with his arms wrapped around his legs. She didn't recognise the man who had inflicted such violence on the vendor.

Ten minutes later, two young male paramedics stepped out of an ambulance with their medical bags and equipment. A young one with a moustache said, "What happened here?"

Eva faced Tomas. "As I said on the phone, this man was assaulted."

The paramedic nodded as he checked his airway and brought an oxygen mask to his face. "He is breathing, but he's in a bad way," he said.

The other paramedic with a slight paunch pulled out a liquid. He turned to Eva. "The police are on their way. Did you see the perpetrator?"

Tomas inched forward. "It was ... was ... my fault. I hit him."

Eva interrupted, turning to the boy whose head bowed. "We're going outside to wait for the police." She gazed over the crowds oblivious to what had happened. Facing the boy, she noticed how he clung to her by squeezing her hand, his eyes misting. "What's your name?"

"Raul." He blinked twice.

The paramedics carried the stretcher towards the ambulance when one of them said, "You will need to speak to the police. They shouldn't be long."

"Of course," said Eva.

Tomas and Eva waited, but she turned away from him. He walked over to the bench, stony-faced and picked at the skin on his hands. She couldn't look at him now.

Standing in front of the area with Raul, she turned to the boy who appeared to be about sixteen. "Are you all right?"

Raul squinted. "He forced me to ... tomorrow I had to ... to ..." He flinched when a couple and one child passed by and headed towards the stall. "This is closed for today." The man nodded in understanding. When more people dropped by, she ushered them away.

Eva patted his shoulder. "It's all right. The police will be here. They will ask you questions and help you." As if she'd spoken of the devil, Officers Sanchez and Diaz walked towards her.

"We meet again, Ms Lopez. What's the situation here?" asked Officer Sanchez, who led Diaz inside the stall.

"This boy asked for help, but I'm not sure what's going on." She pointed to the stall. "Tomas assaulted the seller of this stall, but the man looked suspicious. He's been taken to hospital."

Officer Sanchez nodded. "Give me a moment to search inside the stall, then I'll need to get you two to the station. Please don't go anywhere, and divert any patrons who come by. We won't be long."

"We'll be right here." She had a bad feeling about all this, her heart pining for Tomas but also loathing him.

CHAPTER 51

After giving their statements separately, Eva and Tomas waited in the police waiting area. She sat two seats away from him.

"I am sorry, Eva. I didn't mean to ..." he stammered. "I told them exactly what I did, but the man didn't lay charges. Don't you think that's strange?"

Her body stilled. A part of her wondered how well she knew Tomas. Her chest ached, and she felt as if pins and needles had been jammed into her skull. She never expected this level of violence from a man she cared about. Possibly even loved. But how could she love someone like this? Not again. Why was she attracted to men who liked to inflict violence?

Tomas sighed. "Can you please say something, Eva? Your silence is scary."

She scoffed. "My silence is scary? What about what you just did? Wasn't that scary, violent, criminal?" She pointed in the air. "That man might have been dirt, but what you did to him was inexcusable. He's in the damn hospital because of you, Tomas. Your punches, your anger, your ... your dark, criminal side." She pushed back tears. "I thought I knew you, but I don't know you at all. What you did, Tomas ... I cannot forget that. It will haunt me for God knows how long, and it makes me sick to think you could be like that. What would happen if I made you angry like that? Would you pound me? Would you give me another glass eye?" Tears streamed down her cheeks, and she rubbed them. "No, I've seen a dark side to you, and I don't like it. I can't look at you right now."

Tomas touched her on the shoulder, but she pushed his hand away. "Please, Eva. I didn't mean to let it get out of hand. I am sorry you had to see that. Forgive me."

She looked away. "If I didn't stop you, you would have killed the man, and then where would you be?"

He shook his head. "No, I would have stopped."

"I don't think so, Tomas." She stiffened, her hands sweating and her chest aching as if a deep pit of dirt had grown there. "You are lucky the man didn't lay charges, so I'm guessing what he was up to was illegal. It's still no excuse to hit him the way you did." She exhaled. "I don't want you to call me ever again, Tomas."

He shuffled his feet. "What are you saying?"

Eva's temples throbbed. "We're done." She held back tears and quaked in her seat, a surreal sense overcoming her. Was it her way of coping with the grief of losing Tomas? Her breath caught, and goosebumps spread across her arms. If she looked at Tomas now, she would break down, but she had to be strong. She would not cry over a man she didn't know or understand. She would not fall into the same pattern of violence ever again. It stopped now.

Leandro approached them. "Both of you. Please come with me. We need to talk." They followed him into his office down the corridor. "Take a seat."

Eva sat beside Tomas but inched further away. "What is this about?"

Leandro's eyes softened. "Raul gave his statement. We discovered that this man in the hospital, Javier, was grooming him for a meeting tomorrow. His parents reported him missing, but he's not from Madrid. He lives in the north of Spain." He cleared his throat. "Javier is part of a spiritual group. He planned to teach Raul the business of natural medicine, so those bottles will need to be tested for mercury or other suspicious substances. If it wasn't for you two coming across that stall, Raul would have been lost in the group, never to see his family again. Javier explained how he'd be united with a new family to seek spiritual enlightenment. That he'd be loved and cared for by this group while working the land."

Tomas leaned in. "That's terrible. Is this the same group that Lola was a part of?"

"A few things connect, but we can't be one hundred percent sure until we speak to Javier and get forensics to search the stall. They're searching the area as we speak." He glared at Tomas. "As for you, how could you hurt the man so badly? You are lucky he didn't press charges, but if it was up to me, you'd be in a cell by now. Stupid and violent, and ... I have no words."

"I am sorry, man," said Tomas. "I wasn't thinking."

"I don't care about your past. You should have walked away and called the police. It was not your job to punish him. But the fact he let it go might suggest he's guilty of other things." He angled his head. "How did you even find out about this man, Tomas?"

Eva diverted his response. Why was she saving him from Leandro? "Was Raul sexually abused, Leandro? By Javier?"

Leandro's eyes darkened. "I can't tell you that, Eva. Sorry." He shifted forward. "I forgot to tell you about what you found in Valencia. We've sent the bottle off for prints, but it'll take some time before we get the results.

A police officer will continue to patrol your apartment regularly for a few more days."

"Thanks, Leandro. Can I go now?"

"Of course. Thanks for your help again. You saved Raul and he's re-united with his family thanks to you."

Eva walked off and ignored Tomas as he reached for her. She rushed out before more tears came. It had to be this way.

CHAPTER 52

Tomas, Gonzalo, and Leandro walked past a towering monument opposite strips of shops, a row of tree-lined streets, outdoor restaurants covered by white umbrellas, and sets of apartments to a tapas bar in La Latina.

Tomas' heart felt heavy as he thought of Eva. He hadn't seen her for a week and a half. The deep ache and emptiness in his chest made him want to sleep and never wake up to face the day. That sense of abandonment again, as if he wasn't worthy.

Stepping inside a dark, cramped bar, they found a table in a corner with few patrons around and a waiter greeting them. A group of men nearby shouted and clanked beers together. Why were they this loud when his head was so sore?

"Earth to Tomas?" said Leandro.

He broke out of his thoughts. "What?"

"I asked what you'd like to drink. A beer, wine, something else?" asked Leandro. He turned to Gonzalo but got a shrug.

"A beer."

When the waiter arrived, Leandro ordered the drinks and added a platter of toasted canapes and tomato bread.

Gonzalo rubbed his hands together. "How's the wife?"

Leandro smiled. "She's good, apart from an aversion to certain types of food like fish and rice. She can't seem to stomach those."

"How far along is she now?" asked Tomas.

"Almost six months, and I can't wait. I'll be taking time off to help, but my parents will also be around. It's scary but exciting, too."

Tomas forced a smile. "I'm happy for you, man." He bowed his head, wishing he could feel differently. "Your life will forever change with a baby."

"True. Now, what's going on with you, Tomas? Come on, spill," Leandro demanded. "Gonzalo here wouldn't tell me anything."

His friend held out his hands. "I thought you should tell the man."

Tomas took a breath. "Eva broke up with me."

"Is this because of the guy you assaulted?"

Tomas nodded. "He was being sleazy with the boy, Leandro, grooming him. I saw it with my own eyes. It made me sick. I couldn't stand there and watch, but going overboard was not my plan. He triggered something in me, and I lost control."

"You need to get rid of those triggers of yours. You can't keep letting your anger control you, my friend," said Leandro.

Their drinks and food arrived, and instantly Gonzalo picked up a salmon canape and bit into it. Leandro picked up a piece of tomato bread.

Gonzalo leaned forward and licked his fingers before wiping his hands on a napkin. "Eva needs time, that's all. She cares about you. A lot. Don't give up on her."

"I'm not, but it hurts like hell to be away from her. I can't stop seeing her in my head day and night. It's even affecting my work." He touched his aching chest. "I'm making mistakes and I feel like shit. I hate this time apart, but I need to do what she wants." He grabbed a piece of bread and chewed. "Let's change the subject." He perked up and brushed his pain aside. "Any news about Javier? Is he connected to this cult?"

Leandro's eyes darkened. "He won't talk, and that's all I'm saying."

"What about that property you visited? Was there anything incriminating?" Tomas threaded a hand through his hair.

Leandro huffed. "Let us worry about this case, not you."

Tomas flailed his hands around, wanting to help. "Come on. I am most likely going to help as an EMT when you go next time, so tell me."

"Nothing tangible yet. All we saw were groups of men, women, and children worshipping in a chapel, cleaning cabins, doing household tasks, and cooking large amounts of food. But something didn't feel right about the place."

Gonzalo scratched above his mouth. "What do you mean?"

"It felt forced, with few people in charge. They were too polite. It seemed unnatural. It was as if the residents had a rehearsed script."

"You should be able to go there when they're least prepared," said Tomas.

"You're right, but to do that we need probable cause and so far, we don't have enough for a warrant. We'll keep digging."

"Did you ask about Efren?"

"We did, but they claimed to not know the boy. I doubt they were telling the truth. But we won't give up."

Eva, Daniela, and Blanca climbed down the multiple steps of the Prado Museum towards a cobblestone path to sit on a concrete bench. The mild sun warmed their cheeks, and scattered trees behind them provided little shade as Eva stared at the orange sign, *Museo Del Prado*.

The large space was busy as people entered and left the museum, some pausing to snap pictures of the museum and monuments. At a grassy knoll, an umbrella-shaded stall sold artworks. Nearby, a National Police car was parked.

Daniela sat beside Eva and grabbed her hand. "Penny for your thoughts, sister."

She chuckled. "I always love visiting the museum. It inspires me for my writing. It makes me creative." Despite the positive words, her tone fell flat. She was missing Tomas like crazy and wondered if she'd made the right decision. Had her decision been impulsive?

Blanca turned to her. "I love it, too." She placed a hand across her throat. "How are you doing without Tomas?"

"I'd rather not talk about it, Blanca. Please."

Daniela crossed a toned leg over her frilly skirt. "We understand."

Eva's throat felt parched. "At least we saved that boy, Raul. Who knows what would have happened to him if we didn't go there." She lifted her shoulders. "I know Leandro can't tell me, but I'm sure this guy, Javier, was related to the cult. The expensive prices of those medicines, the grooming of that poor boy, and the flyer about spiritual harmony. They were red flags."

Blanca added, "It's funny about cults. A lot of people seem to think there's always one main leader, but it's not necessarily true." Eva waited for more. "These cult leaders can come in packs and might even have full-time jobs. They might visit a few times a week and not even sleep on the property. But they still have so much control it's scary."

"Part-time cult leaders who share their responsibilities?" Daniela asked.

"Exactly," said Blanca. "And not only that, but these leaders might alternate so there's always someone watching over the members to make sure no one escapes. But no doubt they'd have loads of cameras. The members live there for whatever spiritual or religious bogus purpose, but the leaders don't always stay there."

"Interesting," said Eva. "That means we might have cult leaders next door or in our local community, despite the group residing in another part of Spain."

Daniela flinched. "I am getting goosebumps thinking about this. And it's even scarier now that two people have died. That we know of. Who knows how many more have died?"

The silence between them gave them time to process, and Eva started to think that these leaders might be closer to home than she had thought. She ignored the chill travelling up and down her back.

CHAPTER 53

Eva hugged the blankets tight around her, having spent most of the night tossing and turning in bed. Every time she fell asleep, nightmares flared like wildfire. She was chased, or stood handcuffed to a table, felt hot coals underneath her feet, and was on the brink of death. What did this all mean?

She pressed a hand against her heart to stop the pain in her chest, but it escalated until she closed her eyes and took deep breaths. Had she overreacted with Tomas and his show of violence last week, or had she made the right decision? Why did this sense of emptiness in her stomach make her want to pour her tears out and scream at the world for falling into the same pattern again?

Rising out of bed, she rubbed tears from her eyes and tried to shake out her ache. She had to focus on Lola and getting justice. But as she headed into the shower, her shoulders fell and her throat burned as if she hadn't drunk water in a week. Even her legs felt heavy inside the shower. The warm water soothed her sore neck and legs.

As she concentrated on her day at work, Eva's mind kept flashing to Tomas and the tender way he'd made love to her. The way he'd kissed her as if he couldn't get enough of her. It wasn't only their physical connection but their emotional one. They both loved to help others and wanted fairness in the world. They were close to their mothers and had fathers who had let them down. She and Tomas enjoyed the same books and films, and they even loved children, particularly Samuel.

How could she stop remembering his beautiful face, his gentle hands and broad physique? But she had seen a different side to him that day, and it had scared the hell out of her. No, she couldn't be with someone like that. Never again.

As she turned off the tap and made her way out of the shower, her phone on the edge of the basin buzzed. Towelling off her body quickly, she picked it up and checked the notification. It was a text: *I am so sorry, Eva. Can we talk tonight?*

Eva's shoulders sank. She responded: *I am busy tonight. Please give me space.* A lone tear fell down her cheek as she towelled herself dry. She needed time to shut out the tension from her heart. She could feel it beating faster than usual. Her gut-wrenching pain kept her awake overnight, too.

A knock on the door broke her out of her reverie. "Eva. Are you all right? You've been in there a while," said Francisca.

She sniffed and dried her tears. "I'm good. I'll be out in a second." She rose and quickly got dressed before opening the door.

Walking towards the kitchen, she found her friend sipping on an espresso with a piece of buttered toast on the side. "What happened?"

Eva sat down with hunched shoulders. "Tomas and I broke up."

Francisca's eyes dilated. "Why, girl?"

Eva broke down and cried as she sank into the chair opposite, her body quaking. She didn't think she could work today. "It's a long story, Francisca."

She held out her hand and squeezed Eva's arm. "Oh, honey. Tell me what happened." She came around and put an arm around her shoulder, then dragged a chair beside her. "I've got time this morning."

Eva explained. "Do you see why I had to finish it?"

Francisca didn't say anything for a minute. "I get that, but..."

"But what?"

"Have you spoken to him about what triggered him?" She shook her head. "Do you know much about his childhood past? It could be relevant."

"Not really. Only how his father worked him to the bone, but what does that have to do with violence? It's inexcusable."

"Did you at least talk to him?" Eva was silent. "Oh, Eva, darling. You need to talk to him and not make such a rash decision. I'm right. Talk to the girls. I'm sure they would agree with me."

Eva swallowed and averted her eyes. "I don't know. I was scared and might've jumped to conclusions. But I'm confused. I need to think."

"Of course you do, and if you need time, then process what happened, but talk to him. When you're ready. Why don't you take the day off?"

Eva nodded. "I think I will. I'm not in the headspace to work. Can you let Ignacio know?"

"Of course, girl. You work hard enough as it is, so take the time you need." Francisca devoured her toast and drank down her coffee. "Are you feeling better, or do you want to talk a bit more?"

She waved her away. "No, you go. It's all good. Thanks, friend."

Francisca got up and gave her a reassuring smile. With a wink, she rushed to the bathroom before heading out.

Eva didn't know how long she'd stared into space before making herself toast and coffee when a loud thump across the living room window made her jump. She snuck towards the window, chills running down her spine. Eyes over her shoulder, she imagined someone coming up behind her, but it was crazy. Laughing to herself, she shook her head when seeing no one outside the window. It could've been next door, as sometimes whatever happened there sounded close.

Eva sat on the couch and turned on the morning news, but her mind wasn't on it. Then she heard what sounded like a muffled voice coming from her laundry. She wondered if her neighbour's children were walking past on their way to school.

Her eyes darted around her to make sure no one would sneak up on her. Goosebumps spread over her skin as the voice grew louder—a child's voice. Chills ran up her arms as she hesitated to open the door. Why was she hearing a child's voice? It had to be a joke, as only she and Francisca lived in the apartment.

Eva steeled herself and took one further step before turning the knob and opening the door. She jumped at the sight before her.

CHAPTER 54

Eva sat on the couch and took deep breaths, the vision stuck in her mind as if it would be constantly etched into it. She swallowed as the ache in her heart intensified.

Leandro approached the two uniformed policemen. "I want you to check CCTV footage, then question the nearby residents who might have witnessed anyone suspicious lurking by." He held out the photos inside a sealed plastic bag and turned towards Eva. "I'll take these photos to be tested for fingerprints. Now are you okay?"

She nodded. "I will be. Thanks, Leandro, for coming fast. I don't know why I'm being targeted." It made her sick to see that image in her head: a blood-soaked neck and Isabela's dead eyes openly staring at nothing.

"We are close to finding answers. It's a matter of time and slip-ups, but for now you should make sure you're not alone. Keep yourself safe."

Eva nodded. "All right." She winced at the image in her head. "Tell me the truth, Leandro. Was that how Isabela died? A slash to the throat?"

Leandro hesitated and angled his head. "It was, but I want you to get that image out of your head. We're dealing with dangerous people who most likely don't want their secrets coming out. You need to always be cautious and vigilant. If you see anything suspicious, please call me."

"I will, and thank you. I know you're doing everything you can."

Leandro squeezed her shoulder. "I had better go." He made his way to the door then quickly turned around. "About Tomas. He's my friend and all I want to say is not to judge him too quickly. The poor guy's been through more than you know. Hear him out." Before she could reply, he opened the door and stepped out.

Her face stung with new tears and her body trembled. She missed Tomas, but she couldn't think straight with Lola's case in the wind. Why would anyone send her photos of Isabela in death? With a quick intake of breath, she decided to head to work for at least half of the day, not wanting to be home alone.

***

Later that day after everyone else had left the school, Eva sat opposite Ignacio, who touched her shoulder and gave a reassuring smile. "I heard about what happened earlier today. Are you all right?"

"Sorry? How did you know?"

"Oh, I have my sources. But how are you doing? Do you need time off?" His tone was almost cold; different. What was going on with him?

A chill ran down her spine, sensing something was off. After staring at the ground then turning back to him, she was sure he'd had the briefest of smiles. It had to be her imagination, for why would he smile when she'd seen the brutality of Isabela's death? "I wish I knew who would do this?"

He clenched his hands, gazing past her. "I heard about the gentleman who got beaten up by your boyfriend. What he did to that boy. Can't imagine." His eyes glazed over her as if he was thinking of something else.

Eva stood up from the chair and neared the door. She didn't like the odd look in his eye. He appeared like a different person. "Right, and how would you know?"

Ignacio rose from his chair, limping as if he had leg pain. "Let me drive you home."

"I have my car here." Something flickered in her mind. *The priest*. Hadn't he mentioned seeing someone limping? But no, anyone could limp from acute pain.

Again, Ignacio clenched his hands, his eyes scanning her from head to toe. "I insist you come with me."

Eva's stomach turned hard, and her legs wobbled beneath her as she opened the door. Why had he closed it in the first place? "No, I am fine. I'll see you tomorrow, Ignacio." She had her back to him, but his arm wrapped around her waist with surprising strength. Her power didn't equal his grip tightening against her waist, restricting her breathing.

"You are coming with me, Lopez."

Eva's heart raced a mile a minute. Her hands began to sweat as he gripped one of them tight against his own. "What are you doing?"

Ignacio pressed something hard against her back. "You try to escape, and I'll shoot you, so no funny business."

She turned to see a gun aimed at her face. "Why are you doing this? What do you want?"

"You don't get to ask questions here. I'm the one in control, so get moving before I shoot you."

Her spine chilled and her heart raced. "What do you know about Isabela's death?" Body quaking, Eva moved slowly in an attempt to stall him. But who would come to save her when everyone had gone home? "Ignacio, please. You know me." He shoved her forward down the dark corridor lined with student lockers. "What do you want from me?"

"Shut up and move. Now." He poked the butt of the gun into her lower back hard enough to cause a bruise. She realised that if she continued to speak he would most likely lose his patience.

He prodded her forward while her legs felt like jelly and her head throbbed as if a jackhammer was trapped inside. Gasping for breath, she made her way forward as he pushed her towards the driver's side of his car. "We are going somewhere private and isolated. The best part of my job." After unlocking his car, he handed her the keys. "Get in." His eyes appeared to glow in the moonlight. His shuffle along the concrete unnerved her even as the sounds of crickets and birds overhead gave her an odd feeling of calm.

Eva fell into the driver's seat while Ignacio sat in the passenger seat with his gun trained on her. His eyes didn't leave her. "Now what, Ignacio?" Her lip trembled, but she steeled herself, not wanting him to see how scared she was. Would he be capable of killing her, and why was he doing this? Eva's vision blurred and dizziness set in. "Are you going to kill me?"

Ignacio hesitated. "Start the car."

She gasped, her eyes darting around the parking lot for any sign of life, but it was deserted. A strong wind howled and a flock of crows flying past gave her an uneasy sense of a bad omen. "Where are we going?" He wasn't going to kill her, was he?

"I'll direct you, but if you veer off my directions, I'll shoot you point blank in the middle of the eyes. Don't think I won't."

Eva froze. "Were you the one stalking me?"

He scoffed. "Don't think you can stall, but yes."

"And the church, distributing flyers?"

He nodded. "Enough with the questions."

Tomas flashed in her mind, as well as Daniela, her mother and friends. Was she going to die by the end of the night?

CHAPTER 55

Tomas walked to his car in the underground car park close to home when his phone vibrated. It was a number he didn't recognise. "Hello."

"Help ... help me ... Tomas."

His body froze. "Samuel. Is that you?" Silence. "Samuel? What's wrong? Tell me." The line disconnected and his mind reeled. What the hell just happened? Was Samuel being attacked again? Were they going to hurt him?

He took a calming breath and called Andreina, but no one answered. He rang Leandro, his hand shaking. "I think I might have heard from Samuel. He asked for help, then the line went dead."

"Come to the station now. Are you sure it was Samuel?"

"Mostly sure. It was a child, and I can't imagine any other child ringing me."

"I'll head over to his home now with back-up. But I'll see you at the station when I get back." He sighed. "Let's not jump the gun here. It could have been a prank with a child's recorded voice on the phone. We can't assume anything yet."

"Okay." Tomas ended the call. He jumped into his car and raced out of the underground space. But then he realised he could reach Andreina's house before the police would. He had to go there. What if Samuel only had precious minutes? He'd never forgive himself if he didn't try to save him.

Traffic was light this late, so the drive didn't take long. It gave him a few minutes to ring Eva on his Bluetooth, wondering if Samuel had tried to call her also. But it went straight to voicemail. He left a message.

His heart was pounding as he parked close to Andreina's building. He looked up at her apartment, but couldn't tell whether anyone was home. He rushed to the elevator, pressing a hand against his forehead as a headache arose. When he reached Andreina's door, he breathed a sigh of relief to see it closed. They might be inside. It was still early enough for them to be awake. He knocked on the door, but no one answered. He banged on the door and screamed their names, but still heard nothing. Other tenants opened their doors to shout at him to stay quiet.

Tomas walked towards a man wearing a singlet. "Did you see them leaving? Can you tell me if you saw any visitors?"

The man scratched his arm, as huge as a tree trunk. "I was going out when the boy and his mum walked outside with two men. They mentioned being cousins taking them on a trip."

"Cousins?" Tomas didn't buy it. "Did Samuel or his aunt look scared to you?"

He shrugged. "Couldn't tell. They rushed out of here." The man returned to his apartment.

All Tomas could do now was wait for Leandro and the police to arrive. They had to find them. This was getting out of hand. Efren was still missing, and now Samuel, too. Somehow, Tomas didn't believe the cult would hurt him. They'd left him alone all this time. The question was, why now? Why not kidnap Samuel and Andreina earlier? Were they worried because he had started to speak? But they'd only know that if they were watching him.

He sat with his back against the wall, rising when Leandro and two uniformed officers arrived. The anger was obvious on his friend's face.

"What in the hell are you doing here, Tomas? Are you trying to get in trouble?"

He sighed. "I figured I'd get here quicker than you guys and I was right. There's no one home. They've been taken, Leandro."

He shook his head. "All the while you could've put yourself in harm's way. Step aside. We're going in."

"You do have probable cause," said Tomas.

Leandro moved back, and with a swift kick, broke open the door. He turned to Tomas. "Go home. We've got this."

"I'll wait." He leaned back against the corridor wall, his hands fidgeting and his mind reeling. Whoever hurt Samuel would have to deal with him. Something must have spooked him enough to talk.

Leandro soon came out of the apartment, barking orders to the uniformed officers. "Diaz. Talk to those in this building who might have seen them leave." He turned to Officer Sanchez. "Wait for forensics to do a sweep of the place. We don't know if anyone's coming back here, but monitor just in case."

He faced Tomas. "I will be glad when this case is over." His phone buzzed and he answered. "You've found the original owner of the property? What else?" His eyes dilated. "Great work." He ended the call.

Tomas neared his friend. "You look like you've seen a ghost. What is it?"

He frowned. "Eva didn't come home tonight. Her friend, Francisca called the station."

Tomas' spine chilled. *No, no, no.*

"You go home," Leandro ordered. "I need to leave."

Tomas couldn't breathe. "No, I'm coming with you." He put up a hand. "If Eva's in trouble, I need to be there. I can help. Please, Leandro."

The detective exhaled. "We've got an address, and I don't have time to argue with you, so come on. I'll explain on the way."

Tomas quickened his pace behind Leandro until they reached his car and sped off. "Are you going to tell me who we're visiting? Speak up, man." His body sweated, and a headache felt like pins in his head.

"We're going to the school principal's home. We found out he's the original owner of the property we recently visited. It was covered up under a few aliases, but we followed the money and found him."

"Do you think he's home?"

Leandro shrugged as he made a swift turn to the right, cutting in front of a slow driver that blocked his way. "I hope so. But I'm worried he might be the one stalking Eva. It makes sense if he's one of the cult leaders and doesn't like Eva's connection to Samuel or her snooping around."

Tomas lay his head back, closing his eyes. "Oh, Jesus. Please let Eva be okay." He hated how they'd distanced themselves from each other when he should have been protecting her, but she didn't want anything to do with him. He had honoured her wishes. But at what cost?

"It's in here," Leandro said, as he parked by the kerb and turned off the motor. "You wait here. If I'm not back in five minutes, come out."

"Fine." The driver's door slammed as Leandro jogged down an even concrete path that led towards a brick veneer home with the lights on. Tomas took quick, deep breaths to calm himself. He tried to call Eva again, but still got no response. His lips trembled, and he shook away his nerves, needing to believe she was okay.

A few minutes later, Leandro rushed back in and started the motor. Tires squealed as he pulled away. "Ignacio is not home, but he could be working late at the school. That's where we're heading next."

Tomas curled a brow. "The school? What if Eva was there with him? You don't think..."

"I won't speculate, but we need to find him. He's a dangerous man who has a long list of priors and identities."

Tomas rubbed his chest and exhaled. *Please let Eva be okay.* He would not survive if something happened to Eva. *Dear Lord.* He loved her.

CHAPTER 56

The keys slipped from Eva's hands to the floor. "Sorry." Slowly picking them up, she took a breath and started the motor after adjusting her rear mirror. The back of her neck sweated and her hands quivered.

"Hurry up or I'll shoot you dead. Who cares about the mirrors? I need you to drive."

Eva turned to him. "Please, Ignacio. I thought we had a rapport. That you cared. You said I was one of your best educators. Was that a lie?"

He scoffed. "No, it wasn't. But you're a threat so we can't let you live."

Eva's vision blurred as her body froze. *Kill me? Do something. Stall.*

He slapped her hard across the cheek. "Fuckin' drive, bitch. You're pushing your luck."

Eva nodded. "All right." But when a set of headlights charged towards them and Ignacio squinted, his hand loosened on the gun. Seeing an opportunity, she activated her self-defence training and smacked the gun out of his hand. Stomping on the brake, she jabbed Ignacio hard in the face with her elbow, threw the door open and dashed towards a tree.

"You bitch. I will kill you!" He swung his body out of the car, gun in hand again, and ducked behind his vehicle as the oncoming car stopped in front of his own, followed by two marked police cars.

Leandro jumped out of the first car. "This is Senior Sergeant Leandro from the National Police. We would like to speak with you, Ignacio. No one needs to get hurt. Please put the gun down."

Ignacio fired wildly, shattering the windscreen of one of the police cars. Leandro and the officers from the cars opposite him returned fire. Ignacio shifted behind his car, which rocked as bullets hit it. "I'm not going to prison and will kill you all, so back off," he screamed.

Eva peeked from behind the tree and could have sworn she saw Tomas hiding behind the open door of Leandro's car.

"We only want to talk, so put the gun down, Ignacio. We can work this out. This will only get worse if you don't comply," Leandro called.

Ignacio shook his head, eyes blazing as he stepped back from his car in an attempt to escape. He dashed around the side of the school building and ran, the policemen tearing off in pursuit.

Slowly, Eva crept away from her hiding place as Leandro and two police officers chased Ignacio. Her body quaked as she pressed a hand across her chest and focussed on her breathing, flashing back to the gun pointed in her face.

Footsteps towards her jolted her out of her reverie until inching closer, Tomas wrapped an arm around her waist and pulled her in for an embrace while stroking the small of her back. "Thank God you're okay." He broke away, gazing at her. "Are you all right?"

Eva's heart raced and the tingle in it proved that she cared about Tomas more than she wanted to admit. "I'll be fine. What are you doing here, with the police?"

"Samuel and his aunt were kidnapped, then Leandro got a lead. He didn't want me to come, but I had to make sure you were okay."

Eva's heart warmed, realising how much he cared. "My goodness. Poor Samuel. Is there ever any end to his trauma?"

Stomping steps behind them broke their conversation as the police returned, with a handcuffed Ignacio between them. He glared at Eva. "This is not over, Eva. You can't stop this." He chuckled. Leandro slapped the back of his head and pushed him towards the police car that was still intact.

Eva's bottom lip trembled. "What are you talking about?"

"Don't believe you're safe," he shouted over his shoulder.

Leandro pushed him into the back of the police car. "Get inside and shut up. You'll be going away for a long time, Ignacio." He closed the door, and Officers Sanchez and Diaz drove him away.

Leandro gestured at Tomas and Eva. "Come with me." He led them to his car. Eva and Tomas climbed into the back seat. His eyes remained glued to her until Leandro started the motor. "I'll get someone to drive your car home tomorrow, Eva. For now, I'll need to get you to the station for your statement. But also, to make sure you're safe," Leandro said.

"Thanks, but hopefully Ignacio will tell you who else is involved. Do you know where Samuel might be?"

"Not a clue at this stage, but we might get something out of Ignacio," said Leandro.

"I hope he's all right. He has been through too much. What twelve-year-old should go through all the trauma he's been through?"

"I know," said Tomas who carried on caressing her hand when Eva tried to pull it away.

"We'll find him," said Leandro.

She nodded. "I hope so."

Ten minutes of silence unnerved her. She felt uneasy about this case. Was Ignacio right about her being in danger? Surely, he would talk to the police if he had an ounce of humanity inside him.

Leandro's phone buzzed. He pulled over to the side of the road and answered it privately. He gasped then nodded and nodded again. "Okay. Thanks for letting me know." He bowed his head and slammed his hand against the steering wheel. "Damn it. Damn."

Tomas unbuckled his belt and leaned forward. "What is it, man?"

He shifted his shoulders and slowly turned in their direction. "Andreina's in the hospital with stab wounds to the chest and stomach. We don't know if she's going to survive. She's in critical condition."

Eva's shoulders sank, her mind racing. "Samuel?"

"He's okay. The men who were after them have been killed, which doesn't help our cause because we don't know who sent them."

"How did they find them?" Tomas asked.

"A witness at a local petrol station called the police about a boy and woman frantically waving to him in fear. Andreina mimed the word, 'help' to this witness. But when the nearby police arrived and started shooting, Samuel ran off and one of the men shot at him, which is when the officers shot him dead. The other took Andreina hostage. The policeman tried to talk him down, but he refused to let go of Andreina. The bastard must have stabbed her out of spite before the officer shot him dead." He rubbed his eyes then shook his head.

"Oh, Jesus," said Tomas.

Leandro started up the motor again. "Samuel's been taken to a safe house."

"That's a good idea," said Tomas.

Eva stared out the window, lost for words as she pondered what Ignacio had said again.

CHAPTER 57

Efren's head drooped, his eyes tired and his arms weighing like lead above him. These damn handcuffs were cutting into his skin. He was hungry and thirsty, but he refused to eat until they let him go. After his failed attempt with Juanita, they had brought him back to the barn. But how could he get an erection when his life was in danger?

Voices made him alert. Ana and Cesar, another one of their leaders approached.

Ana leaned in towards Efren, her eyes red as they blinked a few times. "We're trying to figure out what to do with you."

Cesar faced her. "We need to be careful, Ana. That bastard Marco's been arrested. The police might come back if he talks. We need a new plan."

"Marco's not high and mighty anymore, is he? What do you suggest?"

"Let's get Efren out of here and set up elsewhere, eventually overseas. I've got connections in the U.S., and they're happy to buy him and our other youngsters at a high price when we move over there. There's a smaller property we can use temporarily to avoid police."

Sell me? Bile rose in Efren's throat. He wanted to be sick.

"Understood," she said.

"How are we supposed to sell him when he's all skin and bones? He refuses to eat."

Ana scoffed. "The prick will eat." She glowered at him. "If I threaten the life of his dear mother, he'll eat then."

No, not his mother again. He'd kill them with his bare hands before they did that. "I will eat. Of course I'll eat," said Efren.

Cesar ignored him. "Sounds like a plan. But what about the others?"

"If you mean Eva and Tomas, they'll be disposed of very soon. We'll get Samuel back and he can be of service to us again."

Cesar shook his head. "But you had your chance to bring Samuel here. What happened?"

"They killed our men. I told you not to send those bozos. My little finger has more grit than them combined. But we'll find Samuel. At least his stupid aunt's injured. It's not looking great for her."

"Right. But if he talks."

"He might talk, but by then we'll be long gone. Like you said, overseas to start fresh. Let's take care of Ignacio then go after the others."

Efren took a breath. Who was Ignacio?

***

Tomas made his way up to Eva's apartment but felt a crick in his neck. Ever since they'd broken up, he hadn't been sleeping. But despite that, he smiled at Eva agreeing to see him so he could share their good news.

It had been a week since that intense night when Eva had been kidnapped, and now his spirits rose knowing they were safe.

He rang the doorbell and waited, the door opening a minute later. "Hi Eva."

She swung open the door. "Come in." She averted her eyes as she led him to the couch and took a breath. "Can I get you a drink?" He shook his head. Her nails dug into the palms of her hands, and she stared down at the floor. "What's the good news?"

"The police were able to get a warrant for that property near Corral del Sastre, and found promising leads. They believe they've moved everyone to another property after what happened to Samuel and Andreina. Ignacio's not talking, but something he said gave them a clue as to where they might be. It's a matter of time before they arrest them."

Eva grinned. "That is great news."

An awkward silence settled over them and he hated this tension between them.

"I need to talk to you about the day I assaulted that man, Eva." He exhaled. "The bastard reminded me of my father. The time he ..." Tomas rubbed the back of his neck and swallowed. Her eyes softened. "I was sold to a paedophile for a high price. My father knew this man from the community. He was wealthy." His body ached. "My dad knew what kind of person this creep was and sold me for money. For his pleasure. He didn't care about me."

Eva's body stilled, her eyes dilated. "Oh my God, Tomas. I am so sorry."

"The man took me to his caravan where he ... touched me." His eyes misted. "I felt sick to the stomach. I vomited in his lap and the bastard had the nerve to slap me. He pounded into me until I passed out. When I awoke, I was in the hospital."

She reached for his hand. "What happened?"

"A friend of my mum's told her she saw us going into the caravan, so my mum was worried. She didn't know why I was meeting a strange older man. My mum and her friend got into the caravan and saw this man undressing me while I was unconscious. The man saw them and picked up a knife, but my mum grabbed a vase. She smashed it over his head. The bastard didn't die, but he was injured badly and got arrested. She claimed self-defence; explained how she was protecting her son from abuse or death."

Eva wrapped her arms around him and cried. "I can't imagine what you went through, Tomas. The pain you suffered as a boy. The humiliation and self-disgust you must have felt."

Tomas pulled away and held her hand. "This man, Javier, was too friendly with Raul, and I knew in my gut what was going on. It scared the hell out of me. I had to protect him." He shed a tear. "I don't know what came over me. But I've started counselling to address these issues, my anger especially. It's helped." He gave her a reassuring smile. "I know if I see something like that again, I'll manage my triggers and ground myself. But I am not usually a violent person. Believe that."

Eva shed her own tears and looked past him. "I know, and I am sorry for judging you without knowing the facts." She stroked his cheek and threaded her hands through his hair. "You've never hurt me, and I know you never would, but I was triggered too, Tomas. The violence I've experienced over the years, and the kidnapping." She waved a hand. "The kidnapping story's for another day. But the point is that I failed to trust people, so I am a work in progress, too. Please believe that."

"I do, and thanks for sharing that part of your life. I hope you understand why I did what I did. I would never intentionally hurt you, physically or otherwise. Eva ... I..." He got up. "I have to go."

Eva's heart constricted. What was he about to say, and did she want him to leave? "Okay then. You go," she said unconvincingly. Walking behind him, she reached for his hand as he opened the door. He turned, closed the door, then pushed her back against it, his mouth devouring hers. With a soft touch on the inside of her arms, he planted them high above her head as his tongue tangled with hers when his lips travelled down to the centre of her chest. Eva's moans aroused him further as he sucked on a nipple, savouring the way it became erect. Rubbing his hand over it, he licked her other nipple and placed her breast in his mouth, sucking voraciously. She was undoing him, and he couldn't get close enough to her. He needed to be inside her and couldn't wait to get to bed.

When her arms fell, she pressed her hand against his penis then undid his jeans. Tomas' hands roved over her body. Goosebumps, shortened breath, and a deep love he'd never felt before made him slow down their intimacy until it got hot and heavy again. They moved to the bed and made love.

He was so in love with this woman; it scared the hell out of him.

CHAPTER 58

E va slowly opened her eyes and smiled to herself as she thought about the three times she and Tomas had made love last night. He had sent her to heaven and back, and she had almost told him she loved him. Had he been about to say it to her yesterday?

She turned to his side and her mouth fell when she saw the bed was empty, save for a note. She read it quickly.

Sorry. Had an early shift at work this morning and didn't want to wake you. You looked like a beautiful angel in sleep. I had an amazing time and hope to see you again tonight. Love, Tomas.

She placed the note against her chest and breathed it in as if she could smell his scent on the paper. He had said the word "love," but was it in the intimate sense or as a close friend? Who cared? She was on cloud nine and wanted to savour this feeling. No other man could ever measure up to him. Never again. He was her man.

She quickly showered, dressed then headed to the kitchen. She settled for a cup of tea for breakfast. Francisca had gone away for a few days for work, so she had the place to herself.

While she was enjoying her tea, the doorbell rang. Walking to the door, she angled her head at her surprise visitor whose face appeared ashen. "Esmeralda? What are you doing here? Is everything all right?"

Esmeralda swallowed, her eyes darting over her shoulder. "Can I come in?"

She swung open the door wider. "Of course." She led her to the kitchen table and sat opposite her. "Would you like a drink? Tea? Coffee?"

Her visitor stared into her hands. "I think I'm being followed, Eva. All this stuff with the cult and Ignacio being arrested. Who would have thought our own principal was one of the cult leaders? Not to mention everyone dying around us. Poor Lola, then Isabela, and now I think I might be next." Her lips trembled. "The past few days I could've sworn someone was watching me at home. I even found a note on my car's dashboard, telling me to watch myself. But I have done nothing wrong, Eva. I don't know why they're after me."

Eva looked into Esmeralda's eyes and saw genuine fear there. "You don't think they followed you to my apartment, do you?"

"God, I hope not. I looked carefully before I came here."

She was curious. "Why did you come here, though? How can I help?"

Her hands fidgeted, and she squared her shoulders, her eyes darkening further. "I'm worried about Samuel and him having to move to a safe house. I wanted to see if you were okay after what happened with Ignacio."

Eva flinched. "How did you know about that? As far as I know, only Tomas and I knew what happened." She had said nothing at work over the last week.

Esmeralda smiled. "I hear you, but I visited Ignacio in jail. That's how I know what happened." She cleared her throat. "I wanted to understand how he could deceive us. I needed to know if he killed Lola and Isabela. He refused to say anything to the police."

"Right. Did he say anything to you?"

"Funny thing is that he died this morning. Poisoned apparently. Karma's a bitch."

Eva's spine chilled. Something about this didn't feel right. "But if he didn't say anything..."

"I agree. It's strange how someone would kill him when the police knew nothing." She fingered her temple. "It's possible that whoever killed him might have been worried he'd talk, eventually. Play it safe."

Her heart raced. "Why would you visit him, Esmeralda?"

"As I said earlier, to get answers. Understand why he turned against everyone and hurt innocent children. How could the bastard hurt them like that?"

"When did you visit him?"

"Yesterday." She clasped her hands together then rose. She wrapped her arms around Eva. "If ever you need to talk, please give me a call. I care about you, Eva. I..."

The front door burst open. Eva looked past Esmeralda at a bulky figure: a man pointing a gun at them. A scar lined his cheek, and his crewcut made him look like a gangster. "Get on your knees now."

Esmeralda's body shook. "No, he found me." She turned to Eva. "I am so sorry."

Eva fell to her knees and Esmeralda did the same. But why did Esmeralda smirk? Was this planned?

The man took a rope from his pocket. "Tie the bitch's hands behind her back."

Esmeralda nodded and looped the rope several times around Eva's wrists, then tied a tight knot. But who was going to tie her up while the man handled the gun?

"Get on the couch."

Eva walked to the couch, her heart pounding. Was she going to die? What did this man want with her? Was he connected to the cult?

The man inched forward and kept the gun trained on her until Esmeralda moved.

He pointed the gun at Esmeralda. "You. Get on the couch, too." She did as he said with a darkness in her eyes. "Lean back against the couch."

Esmeralda put a hand over her mouth. "Don't hurt us. Please."

The heavy-set man held the gun to Eva while his other hand trailed the outside of Esmeralda's thigh until leaning in to kiss her hard.

She rested her head back. "Oh, yes. I love the way you kiss, Juan. Yes, yes." The man leaned in and deepened the kiss before she pulled away and laughed in Eva's face.

Eva felt like such a fool.

CHAPTER 59

Tomas sat across from Leandro in his office at the police station. "I told you that Eva is missing again. We were meant to see each other tonight, and she wasn't home. Her door was unlocked, and her wallet, keys and phone were inside the apartment. Does that sound like someone has gone out?"

"Jesus. They must have taken her. That old property was cleared out, so they might've taken her to their new residence. We are close to getting that warrant, but please be patient."

Tomas got out of his seat and paced up and down the floor, his heart racing and his body sweating. "My God. They're going to kill her, aren't they?"

"No, they won't. They'll most likely have a plan, and she might be a part of it. We won't jump to conclusions yet."

He scoffed. "Oh, that's so reassuring, Leandro. You need to save her. Please."

A stocky police officer knocked and entered. "We've got the warrant to search."

"Thanks. Get everyone ready and we'll meet you guys out back. Remember the plan." The officer nodded then left.

"I'll call Gonzalo, and we'll follow you in the ambulance," Tomas said. "If people are hurt, we'll need to give medical assistance."

"I know you love Eva. It's obvious. But you're coming only in a professional capacity, so always stay behind us until it's safe to come forward. Otherwise, I'll arrest you, Tomas. Eva will kill me if you get hurt."

"I understand."

Later that evening, Tomas buckled himself into the passenger seat of the EMT van with Gonzalo driving, his concerned gaze escalating his despair. He closed his eyes and prayed for Eva's safe return. He couldn't imagine anything worse than that not happening, and hoped they'd consider her more valuable alive. At least Samuel was in the safe house and Andreina was recovering in hospital.

Gonzalo exhaled. "We're nearly there, Tomas. Open your eyes."

After a bumpy four-hour ride, his friend braked outside a sprawling compound in south-east Spain. Bare trees spread around a barren square portable building with smaller cabins scattered in the near distance amidst mountainous terrain.

Tomas stepped out of the van with his friend as they hefted their supplies. The uneven ground, dirt, debris and boulders created obstacles, but the sunken white building in the middle appeared deserted. A barn nearby was padlocked, and a vegetable patch contained by edgings looked weathered. "Looks like no one's here, unless they're in those cabins down there."

Gonzalo nodded. "I hope they haven't been tipped off, or we'll miss out on saving these people and arresting these creeps."

Leandro stepped out of the car to join a crowd of uniformed officers and detectives. Using hand signals, he directed the men to surround the white building. As the men took their positions with their guns drawn, he turned to Tomas and Gonzalo. "You always stay behind me. If I tell you to stay back, listen."

"Yes, boss," said Tomas.

The men crossed the uneven ground, avoiding stones, rocks, and leaves in their path. Slowly, they walked behind the police until they reached the entrance to the white building. As he drew near, Tomas could see its advanced state of disrepair. Was the cult hiding in there? It looked deserted. His heart raced a mile a minute as he paced through the long blades of grass and dirty terrain.

The slowly setting sun cast long shadows on the ground, and Tomas squinted into the low light. Disturbed dirt on one side appeared to be in preparation for new buildings to be constructed. Was the plan to build more cabins if they were still here?

Picking up his pace alongside Gonzalo and behind Leandro, he watched as others entered other parts of the building. It was dilapidated and divided into tiny rooms with a few bunk beds. The walls were made of cheap plywood. But what he saw next made his blood boil.

Eva's eyes drooped from dehydration. Her hands felt numb because of the cuts on her wrists and the tightness of the rope tied to a hook suspended from a steel bar. She yearned to bring her arms down. There were no windows inside this cabin, so she didn't know how long she'd been there.

Steel shelves held stacked boxes and a haphazard pile of guns. Crates of bags of white powder lay around her, as well as row upon row of discarded clothing and shoes. Were people abused in this building, or were those accessories for new cult members?

She felt stupid for not realising Esmeralda was one of the cult leaders, letting her into her home and allowing that brute inside. They were obviously in a dysfunctional relationship. They drugged her, and the next thing she knew she was in this huge cabin. No doubt they must have transported her at night when there were fewer people around.

Surely the police had leads about this place. If not, she was doomed and would most likely die a gruesome death. Already, they had tortured her with thirst and hunger. She hoped Tomas was okay, and they hadn't kidnapped him, too.

The clack of heels broke her reverie. "Well, well, well. My favourite person in the world. Hello Eva," Esmeralda said.

Eva scoffed. "You bitch. How could you do this to Samuel? To those poor kids?"

Esmeralda raised a brow, then ran a hand over Eva's face. "My darling, Eva. I did like you, but you got too involved and couldn't mind your own damn business. Had to fall for Tomas, who got you deeper into this. If I don't have my way with him, he'll be next, don't worry. We'll make sure you die a quick death. Not a problem."

She couldn't breathe. "Please, Esmeralda. Don't do this. Save yourself."

"Why would I?"

"Why are you doing this? How could you be so damn heartless?"

Esmeralda toyed with the collar of her shirt and walked around her, watching her from every angle, beaming, with bright eyes. "For the money, of course. And the thrill I get from people's suffering. I can't help it if I need to get my revenge, too." She neared her while stroking her cheek again. "I loved getting back at those teenagers who raped me back in school. The ones who thought they could control me. Now, I control them. Use them while they're of value. I've learned to love sex, so long as I'm in charge."

"You're sick to take out your pain on poor innocent children," Eva spat.

"They're all the same. People in general are out for themselves. No one to trust unless you threaten them. But I'm smart. I get to have all the power, and you don't. You don't get to judge me when you're too piss-weak to fight off your father or your ex-boyfriend. I knew how to make you trust me, and you told me everything about your life. What I said was a bunch of bullshit, and I didn't believe any of it. But you know what? Once you're six feet under, I'll get the pleasure of seducing Tomas and making him fall in love with me. He'll be grieving. He'll be vulnerable, and he'll reach out to me. Oh, yes. Sweet, sweet Tomas."

Eva shook her head. "No, he'll never be fooled by you. He's too smart."

"Possibly, but you weren't smart, were you? Shame. We could've been the best of friends if you believed in my mission, but you don't." She put a finger across her throat. "Did he make you come? Tomas, I mean? Has he gone down on you? Ooh, that's what I'd love from him. Oral sex is the best."

Eva spat but Esmeralda dodged it. "How can you use children as your sex slaves? No doubt you've killed people, too."

"Oh, spare me your righteous indignation. I can't stomach it. At the end of the day, I hate people. Always have. Just born that way. Sorry, my darling Eva." She leaned in and touched a strand of her hair. "Take care, my darling. We'll see you soon."

"I will haunt you if I die. Bet on that."

Esmeralda laughed. "Ooh, I am so scared."

"Wait. Did you kill Lola and Isabela? Ignacio?"

Her enemy turned around, her eyes gleaming in the glowing bright light. "I killed Lola and Isabela, but one of my men shot Lola first. Later, I had the pleasure of slashing her throat. Isabela's, too. The bitch grew a conscience after knowing how the minors had sex for procreation. She wanted out. But Isabela was one of our best recruiters. Online and face-to-face. Shame, really." She licked her bottom lip. "Oh, the excitement you get when seeing the light drain out of their eyes. It's magical." She stared past her. "As for Ignacio, or should I say, Marco, his alter ego in the group, we paid off a policeman to poison his food. It's funny how money talks a lot in this country—and everywhere else."

"I hope you get what you deserve, Esmeralda. For all the pain you've caused. What about Efren? Is he all right?"

"You've asked enough questions, bitch. I hope you enjoy the other side."

She glared, then walked off, the sound of her heels grating on Eva's nerves.

CHAPTER 60

T omas stopped in his tracks. One stocky old man gyrated in the middle of sex with a girl of about fifteen, while an even younger girl wrapped her mouth around another man's penis. Policemen wasted no time in identifying themselves, pulling the children away, and handcuffing the two men. Detectives read them their rights. The two girls had bruises over their faces, cuts along their naked bodies and cigarette burns on their breasts.

These bastards. Ignacio had the nerve to do all this. But who else was involved? His stomach heaved as he looked at the spots of blood on the dirty ground, and the stench of faeces in the room. There had to be more to arrest. But where was Eva? Efren? Were they still alive? They had to be.

Tomas rushed in to treat one of the girls. He set her down inside the ambulance, draped a blanket over her body, pulled out his medical supplies and wiped her cuts with disinfectant. Gonzalo checked over the other girl, who cried as he placed gauze over her cuts. Stopping what he was doing, he drew her in for a hug before continuing to treat her.

Leandro, other detectives and police stalked away with their guns at the ready and hands over their holsters. But he had to follow. Others might need help, especially Eva who would break his heart into tiny pieces if she died. His heart clenched tight, not knowing how to live without her.

He turned to Gonzalo. "Will you be okay with the girls?"

"Yes, but be careful. Remember what Leandro said."

He hefted his medical bag. "I will, but I need to go or I'll miss whoever needs help in those cabins."

Tomas scurried after them in the darkness, lights brightening up the cabins down the path. The sound of gunshots made him squirm, so he ran as fast as he could to one of the lit-up cabins and passed the police.

Leandro grunted. "Hold up, Tomas. Don't go without us. Wait up."

He ran and yelled out behind him, knowing in his gut he had to be there. "Too late!" Tomas was not going to lose Eva without a fight. If he had to die, so be it, as long as she lived. He would gladly sacrifice himself for the love of his life. No, he had to save her, and time was not on their side.

Eva gasped when she saw Esmeralda coming closer with the bulky invader of her apartment and a shorter, bald man. Both men held guns. Was this her time to die? No, she wouldn't die without a fight.

"Sorry to say gorgeous, but our time together has come to an end. I regret that I must say goodbye to you." She moved closer to bulky man and kissed him hard on the mouth before leaving. "Make it quick, darling."

The men approached. "Any last words, lady?" said the bald man.

No, she had to fight. "I know I'm going to die, but at least let me die with dignity. Please let me down. Don't let me die this way. I need to be free. My wrists are killing me. Let me decide how I die."

The bulky man shook his head. "Who gives a shit? You'll be dead, anyway."

She pleaded with her eyes. "Please. Give me my last wish. The police might make it easier for you if you showed some mercy. Esmeralda's not here to tell you what to do. Please." She put all her feelings into her expression in hope they might set her free. "You guys have guns, so I'm not going anywhere. Please grant me this one wish. One of you can untie me while the other has his gun on me, so it's not like I can do anything."

Bulky guy hesitated, appearing to think. "Fine. Baldy, you stay on her." He nodded.

The man reached over for the knot on the rope and untied it with difficulty. When Eva's hands were free, she rubbed the deep grooves around her wrists. Red and raw. It would ache for days. But if she was dead, who cared?

But none of the three had planned for Esmeralda to return in a huff.

Bulky man neared her. "What's wrong, sweetie?"

"I found out where Samuel's staying. I want you there after you kill Eva. The police might move him again." Esmeralda looked to Eva. "Why isn't she dead yet?"

"She wanted her wrists to be free," said the bald man.

Esmeralda smirked then approached her. "This is the end of the road for you, sweetie. It's been grand, but all good things must come to an end. I'll still leave you to these brilliant men who will give you a quick death. Now kill her." As she was about to turn, Eva threw herself forward, shoving Esmeralda into the arms of the bulky man. She hit the ground and knocked her shoulder hard when the shorter man's shot missed. She ran behind the steel shelves.

"Oh, Evie," Esmeralda called. "You can't get out without passing these men with guns. There's no other way out, so just give it up."

Eva felt light-headed. She could reach one of the guns on the shelves, but most likely they weren't loaded. She couldn't find anything sharp to use here, so she was doomed. Running down the length of another set of shelves, she found more boxes with bags of white powder in them. That could be something. If she opened those bags and threw them into their faces, it would blind them for a few seconds and give her time to get away.

Reaching for a few of them, she heard footsteps coming from the two opposite directions. *Oh, no.* How would she fight them both at the same time? But one of them breathed so hard, she thought he might pass out.

"I'll leave you with these two men, Eva. They won't need me." The door banged closed. She breathed a sigh of relief. One down and two more to go.

Eva pulled open one bag and snuck around the corner. The bulky man spotted her and she quickly threw the bag in his face. He doubled over and dropped his gun. Dashing forward, she scooped up the gun and ran for her life around the shelves, where the shorter man stood with his gun pointed downwards. *Stupid man.* She aimed the gun towards him with shaky hands but rather than use it, she gave him a swift kick in his groin. Why not use her defence training when she felt sick having to shoot someone? The gun was a deterrent.

He moaned, wrenched backwards and fell against the shelves. She ran for her life towards the door. But as she opened it, she glanced over her shoulder to see the bulky man approaching. Eva dove back behind a shelf, as searing pain crossed her shoulder. She fell over, the stabbing pain making her dizzy. Bulky man grabbed her ankle and dragged her further inside. He pounded into her shoulder and slapped her across the cheeks, his gold ring scraping her skin, making her wince in pain. Bald man stood beside him. She dropped the gun, and it slid over to him.

He reached for the weapon. "Sorry, lady, but this is your end. You have to die." The bitter, twisted smile of the shooter gave her chills, and she blinked twice, knowing she would die. She was staring down the barrel of the gun, flashing back to Tomas, her family, friends, Samuel. *This is it. Nothing more to do.* She closed her eyes about to meet her fate.

Gunshots and trampling footsteps in her mind confused her. She didn't feel anything. Had she been shot, having made it to the other side without feeling pain? Was she dead?

Slowly, the background voices caused her eyes to open. "Eva. Oh, Eva." Tomas leaned over her. "Your shoulder. But thank God you're alive. Thank God." Around them was mayhem. She saw Esmeralda was being handcuffed, and the two killers were lying dead. Gonzalo arrived, and they carried her on the stretcher. "It's over now, my darling. You're safe." She could only breathe and smile as she closed her eyes in excruciating pain.

Tomas watched as more ambulances arrived to treat those who'd been hurt. People yelling, running their hands through their hair, looking confused, while some cowered when being taken away. Others raised their hands in joy whilst a tall man wearing a white robe, looking like a leader, attempted to run off. Two police officers caught up and handcuffed him.

The screams, laughter, and stomping of feet were bittersweet, even if his head was spinning. It was chaotic, and he got dizzy with the pitter-patter of feet across the uneven ground, and cult members stepping into waiting police vans.

Tomas ran inside a barn with Leandro, and found two young boys strung up like sausages. Their eyes were bloodshot, and they were both shirtless with grubby skin, cuts, and bruising. One of them had his eye partially shut, no doubt from endless punches.

"You're safe now," he said as he watched Leandro use bolt cutters to remove the handcuffs around their wrists. He helped one boy lie on a stretcher as he winced in pain. "What's your name?" Leandro helped cut the other boy free.

"Efren." His eyes lit up. "Thank you for saving us." He pointed. "That's Miguel, my friend. He's grateful too, I'm sure."

His companion, Miguel laughed when Gonzalo helped him up and lay him gently on the stretcher. "Got that right." He moaned in pain as he struggled to cough. "Hey man. See you on the other side."

Efren grinned. "See you, Miguel," he said as he was being wheeled away.

Tomas pushed him towards the van. "I have heard about you, Efren. I spoke to your mother, and she's on her way to the hospital. She'll be happy to see you."

"I miss her so much. Thank you."

Thank God for small mercies. They had saved hundreds of people from long-term pain, suffering, and even death.

CHAPTER 61

Eva held Andreina's hand and smiled. "I am glad you're okay." She turned to Samuel, who beamed at her, then turned to his aunt in the hospital.

Samuel perked up. "Aunty. I love you."

Andreina cried. "Oh, I can't believe he speaks now. Blessed. I love you too, Samuel. We are family."

"I know, Aunty."

Eva looked behind her at Tomas, Francisca, and Leandro. She lifted Samuel onto the bed so he could give his aunt a kiss and hug. It warmed her heart to see how close they'd become.

Leandro looked at Francisca. "Can you take Samuel out for a few minutes? I need to speak to Andreina."

"Of course," said Francisca. She grabbed Samuel from the bed and held his hand as they walked out of the ward.

Andreina stared with a curious look in her eyes. "What is it?"

"I thought you'd want to know that Samuel's father, Adan, was killed. Apparently, he had abused his ex-partner, whose brother didn't take too kindly to it."

She nodded. "I am not surprised. He always had a black heart. Did he arrange the attack on Samuel?"

"He admitted to getting a friend of his to kidnap Samuel so he could develop a rapport with his son. He thought his past would catch up with him and affect custody of Samuel," said Leandro.

"Such a sorry excuse of a man," Andreina frowned. "Please tell me about this cult. Have they all been arrested?"

"Yes," Leandro said as he spoke to the others. "Esmeralda, the school psychologist; also known as Ana in the cult, and Ignacio, who they knew as Marco, were the founders of the group. Alongside more of their cronies and leaders who were arrested a few nights ago. We found many children being abused, with the plan to sell them to the highest bidder in the United States. Sick people. Children having children as parents after their acts of procreation. We are now investigating their connections in the United States, which is bigger than we first thought."

"Esmeralda told me she murdered Lola and Isabela," explained Eva.

"Yes. She'll be severely punished," said Leandro.

Andreina's eyes darkened. "What about that dear missing boy, Efren?"

Leandro inched closer. "We found Efren strung up like a sausage in the locked barn. They planned to keep him and another boy, Miguel, there to die a slow death. They'd been injured and were dehydrated, but otherwise they're recovering. We've arrested those involved in the mercury markets, and all those committing paedophilia." He took a breath. "It's been going on for years, but now they've been dismantled here. We won't stop with those overseas."

Tomas nodded. "Great work." He took a breath. "I spoke to Efren earlier. He read the news article about all those killed in the group, including Isabela. He recognised her in the cult. Mentioned she was arguing with Esmeralda, or Ana as he knew her, overhearing their conversation. She wanted to leave but Esmeralda played nice and lied to her about their true mission."

Leandro stared. "What could he do? He wasn't to know. I'll speak to him again." He leaned in. "But you were too busy playing Rambo and could've got yourself killed. Wrestling the big guy for his gun could have easily got you shot. You were lucky we got there in time."

Eva shook her head. "No, he saved me. If he hadn't come, then they would've shot me dead. He bought you time." They locked eyes and her heart stirred.

Tomas clenched a fist. "Was Ignacio her stalker?"

"Yes. Esmeralda admitted everything. Javier worked for the cult and has been arrested, too. He is also facing charges of molestation against Raul, so luckily you saved him."

Eva squared her shoulders. "Thank you for your help, Leandro. I'm wondering why Samuel wouldn't talk. Was he threatened?"

Leandro gazed at Andreina whose eyes appeared tired. "Yes, he never got to see Ignacio the few weeks he stayed in the cult, but Esmeralda threatened to kill his Aunt Andreina if he spoke up. She had him kidnapped after hearing he'd started to talk and thought he might say something."

"Two boys without their mothers," said Eva. "It's sad."

Leandro nodded. "I know, but justice has been served." He lifted his hand. "Anyway, we'll let you rest, Andreina. Thanks for your statement."

"We'll come and visit you and Samuel at home, Andreina," said Tomas.

"I know Samuel would like that."

EPILOGUE

ONE MONTH LATER

Eva lounged back against Tomas' couch at his apartment while he massaged the back of her legs. She felt safe on his couch and wanted desperately to be with him always. She loved him.

Tomas stroked her cheek with his fingertips. "I wanted to tell you long ago, Eva, but I ... I love you. So much."

Tears fell down his cheeks, and she wiped them away. Her heart warmed. "I love you too, Tomas. I wanted to tell you earlier, but I was scared. I'm not scared anymore."

"I hate it when we're apart, Eva. I can't stop thinking about you when I'm with you and when I'm not. Hell, I even dream about you every night. I hate it when you go home. I almost lost you."

She squeezed his hand. "But you didn't. I owe you my life, Tomas."

"No, I owe you mine. You've given me light in the darkest of my days. You've healed me in my soul and made me the best version of myself. I love your huge heart. I love the way you're there for others, your kindness, your beauty, and your wit. You're my everything Eva, and I never want to let you go. Be with me, always."

She chuckled. "Darling. We see each other most nights."

"It's not enough. I can never get enough of you."

Eva angled her head, curious by the grin on his cheeky-looking face. "What are you saying, Tomas?"

He leaned away from her and reached for her glass of port. "Have a drink first, my beautiful. You're going to need it."

Strange. What was he going to do? Ask her to move in, or did he want to move in with her? But the limited space would make it a challenge. "Please tell me."

He beamed. "I will, but drink your port first. Trust me on this."

She exhaled. "Fine." She took the glass from him and drank it down, the intensity warming her throat. When she got to the end of the port, something sharp and hard fell into the side of her mouth. She spat it out into the glass. "What is this, Tomas?" She lost all breath. "A ring?"

He leaned in and kissed her hard on the mouth. "Will you marry me?" Eva stared into his eyes, speechless. "Marry me, Eva."

Tears spilled down her cheek, overwhelmed by the love in her heart. "Oh, Tomas. Of course I'll marry you. I love you so much."

"I love you too, Eva. More than I can say." He leaned in, bit her bottom lip, then kissed her passionately until they were spent. She couldn't imagine having a happier day than this one. She was finally safe and loved.

ABOUT THE AUTHOR

Lucy Appadoo is a prolific author who writes contemporary romance and romantic suspense novels about strong women who manage adversity with strength and heart.

She is the author of the Women of Strength series and Friends in Crisis series in the romantic suspense genre, and the billionaire romance series in the contemporary romance genre.

After a childhood spent reading and imagining escapist worlds, Lucy has put her imagination into stories. Her work as a rehabilitation counsellor, and former work as a counsellor in private practice, have led to an interest in writing inspirational stories about authentic, driven women who struggle with a stalker, villain or new love interest.

Lucy enjoys plotting the next love or suspense story, travelling for fun and inspiration, researching crime stories and news to inspire her work, watching romance and suspenseful movies, reading. meditating, and spending time with friends and family. She also appreciates her Italian background, which has inspired her to write imaginative stories about her parents' childhoods that have led to The Italian Family Series novels.

Check out Lucy's website and sign up for a free exclusive suspenseful novella with romantic elements:

https://www.lucyappadooauthor.com.au

Check out:

https://linktr.ee/lucyappadooauthor

Follow me on social media:

Tiktok:

https://www.tiktok.com/@lucyappadooauthor

Instagram:

https://www.instagram.com/lucyappadooauthor/

Goodreads:

https://www.goodreads.com/author/show/14186931.Lucy_Appadoo

Bookbub:

https://www.bookbub.com/profile/lucy-appadoo

Facebook:

https://www.facebook.com/profile.php?id=10000923
4984607

Linked In:

https://www.linkedin.com/in/lucy-appadoo-ba986ab
5/

Twitter:

https://twitter.com/LucyAppadoo

ALSO BY LUCY APPADOO

In Rio's Shadows (Book 1):

https://books2read.com/u/mq1qP8

Shadows Of The Past (Book 2):

https://books2read.com/u/3JZe1X

Secrets In The Shadows (Book 3):

https://books2read.com/u/ml88kv

Friends In Crisis Series - Romantic Suspense/Thriller

Haunted By The Past (Book 1):

https://books2read.com/u/bw2ZeY

Twisted Obsession (Book 2):

https://books2read.com/u/4DW8pk

Web Of Lies (Book 3):

https://books2read.com/u/3JXazE

Love-Obsessed (Book 4):

https://books2read.com/u/4jPKGX

Fatal Designs (Book 5):

https://books2read.com/u/3nBjy5

The Hearts Series - Romantic Suspense

Rising Hearts (Book 1):

https://books2read.com/u/mZwpoE

Forbidden Hearts (Book 2):

https://books2read.com/u/bQBKr7

Kindred Hearts (Book 3):
https://books2read.com/u/4AJKQK
Broken Hearts (prequel to Forbidden Hearts):
https://books2read.com/u/mgrnOD

Short Story Thrillers
Evening Interrupted:
https://books2read.com/u/3yZDjZ
The Dreamcatcher: https://books2read.com/u/bzaLxn
Red Flags: https://books2read.com/u/bWZ9W1
Collection of Short Story Thrillers:
https://books2read.com/u/bP5vwj

The Italian Family Series - Coming of Age Family Drama/Romance
A New Life: https://books2read.com/u/mqqwZm
The Beauty of Tears: https://books2read.com/u/bpqwk3
Dancing in the Rain:
https://books2read.com/u/bOr7LA
A Life By Design: https://books2read.com/u/3J8ene

NON-FICTION
Grief & Loss
Moving Beyond Grief - How To Shift From Grief & Loss
to Joy & Peace: https://books2read.com/u/mVNzDA

Stress Management & Anxiety

Holistic Spiritual and Mental Health - Building Resilience and Creativity by Conquering Anxiety and Managing Stress: https://books2read.com/u/47kG8A

Career Guidance

Your Holistic Career Path - Create Career Change, Satisfaction, and Work/Life Balance: https://books2read.com/u/bzYDz4